DNAlien

A Novel
by
JIM WEST
2007

Copyright © Year 2024
All Rights Reserved

Copyright by Aurora Publications

DNAlien is copyrighted by Aurora Publications, Inc.

The cowboy on horseback over the state of Texas, either separately or as shown, is the trademark of Aurora Publications, Inc.

The cover art and cowboy logo are the product of Kathleen Godiksen, Studio K, LLC.

The words to the song 'There's Nothing Slim In This Bar But The Pickin's' are copyrighted by Jim West.

ISBN:
Hardcover: 978-1-964289-22-9
Paperback: 978-1-964289-17-5

FOREWORD

No matter what you or I think, no matter what has been presented as fact or fiction, there are always those who believe. Whether it is religion, politics, scientific "facts," or any other issue that is open to various sides of the debate, the issue of unidentified flying objects (UFOs) will probably never be fully resolved until complete disclosure of every single piece of evidence is presented for everyone to see.

Even if total disclosure were possible, there would always be those who refuse to believe due to various reasons. Only time will take the 'known' into the accepted. The following, while certainly not considered "fact," is nonetheless published information readily found in varying formats—newspaper, television, documentary, eyewitness reports, personal knowledge, or hearsay.

The following information is not meant to be considered absolute, nor is it to be considered the final say or the complete amount of information regarding this subject. However, it is a small amount of information from various sources, combined with a certain acceptance of the possible, and blended, sometimes with a liberal amount of Jack Daniel's, within my mind to present one possible scenario.

This is by no means the only possible outcome of what may have occurred with whatever was found at Roswell or Aurora. It is purely a story that might (with a huge stretch of your imagination) be true. Then again, so may Santa Claus and the fairy godmother. You may make that decision.

I would like to express my appreciation to numerous people who have encouraged me and provided helpful (or not-so-helpful) input to enable me to write this obviously fictional work. Please bear in mind that none of the places, while some are real, ever had any of the occurrences (I don't believe) actually happen.

The names of the people, while sounding like people I know, are purely fictitious, and none have ever been involved with unidentified flying objects—at least, they have not told me about it. And no, I don't believe in crop circles. Nor do I think UFOs target backwoods people for their research. No one with the intelligence obviously required to travel here across billions of miles of space would waste their time doodling in the dirt or trying to extract useful information from a hillbilly—just my opinion. You keep yours to yourself or write a book—I really don't care. Thank you, though, for your insightful observations!

ACKNOWLEDGEMENTS

I would like to thank all the people who helped me make DNAlien a book worth reading. From correcting my horrible spelling, terrible verb usage, and many, many other mistakes, they have been most helpful. Even more, they overlooked my obvious slanted look at life and sometimes even found the humor I had strived to provide.

These people include Kay Pratka, one of my favorite cousins (known affectionately as Aunt Kay); Vicki Jean and Renee Mischelle West, my darling daughters; John and Mary Fleenor, two of the best friends a man can have; and Kathy Godiksen, who was also instrumental in the artwork and finally decided that you can't believe all you read.

The numerous others shall go unnamed but certainly provided encouragement and the occasional snide remark or crude comment that found its way into the finished product. I know who you are.

Thank you all!

DISCLAIMER

Absolutely none of the characters in this fictional work are real. The names, while taken from friends, do not represent them, their families, or their actions. They are just names I picked to show them that I will keep them in my mind as long as I shall live.

Most of the places are real, but none of the events took place in them or anywhere else. They are just places, and their only reason for inclusion is that they just happen to be on the map. Having lived in the area for more years than I care to mention, I have come to love the places and their people. A man could not ask for a better place to spend his life.

None of the events are real. Although I have had meals and drinks and have sung and danced at some of the locations, none of the events happened as described in my novel. And no, the crowd did not go wild when I sang.

Finally, remember that the entire book is absolutely fiction and has absolutely no bearing on reality anywhere in the world.

INTRODUCTION

Although this book is obviously fiction, the reader should bear in mind the possibilities that exist for science and technology to develop things we can only imagine. The commonplace today was science fiction only a few decades ago.

What if there have been alien spacecraft visiting our planet? What if there have been crashes? What if our government is using the remains to further its own agenda?

Now, imagine what would happen if the result of one of the secret programs was to become public knowledge. What if a new species of man was to be walking among us? Would you be able to recognize it? What would you do if you were to discover its existence? DNAlien is the story of just such a possibility.

I hope you get as much enjoyment from reading it as I did writing it.

CHARACTERS

Military

1.   General Mike Nelson - Project Revive Commander, Facility commander, and member of Majestic12
2.   General Gary Brown – Naval Air Station/Joint Reserve Base (NAS/JRB) Ft Worth, Texas, Commander
3.   General Paul Modelle - White House/presidential staff adviser and member of MJ 12
4.   Colonel Rick Erickson - Facility Deputy Commander and Operations Officer for Revive
5.   Colonel Karyn Lynch - Communications Officer for Revive and the Facility
6.   Colonel Amy Moore - Facility Laboratory Commander
7.   Lieutenant Colonel Mark Mallory - Facility Security Commander
8.   Major Jerry Fleenor - White House liaison
9.   Major Cory Romine - Facility engineering
10.   Lieutenant Colonel Don Pratka - a friend of James and Vicki Grubbs, also works in security at the Facility
11.   Lieutenant Colonel James Grubbs - Vicki's husband; once chief of security at the Facility
12.   Kathy Blevins - General Nelson's secretary

Civilian

1.   Ray and Myrtle Downey - first hired Gene
2.   Butch North - owner of The Equestrian Center of Aurora Vista
3.   Mischelle and Jeannie North - Butch's daughters
4.   Steve and Sheril Rose - stable manager at The Equestrian Center of Aurora Vista, and his wife
5.   Mike Jackson - owner of Bowie Livestock Auction
6.   Kay - waitress at KK Restaurant in Boyd
7.   Stacy Hyden and Leslie Barber - met at Red's and took Gene home
8.   Vicki Grubbs - nurse and Gene's closest friend at the Facility
9.   Nanette Bost - the owner of Southern Delight Restaurant in Boyd

Page Blank Intentionally

CHAPTER 1

Vicki Grubbs was dying, and there was nothing that could be done. Here she was, working in the most advanced medical Facility in the world where ultra-secret military and scientific research was being conducted, and she had absolutely no hope. Her death was inevitable and would come in mere weeks—certainly less than two months, she was told repeatedly by both the doctors here and throughout the civilian medical fields.

Unfortunately for Vicki, the purpose of this particular Facility was not in saving lives; it was specifically designed and operated with one singular purpose: The creation of life!

The cancer that had been diagnosed over a year ago during her annual breast exam had begun to metastasize and now was throughout her fifty-odd-year-old body. Following a radical mastectomy, radiation, and bouts of chemotherapy, the inevitability remained, and the results that had arrived just last week were nothing more than a death sentence with a nonnegotiable execution date. No extensions are possible.

Vicki was currently stationed at Naval Air Station Joint Reserve Base (NAS/JRB) Fort Worth, formerly known as Carswell Air Force Base and before that as the Fort Worth Army Air Corps Base, during and immediately following

World War II. She had completed advanced nurses' training for the U.S. Air Force in 1962 and served one tour in Vietnam. There, she had been highly decorated, and upon her return to the United States, she had been offered her choice of assignments. She wanted to come home to Texas, and any assignment in the state would satisfy her longing to be close to her mother and father, then in their fifties. After their deaths, she only wanted to remain in what she considered the most desirable place on Earth to live—Texas.

While serving in Vietnam, her exemplary service and outstanding dedication had been noticed by one of the fighter pilots flying F-4 Phantoms out of the base where she had been stationed. Then, Captain Mike Nelson had met her while he was getting his annual flight physical and also when visiting one of his squadron's pilots who had received some minor injuries during a mission over Hanoi. Her constant smile and obvious desire to ensure her patients' comfort and care impressed Captain Nelson, Mike, was a man whose later career would be able to reward Vicki in ways she had never imagined.

Mike Nelson, a new Colonel at Carswell AFB, met her again shortly after she returned from her parent's funeral. After their brief reunion, they remained in touch and Vicki came to Mike and his wife's home frequently for dinner or just social drinks after work.

Colonel Nelson had been instrumental in securing her assignment in a program she knew only as Project Revive. She had undergone intensive screening procedures, been granted the highest security clearances, and was approved by officials at the very top of both the military and civilian chains of command. She knew the project she was involved in was cloaked in secrecy so deep that even knowledge of its existence was limited to the very few with an absolute need to know. She also knew that this project was of a most controversial nature yet critical to an extremely important issue—the security of the United States of America.

It was while serving within the deep underground facilities of the program, located clandestinely at the NAS/JRB, that she met her husband, James Grubbs, a Captain in the Air Force stationed at the same Facility. James had graduated from Texas Tech University under the ROTC program, had attended initial training in security at Sheppard AFB, and was stationed at Carswell AFB's security office.

After serving one tour with the base security office, his superior performance gained him both recognition and his choice of follow-on assignments. Being a third-generation Texan, he expressed his desire to remain somewhere in the state, just as Vicki had done. He was given the same security screening and approval process, passed every facet of the intense investigations, and was ultimately assigned to the 'Facility' as it was called on the base.

Once assigned, James was only told how the security systems were to be managed, who to contact regarding any questions of security and to never ask what any other member of the organization did nor what section of the project they were involved with. All he ever needed to know, he would be told. Any questions or suggestions regarding his specific area were to be directed to his immediate superior. Contact with anyone outside his area would result in immediate termination. James was fully aware of what that meant.

Each area of Project Revive was completely compartmentalized. A strict need to know regarding any information was rigidly enforced.

Infractions were swiftly and rigorously enforced. The overall mission, known only to the very top officials, headed by newly promoted General Mike Nelson, a current member of MJ 12, and his staff, was unknown to anyone else outside the laboratories that performed the actual embryonic research. Even the scientists and laboratory technicians only knew that they were dealing with a radical new area of genetic manipulation. Those working with rodent specimens never knew where the genetic material came from. Those dealing with human embryos were told it was an experimental procedure to eradicate specific genetic markers found in normal human populations that were predictors of possible diseases or defects such as cancer or Down's syndrome.

Now seen as a national asset, the Facility and its sole mission, Revive, existed solely to test a premise that had been theorized for years among scientists. This theory was to develop a being using alien DNA combined with a human embryo. This was hoped to create a being that would possess encoded genetic information from the alien intelligence and be passed to the combined result through germ-line manipulation.

The entire project, its true purpose, and the results produced were some of the most tightly guarded secrets in the world. Even the project's name, *Revive,* was meant to be either meaningless or misleading if it was ever used outside the Facility.

To truly understand how this mission reached the point where an entire country would become involved requires some critical background information. The following chapters will provide that information and reiterate how this program was developed and remained virtually unknown until the fateful day of September 11, 2001.

CHAPTER 2

Aurora, Texas, April 17, 1897. Something flying through the air all over north Texas finally hit a windmill north of the small town of Aurora, owned by one Judge Proctor. Among the pieces of the wreckage, a small body was discovered and subsequently buried in the local cemetery.

This happened over five years before the Wright brothers made their first flight.

July 7, 1947. A "spacecraft" of unknown origin crashed on a ranch outside of Roswell, New Mexico. Among the debris, several bodies were discovered. Reports of this event were covered by local newspapers and radio. Initially verified by local officials and representatives from the U.S. Army Air Corps at Fort Worth, Texas, the actual events became widely known.

Almost immediately, officials of the government, in the name of the U.S. Army Air Corps, arrived to secure the crash site and prevent further civilian speculation. The team that arrived wasted no time in establishing a secure perimeter, gathering every piece of material, each body, and any fragment that may have been identifiable as alien in origin.

Word was immediately sent to Washington, DC. All the evidence of the crash was transported to the Fort Worth Army Air Corps Base, Texas. It was there that the future events really began.

The physical remains, both alive and deceased, were immediately rushed into a vacant hangar. All of the metal or inorganic material was placed separately within the hangar and locked securely. Guards placed around the area were ordered to approach no closer than one hundred yards and to detain anyone not authorized to enter the area.

As word of this and the "unauthorized" versions were spreading, a select group of both scientists and top military officials were called to the White House to meet immediately with President Harry Truman.

At this meeting, it was quickly decided that absolutely no information with regard to the actual events was to ever reach the general public. This was due to the idea that an unknown aircraft had penetrated U.S. airspace undetected and the belief that knowledge of alien life would disrupt not only the United States but also every nation on Earth.

The ramifications of both mythological and religious beliefs could possibly throw the world into turmoil that would disrupt countless lives in an unprecedented way. This information had to be controlled immediately.

President Truman and the newly formed council then decided to leave the alien remains at Fort Worth and transfer all other material to an unknown base just north of Las Vegas, Nevada. This base, unnamed as yet, came to be known as Area 51. It has recently been used almost exclusively for testing "black" projects due to its location, remoteness, and basic security, which guaranteed isolation of the "evidence" as well as any new technology developed as a result of the captured material from Roswell.

Upon completing the briefing and ensuring each member's oath of absolute secrecy, the 12 members of the group became known as the Majestic 12, or just MJ 12, in all future discussions.

One of the final decisions of MJ 12 at this meeting was to send a team to Aurora, Texas. Located just about twenty miles north of Fort Worth, the remains from the 1897 crash were to be found and secured. Any evidence still around after fifty years was to be immediately removed or destroyed.

A small team of government personnel went to Aurora to "exhume and confiscate" the remains from the local cemetery. Great care was taken to leave no trace of having disturbed the final resting site of an unknown being whose grave was marked with a simple stone by the citizens of Aurora over fifty years ago.

Visitors and researchers during subsequent years would find no markers and would meet resistance from every official regarding the "alien" buried as well as the location of the crash site in Aurora.

From this date on, MJ 12 would control every aspect with regard to the UFO phenomenon. From placing selected technology into the hands of certain industries to revealing techniques in all aspects of the medical and scientific fields, MJ 12 had complete control.

The benefits to society would be enormous. The breakthroughs in aviation, research in biochemistry, cloning, and genetic research—all resulted from work done for those at MJ 12. MJ 12 reported to no one except the President and only to advise him of their progress and the impact of the various programs.

CHAPTER 3

Constructed deep beneath the sprawling complex collectively known as the Naval Air Station/Joint Reserve Base Fort Worth, Texas (NAS/JRB), formerly Carswell Air Force Base, lies one of the most closely guarded facilities in the world. Even those who know of its existence, outside those working in its depths, do not know the true purpose of the Facility.

The thousands of people stationed at NAS/JRB go about their daily lives with no concept of the underground operation. Very few even know of the ten-story underground complex. Initially built during the mid-to-late 1940s, it was understood by those not directly involved to be an underground bomb shelter. Fallout shelters were springing up across the country as we ushered in the nuclear age. Mammoth projects were underway at virtually every military or governmental Facility across the country. That such a facility existed at the then-known U.S. Army Air Corps Base was no surprise.

The exact specifications for the Facility were never revealed to the workers nor the military commanders stationed there. All orders, budgeting, materials, and contracts were handled directly from Washington, DC. The base commander at the time was ordered to ensure that unrestricted access was provided to the approved personnel. The list came directly from a certain individual or his designated replacement, should the need arise.

No other orders could countermand those received from Washington. Failure to comply or interference of any nature would result in immediate transfer, and the implied threat to their careers made it extremely clear. This project and its purpose were never to be discussed. The only information to be provided was that a fallout shelter was being constructed.

The current Base Commander, during initial construction, lost his position and any future promotions due to one small indiscretion. He happened to mention MJ 12 during a phone call with one of the supervisors of the construction project.

He never knew its meaning, but he sure knew the results of even mentioning the name. Orders for his transfer arrived before the day was over. His replacement, handpicked in Washington, was on the first airplane headed to Fort Worth within minutes of hearing. His orders in hand, he presented himself and orders to the Wing Commander upon arrival. The departing Base Commander, ordered to appear before the Wing Commander, was relieved and given orders to report to Washington on the following day to receive his next assignment. He was retired the very next day.

That lesson did not go unheeded by subsequent commanders. Never again was any mention made of where the orders came from, the purpose of the Facility, nor any contact with the people over at "the dig." Access was provided through a special gate with strict orders as to who and what could approach the construction site.

Every contractor was selected through Washington. A representative of the Facility oversaw the specific job and material requirements, and the Base Commanders left it alone for fear of a repeat of the one slip made before them.

Construction lasted nearly a year. Ten stories deep, constructed of concrete nearly twice as thick as normal, reinforced to five times the standard specifications, the Facility was topped with a layer of concrete five feet thick. No photographs were ever taken. No mention of its location on any map outlining the base and its other buildings has ever existed.

Any records search would show only the hangar built over the Facility. At that hangar, only certain aircraft with specific orders, carrying dates, and time stamps were allowed to use the facilities. A special parking area was located adjacent to the hangar, designated specifically for those working within the hangar.

All deliveries of equipment were done during hours of darkness and unloaded within the closed doors of the hangar. Personnel working within the Facility were given a wide berth by the rest of those stationed on the base. It was a well-rumored fact— just talking to those people could result in immediate dismissal or even a dishonorable discharge. The Facility and its personnel were feared more than the plague. Either could mean certain death.

Over the next few decades, people gradually forgot about the Facility's history and only knew that a classified project was located there, and unless you were directly involved, you stayed away. Only the Base Commanders were allowed communications with the Facility, and they never knew exactly what was taking place beneath the hangar.

The cover story finally listed Air Force Systems Command as the facility owner, and research into bio-chemical defenses was listed in their mission statement. This alone ensured most people remained well clear of the Facility.

CHAPTER 4

The true purpose of the Facility was known only to MJ 12. The embryonic research conducted within what was only known as the Facility was one of the most closely guarded secrets in the world. It was guarded more closely than the experiments which produced the first atomic bomb. Scientists and researchers never even knew where their work was ultimately headed.

Each section, located on separate floors, was autonomous and never interfaced with the other sections. Only the very senior staff members of Project Revive knew the true purpose of the research and the progress being made toward its end.

The purpose—combining DNA extracted from the bodies discovered at Roswell, New Mexico, and the remains exhumed from Aurora, Texas, with human embryos—was the sole reason the Facility existed.

Millions of experiments were conducted after science finally discovered ways to separate individual strands of DNA. Gene splicing advanced at staggering speed as techniques were provided to outside agencies in order to gather as many scientists and researchers as possible without their knowledge of how this research was ultimately to be used by those involved in Project Revive.

Those in the medical areas of the Facility knew only of their assigned role. All of the lab workers were told that the research focused on embryonic fertilization and stem-cell research. The result of their findings was purported to help infertile couples and to help eradicate genetically passed defects.

The DNA provided was never explained to those dealing directly with engineering the donor human eggs. The source of the eggs was never known. Nor was the identity of the human 'host.' The floor where the implanted females were kept was strictly off-limits except for the doctors and nurses dealing with each patient. Even they never knew how the eggs had been fertilized, or the results anticipated.

They only knew of the failures, the aborted fetuses, and when a live birth was successfully attained, they never saw the result. A special team provided by MJ 12 arrived to perform any necessary procedures. The members of these teams never met those working within the Facility other than the senior staff.

Everyone within the Facility and the teams brought in knew that all reference to MJ12 was strictly controlled, security was absolute, and any mention of the group or its purpose was forbidden under any circumstances. The funding, administration, and control were to be carried under what was known as an X file, never committed to written documents and "ears only" when information needed to be passed. All funds were funneled through other "black" projects.

The only public information ever to arise from the work of MJ 12 was Project Blue Book. This group's sole purpose was a method to provide the public with the necessary view that the government was actively researching any phenomena concerning UFOs and that each event was to be explained as naturally occurring or the result of a man-made yet classified program.

The membership of MJ 12 changed throughout the years but never included more than twelve members at any one time and was so controlled that presidential approval was required. Additionally, each new member was submitted for approval by the current membership. Everyone on MJ 12 knew the repercussions resulting from any breach of intelligence. Anyone leaking any information would disappear and never be heard from again.

One special nurse, involved with the project for over twenty-five years, was selected once a viable "product" had finally arrived. The birth of the product and its daily care became her only assignment. She was to be a nurse, mother, teacher, and sole emotional provider as the product grew. Vicki Grubbs was the most important individual to the product.

Every effort, including constant reminders, was made to ensure that any emotional attachment to the product was avoided. It was never to be named, only referred to as the product. It was to be seen only as a scientific experiment, the disposable result of no more consequence than a used petri dish whose contents were toxic. This policy was to be strictly enforced. However, it was impossible in the end for Vicki to remain so detached. This attachment became her ultimate fate.

CHAPTER 5

Genetic manipulation has been in the public domain since the mid-1980s. Tremendous research into the secrets of our DNA (deoxyribonucleic acid) has taken place within the scientific community. Amazing results have been presented to the public. Examples of this, such as the cloned sheep "Dolly," have been reported in various medical and scientific journals over the past few decades.

Basically, there are three means of manipulating the genetic makeup of plants or animals using current technology. Each has its own merits and its unique drawbacks. These three are: 1. Somatic cell manipulation—known as gene therapy, involves inserting specific genes into the cells of an existing plant or animal. 2. Cloning—copying the entire genetic makeup of an existing plant or animal. 3. Germline manipulation—changing the genetic makeup of an embryo by specific gene placement.

These techniques, while revolutionary within the civilian scientific fields, came mostly from previous research and study by one of the most secretive programs ever developed by the U.S. government. Much technology, such as that which produced Teflon and fiber optics, have become common products today and were initially developed by the U.S. government's space program. The use of a global positioning system (GPS) has become so commonplace that our cars come equipped from the factory. Palm-sized GPSs exist for even pedestrians to walk to the nearest drug store or restaurant. Cell phones come with every conceivable option—music, email, GPS, and, yes, communication between you, your friends, or anyone else with access to that particular wave of electronic information. Most of these and today's electronic products were first developed by the government for military use.

The research conducted by governmental organizations has seen dramatic advances in genetic programs as well. Certain aspects of earlier "breakthroughs" have been placed within cooperative civilian research facilities to assist public programs or to increase the number of scientists working on a specific issue. All new developments, of course, must first be presented to a certain governmental organization for evaluation prior to corporate announcement or use.

Of primary interest to the governmental organizations operating deep within the Department of Health and the Center for Disease Control is research in germline manipulation. The true recipient of this information is buried so deeply, with so many layers, and is only noted as an "info to," that tracing the flow of this information to the ultimate user is impossible.

The technologies available to the civilian world could be compared to an iceberg. While an enormous amount of information and technology is apparent, the part hidden below the surface is almost ten times as great. Occasionally, corporate or research scientists will solve a particular problem; that information is immediately incorporated into the government's program.

Germline manipulation is especially troublesome. While the use of animals such as mice or rabbits will provide a new generation in a relatively short period of time, humans procreate much more slowly. Problems that develop after birth, sometimes midway through the life cycle, become apparent quickly in mice but may require forty years or more to present themselves in humans.

Additionally, certain traits are due to multiple combinations of genes, while at other times, a single gene may dictate numerous traits. Also, the interaction between genes varies depending on their exact placement. The problem is not just difficult—it can be compared to solving a jigsaw puzzle of a hundred billion pieces, all white, with only minuscule differences.

However, it has been done. Neither you nor I will probably ever know unless some major problem arises that opens the vault of a most secretive program, and the result of decades of work escapes into our world.

CHAPTER 6

It was while James, then a Captain, was working deep beneath the hangars that he met Vicki. Whether it was the long hours trapped together or the strict security requirements that brought them together, something provided the initial ingredient, and after only one year of courtship, they were married in the base chapel.

Unable to have children of their own, they saw the workers at the facility as their own family, which is typical in any close-knit military organization. They never socialized with the topside military, only those assigned to Project Revive and the people working within the facility. Additionally, the project became their child.

Finally, after nearly forty years of marriage, James died. His death was a terrible blow to Vicki. The family, which had grown immensely during the last twenty years, had lost its closeness. The project, after thousands of failures and disappointments, had finally yielded potential success.

Now, nearly two years after James's death, Vicki was facing her own end. Without a child of her own, Vicki had begun to think of the project and its result as her own child. Even during the early success of this experiment, Vicki had identified with, nourished, and loved the tiny being, which was the first success of the years of work on the project.

Vicki had been there at the birth, had been mother, nurse, teacher, and protector. Of the select few who actually had knowledge of or had seen the final result, Vicki was the most involved in every aspect of the life of the being known only as GENE 1, standing for the first success of the Genetic Embryonic Nucleus Enhancement Program.

Affectionately known simply as Gene, the twenty years of nurturing, loving, and closeness between Vicki and Gene had resulted in a bond as strong as that between any mother and her child.

Now that Vicki knew she could no longer be there to keep Gene safe, she also knew that she had to do something to ensure his future. Over time, she had developed a distrust of those in Washington and of the military as to the use of Gene.

They wanted him primarily as an instrument of science, wanted to use any intelligence to further their attempts at discovering the uses of the mechanical aspects of all the UFO pieces, including ships currently being evaluated deep within the fringes of Area 51.

Vicki also knew that once they had used Gene to the limits of his capacity, he would become a liability and could not remain alive. Knowledge of his existence could never be released, even outside the few at Project Revive, and no one could ever let this information leak. For sure, Gene could never be known to exist.

Knowledge of her impending demise gave her little reason to fear anything they could do to her. Maternal instinct drove her to rationalize what she was about to do. Much as any mother will risk almost certain death to protect her child, Vicki knew she was already dead. Knowing this, there was nothing to prevent her from saving her only child.

With a basic understanding of the security systems and having evolved even closer to one of her late husband's closest friends, she devised a plan that, while not absolutely foolproof, at least stood a fair chance of success. She could never deny knowledge or even hope that she would not be caught. Vicki hoped that no one else could be proven guilty of assisting her.

Presenting her plan to Lieutenant Colonel Don Pratka, the closest friend she and James had ever known, she hoped that he would know how to bypass the security systems to enable her to get Gene out of the facility. Don had been on the security force since before James had been assigned. They had been instrumental in developing most of the systems in use today, and he would know if any chance of success existed.

Even with Don's participation, Vicki had little faith in the success of the escape but knew that she had to try. She could not die knowing she had let Gene become merely a tool for the military and science. To her, Gene was truly her child, and she had to take any chance to ensure his survival.

She had bought used clothes which would help him blend into the outside world. Faded jeans, T-shirts, sneakers, a baseball cap, and an old jacket would provide Gene with a new start. Vicki had saved enough money for Gene to get out of Fort Worth and survive for months, if necessary until he got a job and a new identity.

His appearance, fortunately, would allow him to pass as one of the many illegals working all over the state or nation. Somewhat small in stature, his skin was lighter than most Hispanics, and there was a slightly noticeable Asian look to his eyes, but he probably would never draw sufficient attention to warrant questioning. Although his head was a little large for the rest of his body, with a ball cap on and keeping his eyes down, he could blend with the almost socially invisible illegal crowd.

Shortly after midnight, during the shift change at the security post, Vicki dressed Gene in his new clothes and walked toward the exit point. Don had chosen this shift in order to send the other members of his squad to check different areas of the facility. This left him alone in the central security office.

As Vicki approached with Gene, disguised as a maintenance man in case she was noticed, Don forced an overload on the main electrical system, providing the power to the security systems. During the power surge, both the security cameras and locking systems dropped offline for almost a minute while the electronic matrix searched for the fault, bypassed the overloaded system, and began its programmed power-up sequence.

With the cameras down and the locks released as a safety measure during power outages, Vicki hurried out of the remaining gates and into the empty hangar. Her car was parked in a reserved spot a short walk away, and she hurried to get off the base before Gene's departure was noticed. She knew the entire base would be locked down, and escape would be impossible if she failed to be outside the main gates of the base when the discovery was made.

It would take an extraordinary amount of luck for them to be off base; with more help from above than she thought possible, could they avoid being caught? Her own future set, Vicki only hoped that Don and the rest of the security personnel would not be investigated and punished.

Vicki drove Gene quickly away from the facility. If she could make it through the one guarded gate leading off base, she thought it would be possible to get Gene away from the future that lay in store for him if he remained within the confines of the military base, subject to the wishes of those she had come to distrust.

As she slowed down to exit the base, the guard at the gate stepped from the shack and motioned her to stop. The pole blocking her way out was lowered across the street, and a bright light shone on the area where she knew she would have to stop.

Coasting to a stop, she waited for the guard to approach her window before she turned to look at the uniformed man approaching her car. As he motioned for her to roll her window down, she quietly told Gene to look out the other window, away from the guard.

As she rolled the window down halfway, she said, "Yes, what seems to be the problem?"

The guard looked directly into the car and said, "Your base sticker is about to expire, ma'am. If you plan to be off base for more than two days, you will need to renew it before you leave tomorrow. The pass office will be open today but will close for three days after that."

"Thanks; I'll be back later this afternoon or tomorrow morning at the latest. I'll be sure to take care of it then. Anything else?" Vicki asked. "It's kind of cold, and I would like to get home after I drop this gentleman off. It's been a long shift today."

"No, Ma'am, just be careful, and don't forget about that sticker," the guard replied. Stepping back into his shack, he pushed the switch to raise the gate bar.

Vicki slowly drove out the gate and turned north on Highway 183. Her heart was finally beginning to return to its normal beating, and the sweat running down between her shoulder blades felt ice cold. Keeping her speed as close to the posted limit as possible, she drove on through the residential areas just outside the base.

"OK, Gene," she said, "I'm going to take you up to the Jacksboro Highway, just as we discussed. There is a small all-night gas station there where a lot of men gather to find work each day. I'm going to stop a block short of there; you have to walk the rest of the way."

"No problem," Gene answered. "I'll try to stay away from the crowd and in the shadows until I think I can get a ride out."

"Good, and don't try to contact me," Vicki said. "They will be watching me extremely closely once they find out you are missing. Get as far away as quickly as possible and contact as few people as possible. Any hint of your identification will mean they will take you back, and probably, you will never see the light of day again. I'm serious—they cannot have you or even knowledge of you known to the rest of the world. You have to disappear. Never try to contact anyone you have ever seen again. Your life depends on you becoming just another illegal working wherever you go."

Tears streamed down Vicki's face as she thought of never seeing her child again. Knowing that this was the only way to help Gene live was the only thing that kept her courage up. She no longer cared about the rest of her life, especially since it wasn't going to last much longer anyway.

The streetlights gave only pools of light as they drove north, faint light that provided only glimpses of Gene sitting quietly. With his slightly brown complexion and small stature, he would pass for an illegal Mexican to almost anyone. Even if you looked closely, you would see that his head was only slightly larger than normal for his size. His eyes were slightly sloped, giving him a somewhat oriental look, which disguised their larger-than-normal appearance.

Most people would notice something different but never realize Gene's true genetics. Most would barely give him a second glance. Just another of the thousands of illegal aliens in this part of the country; necessary to provide the labor to keep the economy going, but invisible once the job was done.

CHAPTER 7

As her car pulled over one block from the service station, Vicki knew that this was going to be the last time she could ever see Gene. Her emotions had been kept in check for so long now she could barely find the words to tell him all she felt. She had to let him go in order to save his life, and she had a slim hope that this would ever work.

As she looked at him, so young, with so much to offer the world, her heart was breaking. As the tears ran down her face, she said for the last time, "Gene, you know how I feel about this, but it is the only way. You have to disappear. I don't think I have ever had to make a decision this difficult in my entire life."

"I know, Vicki. It will be hard on me as well. I've never known anyone except you who cared for me as a person. Everyone else just wanted to see what I could do for them," Gene replied. "I guess this is the best I can hope for. Maybe after time has passed, I can see you again."

"No, never," answered Vicki. "You can never let anyone know you were ever involved with anything to do with the facility. You must never mention having been on the base. It will be extremely lucky if you ever get away. Promise me that you will get as far from here as quickly as possible and forget everything you have seen or know. Promise me that."

"I promise, Vicki, but I will never forget you and all you have done to help me. That and your love will remain with me forever," said Gene. "They may find me someday, but I will always have my memories. That they can never destroy."

Gene opened the door and looked for the last time at the lady who had been mother, friend, and teacher since birth. Stepping away into the darkness, he walked toward the lights of Jacksboro Highway and his uncertain future.

Vicki sat quietly, watching him walk away. "God, just let him get away quickly. Let him disappear and live as normal a life as possible."

Approaching the highway, Gene began looking for a chance to get a ride and put as many miles as possible between himself and his old home, the only home he had ever known.

Just ahead, he saw a group of men, ranging in age from teens to middle-aged, mostly Hispanic, in the parking lot of the service station's convenience store. As he watched, a pickup stopped, and a couple of minutes later, four of the men got in the bed, and the pickup left.

Gene walked to the store's side and waited just a few feet from most of the men. Several looked at him but paid him no more attention. As they waited, several more pickups came and went, taking two to four of the men each time.

Another pickup pulled up, the driver saying he needed one man for only a half day's work, offering $50 and transportation back after lunch. Gene quickly stepped to the truck and volunteered. "Go around and get in," the driver said, opening his door. "I need a cup of coffee. You want some?"

"Sure," replied Gene as he walked in front of the truck. "Black would be great."

Gene opened the passenger door and climbed into the seat. Shutting the door, he glanced around to see if anyone was paying any attention to him. Cars continued to pass on Jacksboro Highway without slowing, and everyone he could see appeared to have no interest in him at all.

The driver returned with two cups of coffee and a couple of donuts. Gene leaned over and opened the door for him and took the two coffees. "Thought you might like an early snack," said the driver. "If not, I can eat both."

"Thanks," answered Gene, "I appreciate it. Where are we heading?"

"Just north of Azle," said the driver. "My name is Ray, Ray Downey. What's yours?"

"Gene," he replied, "Gene Morales. I appreciate you picking me up. I just got laid off and need to find something to help out until I can find a new permanent job."

"Well, good luck. I only need four or five hours today. I've got some stalls that need cleaning. My wife just bought a couple of horses, and the barn hasn't been cleaned in years. You spent any time around horses?" Ray asked.

"No, but I think I can clean up what you need. The horses aren't there now, are they?"

"No, they are coming in a couple of days. Gotta have the vet check them out and get all their shots before we bring them here. Don't want any surprises after they get here," Ray said. "Should be light enough in a couple of hours to work outside. Until then, the barn has lights."

They continued on Highway 199 to Azle, turning north of 730. As they approached the edge of town, Ray said, "Just about eight more miles; should be no problem finishing before noon. You ever been up this way?"

Glancing out the window, Gene saw a sign saying Boyd was further north on Highway 730. "Yes," he said, "I've got a cousin up in Boyd. I go up there a couple of times a month. When we finish, could you take me there? It's probably a little closer than back to Fort Worth."

"No problem," replied Ray. "I need to go to Decatur this afternoon. I'll drop you on the way."

CHAPTER 8

Colonel Rick Erickson was visibly upset. The project was now at risk. Worse yet, it had been almost an hour since the discovery, and it now appeared that the "item" had managed to not only leave his quarters but had also escaped the lab, possibly even the base.

"OK," Rick said, "when was the last time he was positively seen, and where?"

The item under discussion, Gene, was the result of years of study and thousands of failures. Finally, after attempting every known, suspected, or educated guess, strands of DNA taken from the Aurora and Roswell donors were combined with human DNA, which actually produced a viable embryo, almost identical to modern man.

Thousands of failures, hundreds of scientists around the world, billions of dollars, and untold secrecy all led to the creation of the Genetic Embryo Nucleus Enhancement, or GENE as it came to be known.

Varying samples from both the Roswell crash and the Aurora crash have been studied and experimented with. Differing degrees of success, some failing to survive beyond an hour, others aborted months after placing the fertilized egg within the donor and unsuspecting female host.

Some had resulted in abnormal creations, having traits more resembling the alien side, others with the normal appearance of a human embryo but abnormal internal organs—the list of failures took volumes of data.

Finally, in 1980, GENE 90437 began life with a normal appearance and progressed through the next year with no abnormal external signs. The following year, he was formally renamed GENE 01, or just Gene for short. The computer model had finally hit on the magic combination. A lot of reference was made to the random collection of primordial elements that resulted in man's first appearance on Earth, the evolution from a single cell to the complex miracle of man.

Colonel Erickson quickly assembled the heads of the labs, security, engineering, facility maintenance, communications, White House liaison, and JRB liaison.

"All right, folks, we seem to have a major problem. Our prime star appears to be missing. The last positive sighting was over an hour ago. So far, no absolute guarantee of being out of the facility, and it is imperative that no information regarding this project, its location, or identity of Gene leave this complex," he told them.

"You have five minutes to prove either Gene is still here or provide me with the data showing the means and avenue of escape. Major Fleenor, you stay here and get your White House operative on the phone. The rest of you, five minutes, and be back here. Let's get going."

Colonel Erickson selected a line on the secure phone in the briefing room and dialed General Mike Nelson, Commander of the GENE project. "General, we have a problem that requires your presence. Potentially, a missing item that must be recovered or destroyed."

"I'll be there in ten minutes. Has Washington been informed?" the General asked.

"As we speak. Confirmation of status in less than five minutes, but it appears the item is gone," answered Rick.

Colonel Erickson listened for another minute, said, "Yes, sir," and hung up. "What's the word from Washington?" he asked Major Fleenor.

"They want immediate confirmation to start. A team of 'Retrievers' is enroute. Local agents are to be used as necessary. The preplanned cover story regarding a potentially dangerous escapee from some local prison will be sent to the press if Gene is proven gone."

"OK," Colonel Erickson said, "let's prepare a statement for the Fort Worth Star-Telegram and local TV. Use the Fort Hood facilities as a base for our escapee. Get me the Hood Base Commander on the line. Call the tower and tell them to stand by for arrival from Fort Hood and most likely from Washington before noon."

"Roger," Major Fleenor said. "When do you want the JRB Commander brought in?"

"Soon," replied Colonel Erickson. "We'll wait until confirmation of Gene's disappearance. But go ahead and give him a 'heads-up' on a meeting about noon."

CHAPTER 9

Ray drove north on 730 out of Azle about eight miles before turning onto an unpaved gravel road. After about two more miles, he pulled into a small ranch area, crossing an overgrown cattle guard, and said, "The barn is just ahead. After you get the stalls clean, if you have time, there is a little clean-up work here at the entrance if you want."

"No problem," said Gene as they crunched along the gravel. "I don't have anything else to do today. I can stay as long as you need me."

Pulling up to the barn, Ray shut off the engine and climbed out of the truck. Gene got out and walked around to the front, looking at the wooden barn and what little of the land he could see. This was his first glance at life outside the facility, other than being escorted to other military locations, always being accompanied by his guards and Vicki.

The thought of her brought on a quick feeling of depression and despair. He had to suppress any feelings he had to make sure no one noticed anything out of the ordinary. Otherwise, he could never escape, and Vicki, as well as he, would disappear forever.

As they walked into the barn, Ray switched on the lights. "There is a lot of old crap in these stalls as well as other junk piled here in the alley. I'll get you a shovel, a pitchfork, and a trailer to use. Just load everything on the trailer for now. I'll dump it when you finish," Ray said.

As Ray walked back out of the barn, Gene wandered down the alley, looking at the wooden stalls, peering into each through the iron bars comprising the upper half of the fronts. Most of the doors were open, showing the dirt floors and debris from years of disuse.

He heard an engine start, and shortly Ray pulled into the barn on a small John Deere tractor with a short trailer behind it.

Once inside the barn, Ray shut off the engine and climbed down. "This trailer should hold just about everything that needs to be removed. There is a wheelbarrow in one of the stalls you can use to move the crap to the trailer," he said. "The tools are in the bed of the trailer. I'll be up at the house for a few minutes. You get started, and I'll be back to see if you have any questions or need anything else."

"All right," Gene said, looking around. The newness of everything still evoked a feeling of fear that he would be found out, and Ray would either tell him to leave or, worse yet, call someone.

Ray turned and walked toward a small brick house about a hundred yards from the barn. As he disappeared into the dissipating darkness, Gene picked up a shovel from the bed of the trailer. The wooden handle and weight of the shovel felt strange, but after a couple of attempts, he began to find the rhythm and position of the blade to scoop into the soft material on the stall floors.

Leaving the shovel, he searched the other stalls, looking for the wheelbarrow. Most of what he saw he had seen in magazines or on the computer during his education back at the facility. Seeing their actual size and weight and learning how to use them was an education in itself.

Finding the wheelbarrow in another of the stalls, Gene pushed it to the trailer. How to get the material from the wheelbarrow onto the trailer posed another problem.

Seeing a couple of ten-foot-two-by twelves, Gene fashioned a ramp from the ground to the bed of the trailer. His knowledge from the lessons on physics and geometry now had a practical application. He was amazed that all the time spent learning what he considered unnecessary information just might prove to benefit his success of escape.

Gene began scooping all the loose debris from the stalls into the wheelbarrow, unloading it every few minutes. The physical exertion was not unpleasant but certainly different from the exercises he had as a daily routine back at the facility.

Ray returned just as the sun was beginning to rise in the east. A faint light began streaming into the barn, highlighting the dust particles floating through the interior. "Gonna be a nasty job. Lotta dust and crap. How's it going? I see you found the wheelbarrow, and it looks like you've found an easy way to unload it onto the trailer," he said. "Not bad for a city boy."

Gene paused with the shovel in his hands. "Not my first rodeo," he answered. "My dad always said, 'Work smart, not hard.' Guess a man can always learn the easy way instead of breaking his back the hard way."

"True enough," Ray said. "If you have everything you need, Mother's getting ready to cook some eggs. I'll come back in an hour or so when it's ready. You are certainly welcome to have Breakfast with us."

"Great. I'll try to have a couple of these done by then."

Ray turned and walked back toward the house. The sun was just now breaking above the horizon. As he walked along the path back to the house, he watched the early morning rays stretching across the dark blue sky overhead. *Another beautiful morning in the great state of Texas*, he thought. *Wonder how anyone could live anywhere else?*

CHAPTER 10

Ray opened the screen door and scraped his boots on the boot scraper his son had made for him out of old horseshoes and a hoof file. The top of the file was worn almost smooth from the years of use. Unless it had been raining, there was never a lot of dirt on the bottom of his boots, but the habit was born from too many times having his wife of forty years yelling at him for tracking her clean floors. A lot of memory in every rake of his boots.

Myrtle called as she heard the screen door slam, "Breakfast in thirty minutes. That hand down in the barn coming up?"

"Yeah, I think so. I'll go get him in a few minutes. Coffee still hot?" Ray asked as he sat in the old leather recliner. He reached for the TV remote and turned the set on as Myrtle came in with a hot cup of coffee.

As Ray looked up and thanked her, he noticed her face turned white, looking at the news program showing an aircraft flying through the sky, heading for a tall building in a large city.

"What's that?" asked Myrtle, watching as the aircraft continued toward the visible twin towers they both recognized as New York City.

Ray watched as the airplane headed straight for the towers, unable to take his eyes off the sight. Within seconds, they watched it slam into the North Tower, leaving a gaping hole in the side. Smoke was pouring out as the news cameras zoomed in.

"Holy shit," he exclaimed. "What in the world was that? How could someone not see that building? What would cause a pilot to fly right into the side of a building in broad daylight?"

Myrtle sat down, mesmerized by the horrific sight, unable to comprehend.

Neither Ray nor she could tear their eyes away. The announcer's voice continued to describe the scene, smoke now pouring from the side of the building, sirens sounding in the background, and the sight of people staring toward the scene.

As they sat watching, the cameras picked up another airplane turning through the sky. Just over ten minutes since they had seen the first tower hit, they watched in awe as a second airplane began to swing around toward the other tower. As they continued to watch, the aircraft hit the South Tower, slicing a gaping hole in the side, flames visible as it tore through the building.

"Something is wrong here," Ray said. "Nobody just runs an aircraft into a building like that. This isn't just an accident. What the hell is happening up there?"

As they sat, hypnotized by the tragic scene, the telephone began ringing. Picking up the phone, Ray answered, "Hello?" Listening for a second, he said, "Yeah, I'm watching. Nope, no idea. Gotta be some bunch of idiots, like those guys that bombed that place up in Oklahoma. OK, I gotta go. I'll let you know if I hear anything. Thanks.

That was Frankie. He's watching the same thing. You better check on your cooking—I think I smell something burning."

Myrtle got up to go to the kitchen. "I'm just going to turn everything off for now. I want to see what happened. Breakfast can wait."

For the next few minutes, they both sat drinking their coffee, watching as newspeople jockeyed back and forth with different camera shots or views as to what had happened. Just over thirty minutes later, news showed another aircraft hitting the front of the Pentagon.

"This is nuts," said Ray. "I just don't believe this. There has to be some explanation. Three airplanes, in less than an hour, hit three different buildings. How could someone get that many people, knowing how to fly those things, to do this?"

Myrtle just sat, too stunned to reply. Her cup of coffee, now cold, was still in her hands. "Thank God we don't know anybody up there," she thought. "Those poor people; how many dead or hurt? Why would anyone do this?"

Ray got up from his chair. "I'm going down to the barn. Not sure what to do now, but I'll tell the boy down there what's happening. He may have friends or family up there. I sure hope he doesn't."

Ray set his cup down on the table as he walked through the kitchen. Picking up his hat, he walked to the door, unsure of his next move. He stepped outside; the sun now bright and the air slightly crisp, he went down the well-worn path toward the barn.

As he entered, he could see several loads of manure, dirt, and other debris on the trailer. Gene was still in the first stall, the wheelbarrow parked just outside the open gate.

A cloud of dust hung over the stall as he heard the shovel scraping.

"Hey, Gene," he called, "come out for a minute. There's something that just came on the news. Not sure if it affects you, but I thought you might need to know."

Gene laid the shovel up against the side of the stall and walked to the gate. "What's this about?"

"There were three plane crashes up in New York and that area. I just wondered if you had any friends or relatives up there. Looks like a lot of people may have been hurt," Ray answered.

"Nope. None that I know of," Gene replied. "Most of my family and friends are down in Fort Worth, some in New Mexico, out around Roswell."

"Well, glad to hear that. I'm going to head into town in a few minutes and see if anyone there knows anything. If you want to keep working, that'll be fine with me. But if you want to knock off, I'll be glad to drop you off down in Azle or where I picked you up this morning," Ray said.

"I think I'll keep working. If you aren't back when I get done with these stalls, what do you want me to do?" Gene asked.

"Well, I guess just go up to the house. I'll tell my wife to pay you if I'm not back. If you need anything, ask her. She knows as much about this place as I do. I'll be sure to have the money sitting on the table. She'll take care of you," Ray told him. "If you still need work tomorrow, and I have time, I'll be glad to pick you up. Have Myrtle give you our phone number."

"Sure thing. I'd be glad to come back out. I'll probably try to catch a ride back to Fort Worth if you aren't back when I finish."

"Tell you what—have my wife drive you back into Fort Worth if I'm not back. She won't mind."

"Thanks. I'll see you when you get back, or I'll call tomorrow if I haven't found something. I appreciate your letting me work."

Ray turned and walked toward the pickup. As he opened the driver's door, Gene stood and watched as he started the truck, turned around, and drove away down the gravel drive, white dust rising off the road behind the tires.

Gene wasn't sure what had just happened, but he thought it just might give him the little break he needed.

Whatever had happened, it would at least take some of the pressure off him. At least, he hoped so. Anything that would give him extra time meant more miles. More miles meant more area they had to cover to find him. He knew that by now, his disappearance had been discovered. Vicki had probably been taken back to the facility and was undergoing a lot of questioning and threats. He was glad she had told him to keep his destination from her.

If she didn't know where he was headed, it would take them longer to figure it out.

Right now, he had to get out of here. The sign to Boyd had evoked some feeling when he had seen it. He wasn't sure why, but he knew he was going in that direction.

CHAPTER 11

The briefing room was filling up quietly. The tension was palpable. Never before had a situation arisen that was as significant as this. A pot of freshly brewed coffee was sitting on a side table. Sugar, cream, and their substitutes were readily available. A dozen plain white mugs rested upside down beside the spoons and napkins. Two boxes of donuts lay open.

Colonel Erickson was talking on the telephone as the last member of his staff entered and took a seat after grabbing a cup of coffee and a donut.

As he hung up the phone, Rick took his seat at the end of the table. "All right," he said, "let's have it. Is Gene gone or back in his quarters?"

"He is definitely gone," said Lt. Col. Mark Mallory, current head of security. "Every possible space has been searched. The videos show him leaving his quarters with Vicki Grubbs, and the electronic locks up to Level 2 have been bypassed by the security office. The video shows them arriving at Level 2, and a couple of minutes pass during the electrical changeover from external to internal power. We are still looking into the power shift, but we suspect someone in security was involved, along with Vicki."

"All right," said Colonel Erickson, "find out who's involved, round them up, and let's hope we can get it done before we have to implement our cover story. How long since he was positively seen in the facility?"

The buzzer on Colonel Erickson's phone sounded, announcing General Mike Nelson. He walked into the briefing room, and every one stood at attention. Motioning for them to sit back down, he took a cup of coffee and sat at the opposite end of the table from Rick.

"General," Colonel Erickson said, "thanks for coming so quickly.

We've just started with security—Lt. Col. Mark Mallory's area. He believes Gene has left and is probably assisted by someone from our group. It looks like Nurse Vicki Grubbs and possibly another person from security assisted in the departure from the facility. We still don't know the reason, but they have been gone at least two hours."

"All right, continue with your briefing," replied General Nelson. "We will talk at the end."

"Yes, sir. Major Fleenor, what is the status of your White House contact?" asked Rick.

Major Fleenor answered, "General Paul Modelle is en route. His estimated time of arrival is 1145 local. He's bringing twelve agents to assist in the search. President Bush has been notified, and General Modelle is to be briefed by noon and make his report to Washington within 1 hour of his arrival. Majestic 12 has been alerted."

"Lieutenant Colonel Mallory," asked Rick, "Have you analyzed the security systems and video to find out exactly how this was accomplished and made damn sure it can't be done again? The other 'projects' may still be at risk."

"Yes, sir," replied Mark. "The entire lock system was bypassed when the electrical system shifted. I have directed the facility maintenance personnel to reprogram the system to lock instead of open as a fail-safe in the event of an electrical problem. I'll provide data on the new procedures later today.

Also," continued Lieutenant Colonel Mallory, "the video cameras of the corridors were set to 'freeze' during a power shift. This left a gap of a couple of minutes, during which the video recorders held their last images, coinciding with the escape. Their power, unfortunately, is parallel with the rest of the security systems. The cameras themselves are on a separate circuit and have internal power. The video CD recorders stopped, held the last image, and then recorded after the power shift was complete. We are also redirecting the power supplies with internal batteries, picking up the recorders should another power shift occur."

"OK, boys and girls, here is what I want right now," said Colonel Erickson. "I want an old-fashioned lock, with an old-fashioned key, put on every goddamned door that leaves any level, section, secure room, or exit. These marvelous little toys of yours that use fingerprints, retinal scans, fecal smears, or any other 'technology' have failed. We cannot have the most classified projects in the most classified facility in the entire world just walk out the damn door because an electron farted. Do you understand? I want Lieutenant Colonel Mallory and Major Romine to get together when we break and present me with the plan. I want the absolute minimum number of keys, each lock to use a different key, and a system to transfer keys between shifts. I don't want a single computer chip, electrode, bit, bite, or anything else ensuring last-ditch security for my facility except brass and steel. Understand? And I want it installed before the sun sets on your happy asses!

All right, Colonel Lynch, what is your plan to get a handle on the publicity angle if we need it, and how far along are you?" asked Rick.

"Well, sir," Colonel Karyn Lynch answered, "I'm working on a story regarding the urgent need to find and capture an individual and that very little information will be available until certain security issues have been resolved. I plan on using an escapee being transferred to Fort Hood to avoid any verifiable base of escape."

"I am also working on a script for the local television stations," Karyn said, "that will be aired as soon as it is approved and taped here in our facility."

"All right," replied Rick, "Have a copy of the draft script ready for me before noon to brief General Modelle."

As Colonel Erickson prepared to adjourn the meeting, the phone rang.

"Rick Erickson," he answered. He listened for a minute and then hung up. "Turn on the television," he said. "Any local station or satellite channel."

Colonel Lynch rose and went to the overhead TV at the far end of the room. As she turned on the screen and selected Channel 4, there was a shot of smoke rising from one of the Twin Towers in New York City. As they watched, another aircraft appeared and flew directly into the other tower.

"Holy shit," said Colonel Erickson. "What the hell is going on?"

The newscaster continued his description of the obviously intentional crashes. As they watched, spellbound, the scenes of smoke rising over New York became etched forever in their memories.

"Major Fleenor," said Rick as his eyes never left the screen, "get Washington on the line and find out what is happening. This meeting is over. You all have your orders, and I'll get back to you as soon as I find out what this is about. Let's stay focused on our problems here. This is not the time to be distracted until we know the impact of the crashes and how it affects our situation. General Nelson, is there anything you would like to add?"

"Not right now, Rick," he answered. "I do want you to contact Colonel Moore and have her come to my office. I think she may have a way of assisting us in our search. Other than that, let's all get to work."

CHAPTER 12

Gene continued to clean the stalls while he thought this latest development over. The crashes in New York would surely dominate the news. He also knew that the facility could not publicly broadcast his disappearance, especially since neither the facility nor its projects were supposed to even exist.

The whole purpose of the facility was so cloaked in secrecy and shrouded in the fog of funding that the final recipient of the money was never known.

Since they couldn't use the media in their search, and attention was diverted to the events taking place so far away, it appeared to him that this was the perfect opportunity to fade into the countryside and create a new life.

He placed the shovel beside the trailer and walked toward the house. He had decided to head north on Highway 730 toward Boyd but needed to provide a little false information in the event he was ever tracked to Ray's place.

As he knocked on the door, he could hear the description of the carnage taking place in New York. Myrtle came to the door wearing an apron with a towel in her hands. "Yes," she said, "can I help you?"

"Yes, ma'am," Gene answered, "Ray hired me to clean the barn this morning, but I think I need to get back to Fort

Worth. I heard about the crashes, and I think I had better be with my family to make sure we have no friends or relatives up there. I don't think we do, but I better go find out."

"Well, Ray asked me to drive you back into town if he wasn't back, but I didn't expect you to be ready for another couple of hours," Myrtle replied.

"No need for you to take me," he said. "I can catch a ride to Azle easily enough, and it shouldn't be a problem to get home from there. I hate to have to leave before I finish, but I really do think I need to be there."

"No, no, that's all right. I do understand. I just wish I could help you get back into town. I know Ray would want me to help, but I've just started preparing some homemade bread, and I can't stop right now. Ray left your pay and our phone number. I'll go get it," she said as she turned away.

"That's OK," Gene said. "I didn't finish the work, so I can't accept any pay. I'm awfully sorry about that, and I hope Ray will let me come back tomorrow and finish. I'll get my cousin to drive me back out in the morning if that's all right?"

Myrtle turned back around and said, "I'm sure that would be just fine with Ray. I know he needs to get that barn cleaned out and ready for the horses, but another day won't make any difference. I'll tell him that you are coming back in the morning. You can work out the pay with him then. Thanks for stopping in and letting me know. Best of luck getting a ride; I sure wish I could be of more help. And I hope you don't have anyone close to you up in that awful mess. What a tragedy."

"Yes, ma'am, sure is. Well, thank you, and I guess I will see you in the morning," Gene said as he turned away and began walking along the gravel road toward the highway.

The gravel crunched beneath his shoes, and he could feel the rocks through the soles. It was a feeling that was a little uncomfortable at first since he had always walked on smooth surfaces or carpeted areas.

He wondered what else he was going to learn. Even the air out here was different. The smells of the dirt and the feeling of gravel beneath his feet were all new to him. He was actually seeing the things that he had only seen in pictures. Even more surprising was the way people were treating him.

All his time within the facility, only Vicki and a few others treated him as anything other than an experiment. They were constantly testing him, a daily routine of taking blood samples and measurements. He knew he was different but had never been told why he had been kept so isolated. He had always assumed that it had something to do with his health. Even his trips to another facility, guarded and always at night, had been in extremely sterile environments.

Arriving at the highway, Gene looked back at the house. He saw no one watching. As he started walking along the road toward Boyd, he inspected the grass along the sides, the fences, and everything else he saw. Cars and trucks rushed past him, never a glance back. He was starting to feel as if he was normal enough to fit in, even if he had no idea how this section of the world really worked. The years of study had provided a basic knowledge of things and what they might look like, but this was real, and it was amazing to be experiencing it. He just hoped he could continue to appear normal as each new thing happened.

CHAPTER 13

Colonel Erickson sat in General Nelson's office and once again glanced around the room. Much like any military officer's office, the walls were covered with photos spanning Mike's career, the so-called I love me décor. There were photos of the various aircraft Mike had flown, pictures of Mike with several Senators, Congressmen, and Presidents. Twenty-plus years of service were represented.

Numerous trophies and statues accumulated through the years sat gathering dust on the shelves and tops of the bookcases. Rick's office had the same type of mementos and family pictures. His years as a fighter pilot were also well documented.

Their careers had crossed paths several times over the years. Rick had first met General Nelson when Mike had been just a Captain and Rick a new Lieutenant, or 'brown bar.' Not only were they associated by profession and mutual respect, they were personal friends as well. Their wives and children had become close over the years, and each assignment together had created a close family bond.

Mike sat behind a large oak desk with only a telephone, message basket, and a single pen rising out of a holder in the shape of an F-4 Phantom—one of his first fighters and still his favorite. You never forgot your first fighter assignment.

The feeling of the power beneath you, the sensation of speed as you skimmed just feet above the surface, was something few ever experienced.

The bookcases held hundreds of books and manuals relating to this current project, with one cabinet devoted to CDs documenting the thousands of experiments. All of it was ready to dump into the heavily insulated burn container at a second's notice. None of the material in this office would ever leave the facility. The procedures and processes used to develop the project were so sensitive that civilian tests were comparatively antique.

"Rick," General Nelson said, "I'm sure you are aware of the ramifications if this project is compromised in the least. Both the mechanical program in Nevada and our program have survived over fifty years of secrecy. Now, if this becomes public, both programs will be in jeopardy. Nobody, from the Pope to the President, could predict the impact on today's world. Current views on religion, whether they be Christian, Muslim, Buddhist, or Jewish, would be proven wrong. People need these beliefs because religion is the one thing that much of the world clings to. Without something like that to cling to, their lives become meaningless."

"Yes, sir," said Rick, "I'm fully aware of that. As soon as the security people from Washington arrive, we will turn over every rock, open every door, and use every asset available. That includes the local police, Texas Highway Patrol, and every sheriff's office in the state."

The phone on Mike's desk flashed a red light and beeped once. He picked it up as he studied Rick. "Yes?" he answered. After listening for a few minutes, he hung up and said, "That was Washington. General Modelle's plane, along with the security forces, has been diverted to Memphis, Tennessee. Air traffic control is closing down the entire national airspace until further notice.

Also, the CIA and FBI have identified a group of Islamic radicals, probably tied to Osama Bin Laden and Al Qaeda, that appear to have been the reason behind the Trade Center crashes. All four of the crashes seem to be related. This information will be released to the public shortly.

OK, Rick," Mike said, "we can't wait on Washington now. Get the staff back together. We need to revise our plans to incorporate this information in our search. This may actually help us in enlisting the assistance and support of our outside agencies.

I've got a couple of phone calls to make. Set the meeting for fifteen minutes from now. Notify me when everyone is present."

"Yes, sir," he answered as he rose to leave. "Do you want the entire staff or just security, communications, and White House liaison?"

"Just you and those three will be sufficient for right now. Also, call General Brown at JRB and have him block thirty minutes for me in one hour," replied General Nelson.

CHAPTER 14

As Gene continued north, he never glanced back nor faced the traffic as you would when asking for a ride with the passing cars. He walked with his head slightly bent and watched the cattle along the fences, noticed the trash along the road, and tried to appear as if he were merely walking down the road.

After walking a little less than a mile, a pickup passed him and immediately slowed, braking to a stop just ahead of him. Gene felt immediately that something was wrong—that he had been discovered and was about to be caught. His fear mounting, he knew that he must not show any signs of distress.

As he approached the pickup, now half off the road in the ditch, he saw the window on the passenger side roll down. Stepping up to the side of the truck, Gene glanced inside.

"Howdy," said the driver, "need a ride?"

"Well," Gene replied, "I'm heading up to Decatur. Are you going up there?"

Since Gene had told Ray he was going to Boyd and Myrtle that he was going back to Fort Worth, he thought he would select a destination farther away in case the searchers who he knew would be coming ever asked anyone he had met.

"Nope, but I can get you as far as Boyd," the driver said. "It should be easy to get to Decatur from there. At least it will save you a few miles of walking."

"OK," said Gene, "I appreciate the lift." He opened the door and climbed into the truck.

"You from around here?" the driver asked.

"No, I'm from Fort Worth, but I have a cousin up in Decatur who told me I might find a few day's work up there."

"Really?" said the driver. "What type of work are you looking for?"

"Well," replied Gene, "my last job was what you might call a stable hand."

"By the way, my name is Butch, Butch North. What's yours?" the driver asked.

"Gene," he said, "Gene Morales."

"Well, Gene, it just happens that my stable hand at the equestrian center is leaving for a three-day vacation to take his wife to Arkansas this weekend. I'm kind of stuck doing all the cleaning and feeding while he is gone. Unless you are certain you have a job in Decatur, I could sure use someone for a few days."

"The job my cousin mentioned sure isn't a guarantee, and I don't know how long it was going to be," Gene replied. "I can always call him later and let him know I'm not going to be there for a couple of days."

"Great," Butch said. "How much do you know about horses?"

"Not much. I just mainly clean the stalls. Will I need to do much with the horses?"

"Not really. I was planning on doing it all myself, but it would help a lot to have someone else do the cleaning. I can take the horses out of their stalls after they eat in the mornings and bring them back from the pasture in the evening," Butch said. "All you would have to do is give them their feed in the mornings, clean the stalls after I take them out, and feed again in the evenings when I bring them in. Think you can handle that?"

"Sure. That was what I did best at my last job. I never messed with the horses. I just cleaned the empty stalls."

"Well, sounds like you've got a job then. My current hand will be around for the next day or so; he can show you just about all you need to know. When you aren't helping him clean, I have a few other little projects you could do. How does $50 a day, a room, and your meals sound?"

"That will be fine," said Gene. "Where is your place?"

"It's about halfway between Boyd and Rhome, just off of Highway 114. The name of the town is Aurora. My place there is the Equestrian Center of Aurora Vista. Ever heard of Aurora?"

Something within Gene's memory struggled to surface. He had the strangest feeling that somehow Aurora meant something to him. He knew he had never been there, couldn't remember ever having heard the name, but something strangely familiar was causing an eerie feeling.

"No, can't say I have," he answered. "Don't know if I've ever heard of it."

"Well," Butch said, "it's not much of a town, more of a community now. It's got some history, though. If you don't need anything right now, how about we go out to the stables? I'll show you where you will be staying, and you can meet Steve. He's the one you will be working with until he goes on vacation."

"That's fine," Gene said. "Would it be possible to get something to eat before we get there? I haven't eaten yet, and I'm starting to get a little hungry."

"No problem. I promised you meals, and since you've agreed to go to work, I'll stop, and we can have lunch. How's bar-b-que sound?"

"That will be fine. Anything sounds good right now."

They were just entering Boyd, and Butch turned right at the only stoplight in town. Going east on 114 about a block, he turned left into a parking slot in front of the Double K Bar-B-Que. "Best bar-b-que in town," he said. "Course, it's the only bar-b-que in town. Still, it eats good."

They pulled into the parking area and got out of the truck. Entering the restaurant, they walked to an empty table just inside the door. As they sat down, the waitress came up and said, "Hi, Butch. Eating, drinking, or just taking up space like you normally do?"

"Oh, Kay, you know I only come in here to see you. I force myself to throw up to make room for more food, just so I can see your smiling face."

"Still full of crap, I see. Dr Pepper?"

"You know me so well, Kay. Are you sure we weren't married once upon a time?"

"Not a chance. All my men have been good-looking. What do you want to drink?" she asked Gene.

"Dr Pepper would be fine," Gene answered.

"OK, be right back with your drinks," Kay said. "You know what you want to eat?"

"Give us a minute. I know, but this is his first time here. Try not to make it his last," Butch said as Kay walked away.

"The sliced brisket sandwich is good," he said. "All the bar-b-que is good. They make pretty good onion rings unless they overcook them."

"That sounds OK to me," Gene said. "Where can I wash my hands?"

"Just through that door. Two rooms, both unisex. I hope they have some towels this time. Gotta dry your hands on your shirt half the time," Butch said, getting up to go to the restrooms.

When they returned, Kay was setting their drinks down. "Ready?"

"Yes, ma'am. Two sliced brisket sandwiches, onion rings, not overcooked," Butch said.

"Be right out," Kay said as she walked to the window and placed their order in the kitchen.

CHAPTER 15

General Nelson walked into the central briefing room and sat down at the head of the table. It was still five or so minutes until the meeting was scheduled to begin. The escape of the product was going to cause more problems than any Mike had ever faced.

To remain detached, Mike had never thought of the product as a person. He knew full well the reason for developing it. To acknowledge it, to even use the name commonly used by those closest to it, meant acknowledging its humanity.

Mike had no qualms about killing. All his years in the military had taught him that times arose when it was vital to his country's security to dispose of the enemy. Sometimes, this was a single shot fired from a distant weapon at a single individual. Assassination was as useful a tool as any and sometimes the only way available.

Sometimes, just killing a single person would save countless others. If you could cut the head off the snake, the body would die, hopefully, before it could bite and inject its venom.

Since being appointed to MJ 12, Mike had held the ultimate secret within himself. Very few could ever know the effort it took to continue keeping this information secret.

Of course, he knew what the results would be if the rest of the world ever found out. After seeing all the information presented as to the extent of alien actions on Earth, he sometimes wondered how normal people would react if faced with the knowledge that every religious document written was false.

He knew that the vast majority of all wars ever fought, the most brutal of all actions committed by man, were in the name of religion. How could something that espoused nothing but good cause so much destruction?

It was now when the possibility that the knowledge of alien life might be brought to light, that he again worried about the results.

Colonel Erickson came into the room with his notebook under his arm and another folder stuffed with loose paper. "Well, sir," he said, "it looks like we are going to have to resolve this problem on our own. The FAA has closed down national airspace. It may be possible to get our people in Washington to get authorization for a couple of flights, but it will take more time than we have to get it going."

"I know," Mike said. "Waiting for Washington's assistance could mean losing our product or having this information break loose. We cannot stand for either to happen. We have to get the product back and make sure there are no traces of him left in the public's view."

Colonel Erickson took a seat immediately to Mike's right, opened his notebook to a clean page, and placed the folder beside it. "Coffee?" he asked as he walked to the table beside the oval desk. He picked up a clean cup from beside the always-present coffee urn and poured it full as he turned to look at Mike.

"No, thanks; I'm not sure my stomach can take any more of that black acid. If this little problem doesn't give me ulcers, that nasty little potion will."

Major Jerry Fleenor entered the room and nodded to both Mike and Rick. "Washington's mad as a hornet. If there was any way for them to have us all stripped naked and whipped with barbwire, I'm sure every living soul up there would gladly agree to beat us and throw us on a fire-ant hill. Can't blame them, though." Leaving his notebook on the table beside Rick's seat, he poured himself a cup and stood against the wall as they waited for the rest of the staff.

Colonel Karyn Lynch arrived, carrying several thick folders and two CDs in her hands. Taking a seat on General Nelson's left, she laid the folders on the table and walked to the disc player mounted just below the television set at the far end of the room.

"I have a few ideas and a sample of the information I think we need to present to the local media," she said as she returned to her seat. "I haven't notified any of my sources yet—waiting for your approval of this program."

Lieutenant Colonel. Mark Mallory entered and took the seat next to Karyn. "Sorry to be the last to arrive. Hope I haven't kept you waiting."

"No problem, but let's get this going. I still have to meet with General Brown at JRB to ensure we have his full support and access to his personnel if need be," said General Nelson. "Colonel Mallory, you're first. What happened?"

"Looks like for some reason, still undetermined, an overload on the security system electrical circuits caused a momentary power failure. This power failure resulted in the camera systems dropping offline, and all locks were spring-loaded to fail to the unlocked position. During the time for the backup power to analyze the failure, check the circuits for fault, and accept the load, our product was removed," he said.

"I know how it was accomplished, and I know who actually removed the product, but as of yet, I cannot absolutely confirm whether or not there was any other participant. I am positive that the timing of the removal was not coincidental. I suspect that Lieutenant Colonel Don Pratka, a senior security officer on duty at the time, was responsible for the power failure. It is absolutely certain that Vicki Grubbs took the product from his room and was last filmed walking toward the exit. The cameras verified that she was escorting the product.

She attempted to pass him off as a maintenance man, but it is obvious that it is our product."

"I was sure Vicki was involved," said General Nelson. "I know she got entirely too close to him, especially after her husband, James, passed away. I should have removed her from the program right after that. She was an integral part of this program, and without her, much of the education and basic raising of the product would have proven impossible. We needed someone like her to provide the necessary human traits required to make this program succeed.

However, that being said, I bear full responsibility for the failure associated with her being left in charge of that aspect of the program. I saw the growing intimacy long ago and thought it would be to our advantage. I was wrong. Now, I want her picked up and brought here immediately. I want her house gone through until we are certain there isn't a single speck of information regarding this program. I'll make the decision as to her disposition after we get her back and see what she has to tell us."

"OK, Karyn, what do you have?" General Nelson asked.

"Well, sir," Karyn responded, getting up from her chair and walking to the CD player and television. "I have pieced together a strategy to take advantage of the disaster at the World Trade Center and use the intelligence from the FBI and CIA to provide a cover story that should allow us to use the news media and public outrage to help in the search for our product."

"All right, proceed," General Nelson replied, sitting back in his seat. Knowing that it was possible that he alone bore the responsibility for this catastrophe weighed heavily on his mind. *"Damn it,"* he thought, *"Why didn't I see this coming. All the signs were there—losing a husband, knowledge of a certain death within mere months if not weeks. I should have pulled her out long ago."*

Karyn turned on the television, placed one of the CDs on the player, and returned to her seat with the remote. As she opened her folder and passed copies of photographs to the rest of the staff, she said, "These are pictures of our product taken just two months ago. As you can tell, the slight abnormalities are barely enough to draw attention under normal situations. If you compare them with the next photo, taken from one of the FBI pictures of one of the now-identified hijackers, you may not see a lot of similarities."

She paused for a minute while everyone studied the two photos. "Now, put the product's picture down and compare this photo with that of the hijackers. This picture is actually the one of the product, except we have digitally added a full beard and traditional Middle Eastern attire."

Waiting again as everyone studied the new photos, she asked, "Does anyone here recognize the product in the new photo? I know that when you know what it is, it looks like him, but placed beside the photo of the hijacker, would you have recognized him?"

"I'll be damned," Mike said, "I would never have recognized him. He's a little lighter, and his eyes are still somewhat Asian looking, but I think it is close enough that no one else would think differently, especially after looking at the ugly faces of those other bastards. Anyone think this would not work?"

The rest of the staff nodded their heads as they continued to compare both the original photo and the altered photo to that of the hijackers. "Looks good to me," said Colonel Erickson. "What exactly is your plan?"

Karyn turned and pointed the remote at the television and started the video player. "As you watch this, remember, it has been hastily thrown together, and some of the obvious flaws in the background and sound bites can be perfected within thirty minutes or so after approval of the plan."

The entire staff watched as a known local newscaster talked beside a blowup of the altered photo. Then, the screen showed the original photo of the product, replacing the altered one on the screen. The verbal portion of the tape was obviously not in sync with the picture, but the intent was clear. Portray the product as a suspected terrorist, looking like a Middle Easterner, and then show him as he actually appears.

CHAPTER 16

Kay returned to Butch and Gene's table with their sandwiches. "Here you go, boys. Enjoy," she said as she walked away. The restaurant was beginning to fill up with the local crowd. Although Boyd was a fairly small town, a lot of the nearby ranchers and other people came into town for lunch. Having only three places to eat, they were generally all busy at this time of day.

As they were eating, Butch looked up as someone sat down beside him. "Howdy, Mike," he said. "Momma, make you come to town for lunch?"

"Nope," he replied, "just tired of her cooking. Besides, a man needs to look at a different menu every now and then. Can't just eat chicken forever, no matter how much you love it. A little beef now and again keeps the appetite up."

"Yea," Butch replied, "that's kinda why I never bought a restaurant—I like the variety."

"You aren't just talking about food, are you? I know how you are about the women. Never seen you sit at the same table for too long," Mike said. "Me, I gotta slop at the same trough every night."

"Reckon, you made that decision on your own, didn't you?"

"Well, I guess I did get a little prodding to get harnessed to that little filly a few years ago. Didn't need too much, you know, but I never considered how long I'd be hitched to the plow!"

"Mike, this is Gene. He's going to be working out at the stables for a few days while my other hand is on vacation. Gene, this is Mike Jackson. We call him Mad Mike, the grouchiest man in town.

If you ever see him not looking like he's ready to chew your ass out about something, get a picture," Butch said.

"Don't pay him any attention," Mike said. "I'm the happiest man in the county. Got nothing but money and fine clothes. Nice to meet you."

Kay walked over and asked Mike what he wanted to drink as he picked up the menu. "Dr Pepper, Kay, since I know you won't let me have one of those Budweisers you keep hidden back there in the refrigerator," he answered.

"You know I don't have any beer here," she said, "Besides, I've seen you after you have a couple. Last time, you told me you would marry me if I could run your old lady off for you. I know that woman; she would whup my ass with one hand and be calling her lawyer with the other!"

"You got that right. She's not much to look at, but she does have a temper. Gotta love her for that."

"That's just not right, Mike," Kay said. "She's as pretty as a speckled pup in a fresh-painted red wagon. Now, you just order and let me get back to work."

"OK, chicken fried steak, tater tots, and lots of gravy," Mike said, laying the menu down. "And don't burn my steak."

"You're as bad as that boy there," Kay said, tapping Butch on his hat and walking away. "If you didn't like our food, you'd be down the road, bothering someone else."

"Mike, I gotta get out of here and get something done today besides visiting. If I owned an auction company like you, I could sit on my ass and sip cold drinks all day. Tell the missus I said hi and I'll see you later. Gene, you about ready?" Butch said as he got up and took his check to the cash register.

Gene slid his chair back and wiped his face on his napkin, still keeping his eyes from looking directly at anyone. "Nice to meet you," he mumbled as he started to the door."

Gene knew that the less anyone could see of his face, the less likely they could describe him if ever asked. This small town seemed like the perfect place to hide for a day or two, but he had certainly run into more people today than he would have wished. He just hoped they wouldn't remember him past being another of the day workers everybody was used to seeing.

As they got back into the truck, Butch asked, "Do you have a driver's license?"

"No," Gene replied. "I don't think I can get one here. Do I need one?" Gene knew that one of the things most of the illegals did not have was a driver's license. Most of them drove anyway and seemed to be more concerned with Immigration than the local police or traffic tickets.

"No, you don't need one, but I just thought that if you wanted any other work around here, you would need some sort of transportation. Most folks can't provide daily transportation for the hands," Butch replied as they pulled out of the parking area onto Highway 114.

As they drove east out of Boyd, Gene saw a sign for Highway 730, north to Decatur. "How far from here to the stables?" he asked.

"Oh, just a little over two miles or so. You need to stop for anything else?"

"No, just wondered how far it was so I would know how far it was to Decatur. If I talk to my cousin up there, I thought I would tell him where I was, and maybe he could come down some evening."

"It's about fifteen miles; he can either use Highway 287 or 730 south to 114 and then south on Old Base Road for a half mile to the stables. It's about the same distance either way. Prettier scenery on 730, though, especially when the bluebonnets and Indian paints are in bloom."

As they approached a stoplight, Butch said, "This is Farm Road 718, going to Newark. I live just down there where the white pipe fence is. It's about a mile by road over to the stables, so I can be there pretty quick if I'm home and need to get there."

They continued on through the stoplight and quickly came to Old Base Road. As they turned right, he said, "The next road down on 114 is Cemetery Road. There is supposed to be an alien buried there. The story is that back in 1897, a spaceship hit a windmill out here and crashed. The guy flying the thing died, and they buried him over there."

Gene suddenly sat up and looked toward the area Butch had mentioned. Something deep within his body stirred as if he had experienced a jolt of electricity.

He had never really known much about how he came to be at the facility in Fort Worth. He had heard things when Vicki and other lab people were discussing certain things regarding his 'parents.' He had assumed that the few mentions of an alien meant Mexican or some other nationality. Why was he having these feelings now out here? He had read about déjà vu, but the experience was totally foreign to him.

He had to sit back and slow his breathing down. His heart was still racing, and his vision had narrowed until he could only see through a tunnel of dark gray mist. Something within him related to this place, and he seemed to have no control over his feelings.

CHAPTER 17

Karyn stopped the video and turned off the television. "Now bear in mind that was just a quick production. I think we need to get the pictures cleaned up, coordinate with the FBI through our Washington office, and have them put our photo in with the other photos of known or suspected hijackers."

"I think you have a good plan, Karyn. Good work. Major Fleenor, get your contacts on the horn and have them put a bug in the FBI's ear that another suspect has been identified and have someone at either the CIA or FBI 'discover' our photo. Karyn, how long do you need to get these ready?" General Nelson asked.

"Within an hour," she replied. "I have already told the photo lab to be working on them. The beard and clothes will be modeled by one of the technicians, and once both the model and the original photo are computerized, we can have a picture that can't be told from a real one."

"Great. Major Fleenor, you need to leave now and start the ball rolling with Washington. Let me know immediately if you run into any problems," Mike said.

Major Fleenor gathered his notebook and the photos as he got up. "Yes, sir," he answered. "I don't think there will be any problem on my end. I'll let you know as soon as I have coordinated with Washington. Not to bring up another issue, but we probably need to have a name for our terrorist, don't we?"

"Guess you're right about that. Karyn, while you're getting the photos ready, find us a name. Make sure it sounds Egyptian or Iranian or like any other of those ragheaded assholes. Get the name to Jerry as soon as you can. Both of you, get going and brief Rick on your progress. I expect this whole operation to be completed, with the picture on every television in America, within the hour. Got that?"

Major Jerry Fleenor and Colonel Karyn Lynch nodded and left the room as General Nelson turned to Lieutenant Colonel Mallory. "Mark," he said, "Have you got Vicki Grubbs in custody? I want to talk to her right now. And I want Don Pratka locked up away from her until we can either clear him or send him to an early grave."

"I sent a team to Vicki's house with orders to arrest her and bring her back, along with any material they could find in her house. She is on her way right now, and the 'cleaning crew' is going through her house with electronic gear as well as hand searching every square inch. All of her personal bank accounts and credit cards have been red-tagged in case there is any activity on them," Lieutenant Colonel Mallory replied.

"OK, let Rick know when you have things cleaned up and what you have found. Go ahead and take care of the 'accommodations' for our new guests."

"Yes, sir," Mark replied, gathering his notes and getting up. "Colonel Erickson, I'll notify your secretary when I have any new information." Knowing that this lapse in security was going to ultimately bite him in the ass, Mark was going to have to be very aggressive in following the general's orders. He would be extremely lucky if this wasn't his last job with the Air Force.

Security breaches of this magnitude had destroyed many careers before him, and the lucky few who survived never saw another promotion.

"All right now, Rick. I think we have at least a start on getting our project back without having to come up with the bogus escapee. This plan will galvanize the entire nation into helping us. I doubt if there is a single red-blooded American with a television set that's not ready to hang any camel-riding raghead from the nearest tree, especially down here in Texas. These old boys kind of have a history of taking care of problems rather quickly," Mike said.

"Yes, sir. That they do. However, we need to make sure that we are the first, if not the only ones involved in the actual capture. I recommend we have Karyn contact our friends in Washington, who can listen in as necessary and notify us directly if any sightings happen. We do not want any other agency to get our project. Too many questions would come up, and we can't stand the answers," Rick said.

"Right. Tell Karyn to get on it as soon as we have a name to provide. Also, I think we need to provide an alias. I doubt if the project will use any raghead name on his own. And if he happens to see his picture on the news, he will certainly be careful of using any name. I know everyone working directly with him has taken to calling him Gene. I would bet that if he has made contact with anyone this far, that is the name he would have used. He will probably change it after that, but it will at least put us on his trail until then.

"Also, Rick, call General Brown at JRB and cancel our meeting. We don't need his assistance on our plan, and I'm sure he will be getting direction from Washington on how to use his troops regarding the real terrorist issues," Mike said. "Let's get out of here and make this work. When you get back to your office, have Colonel Moore come see me immediately."

"Yes, sir," Rick replied as he gathered his notes and took his empty coffee cup back to the table. "Would you like me to schedule another meeting for the same group again?"

"Not right now. You stay on top of Karyn, Jerry, and Mark. I know they will hustle to get this rolling, but make sure you're coordinating. Let's not let step 2 get ahead of step 1. I want to be sure we have dotted all the i's and crossed all the t's. There can't be any mistakes. And regarding Lieutenant Colonel Mallory, I want you to pay particular attention to him. I know he's sweating his job right now, and for good reason. If you even think things aren't 110 percent in his area, call me immediately. He's not directly responsible, but his folks are, to a large degree. Just watch him is all I'm telling you."

"Yes, sir. I'll be in my office, or my secretary will have me paged if you need anything else," Rick said as he left the room.

CHAPTER 18

Just about one-half of a mile down Old Base Road, Butch turned into the equestrian center. Passing the gates, the gravel road led through oak trees down to the main barn. As he pulled his pickup into the parking area in front of the barn, he said, "Well, this is it. Let's go in, and I'll give you a quick tour so you'll know where everything is. Steve Rose should be around here somewhere. He's the guy who will show you what to do while he's on vacation."

As they got out of the truck, Gene glanced around at the corrals and the horses running out in the pasture. He couldn't help but be amazed at the sight. None of the films or pictures could truly capture the beauty of the horses with their tails streaming behind them as they chased each other across the green pasture.

"Come on into the barn, Gene. The office is just inside, and I'll show you where you can sleep and where the restroom is," Butch said as he entered the open sliding doors. "There is a refrigerator, a microwave, sink—just about everything you need. The only thing that's not down here is a shower. I'll have to make arrangements for you to either use the one in Steve's house or you'll have to use the water in the horse's wash area. It's got hot water but lacks a little privacy."

Gene looked at the individual stalls as he walked behind Butch. Each twelve-by-twelve-foot stall was constructed of two by-twelves with a metal door and steel rods across the front. Each stall had a layer of pine shavings covering the floor, water buckets, feed containers, and a rack for hay. Everything was clean and well-stocked.

"This is a lot nicer than the last place I worked," Gene noted as they walked down the cement alleyway. "It must take a lot of work to keep it clean. It doesn't even smell like the other place."

"Yeah, it takes work, but if it's done right every morning and kept clean, it really doesn't take too long. Steve does a good job and knows the quickest and easiest way to remove the waste and have the stalls ready when the horses are brought in each night," Butch answered as he opened the door to the office.

"There is a couch in here that folds out to make a bed. We have had to use it when we had a mare ready to foal and someone had to be here all night to watch over her. It's not the greatest bed, but fairly comfortable. Just through the door to the kitchen, there is a television. It's also connected to cameras and a video recorder that will tape the entire birth, and if any complications arise, it's available for the vet or the owner to see."

As Gene looked through the door, it reminded him of all the cameras, recorders, and monitors he had endured throughout his life back at the facility. Having every minute of his life subject to monitoring had always been there, and not being under scrutiny was a new experience.

As Butch led the way to the kitchen, he said, "The television only gets a couple of local stations. We haven't needed cable or satellite down here. But you can see the news and the weather. Speaking of news, I guess you saw what happened up in New York. When we find out who did that, we ought to reduce that country's capital city to a pile of mud and ash.

I know not everyone in those countries is responsible, but they are responsible for their government and religious actions. If they don't have the balls to change it, they have to take the punishment," he said.

"Yes, I saw some of it. Unbelievable," Gene answered.

Just then, Steve walked into the kitchen. "Morning, Butch," he said. "Kind of a late start for you, isn't it? Another late night out trying to find your kids a new momma?"

"Nope," Butch said. "Had to go to Azle this morning. We needed a couple of parts to repair some of the automatic water buckets. Damn horses will either eat it, crap on it, or tear it up. This is Gene Morales. He will take care of the cleaning and stuff while you are gone. Gene, this is Steve."

"Hello, Gene," Steve said, reaching out his hand, "Glad to meet you. I was afraid Butch was going to have to finally work for a change. That would mean he can't sleep till noon after honky-tonking all night."

"Nice to meet you," Gene replied.

"Well, Steve, I'll let you take Gene around and show him what to do. I've got to get started on those repairs. My daughters are coming in this evening, and I'll be driving to the airport to pick them up in a couple of hours. Poor little orphan girls; I sure do need to find them a new mama. Just heartbreaking, I tell you."

As Butch walked away, Steve said, "Orphans, hell, those kids are older than you. I think he just likes to chase the women any excuse he can use, but I'm sure he doesn't really want another wife. Just playmates.

I've already cleaned the stalls, so there's not much to do there, but I'll show you where the wheelbarrows, stall forks, feed, hay, and everything are," Steve said as he started down the aisle between the stalls. "Butch is a fair man, but he demands that this place stay clean and all the horses are taken care of. Just do it right, and you can't ask for a better boss."

CHAPTER 19

General Nelson was in his office, talking on the phone, when Colonel Amy Moore knocked on the door. Mike waved for her to come in as he continued to use the phone. Amy remained standing while she looked around the office. She had been in here on numerous occasions, especially when one of the projects had developed problems. None of those visits had been especially pleasant for her.

Amy was in charge of all the labs, and General Nelson held her personally responsible for both the success and the numerous failures. To be honest, Mike was as fair to her as possible, but he was under a lot of pressure to produce results. On several occasions, Amy had explained the difficulties involved, and Mike was well aware of them. Still, she always felt pressured to push harder and faster than the scientists and lab technicians could work.

Mike finally said goodbye and hung up the phone. "Please, have a seat, Amy," he said as he opened a folder lying on his desk.

Amy sat down and said, "You wanted to see me, sir?"

"Yes," Mike answered. "I'm not sure if you have been told yet, but we're positive that Vicki Grubbs took our pet project out of the facility sometime last night."

"Yes," she said. "Colonel Erickson called me a few minutes ago at home and told me to get in here as fast as I could. After I arrived, he gave me a brief description of what he thought had happened. He didn't tell me all the details but told me to expect to see you and be prepared to answer any of your questions."

"OK, well, first, I certainly don't hold you or your lab people responsible in any way. As a matter of fact, you and your people have performed in an outstanding manner. What I need from you and your people is any information that you can provide that might help us retrieve Gene. By the way, we have officially given him the name everyone has been using."

"Well, sir," Amy responded, feeling tremendous relief at this point, "exactly what sort of information do you need? I know his basic genetic makeup, but I will have to pull all the files on his particular program to get any great details. I can have the lab provide a complete set of the genetic material used if that would help."

"What I'm looking for is if you folks think that there may be any way to predict his actions once clear of this facility and the base. Is there any information encoded in his memory, or can you develop a profile of anticipated reactions to being alone for the first time in his life?"

"We have noted some 'residual' memories; however, it's not certain how much was encoded in the alien DNA we used. He did respond during some of the visits to Area 51 when he was questioned about some of the material. It seemed as if certain pieces, and specifically the spacecraft that was almost completely intact, did evoke some responses."

"Do you think he may have any way to communicate with another person or be telepathically?" Mike asked.

"Not that we have noticed. He has never appeared to have any abilities in that regard, but I can't say for certain. Of course, being in this facility, with all the countermeasures for electronic filtering, may have impaired his abilities. That may all change when he is outside in the open air. We never tested him for that ability other than with the psychologists, who used standardized testing for humans since they never knew exactly what he was," Amy answered.

"Do you know of any specific reason to believe he would have that type of ability?" Mike asked.

"Nucleotide base pairs that form the ladder in DNA are responsible for conveying genetic information. Back in the 1800s, it was proven that dominant and recessive traits could be passed. There are millions of ways nucleotide bases could have transferred some dominant gene that could activate encoded memories. If that were the case, those particular genes, even if dormant for a period of time, could be awakened by an outside stimulus and become activated," Amy answered.

"Would this be like the genes that produce the reactions in animals? Such as a herding dog to instinctively want to herd cattle or a homing pigeon to always return to a specific location?" Mike asked.

"Exactly. That is why certain breeds of dogs, such as blue heelers, will always try to push a cow by nipping at its heels. It appears that at some point in the dog's life, this irrepressible desire becomes dominant. It is so inbred that you can never completely stop the activity if the dog is not well trained, and it will still do this if left unattended around cattle," Amy said.

"All right, what I need you to do is determine exactly which genetic material was used in this case and what areas might be affected. If we can predict any behavior, whether genetically induced or influenced by those people who were in contact with him the majority of the time, we may be able to figure out where he will go," Mike told her. "I hope we can get enough information from Vicki when she's brought in to at least point us in the right direction."

"Yes, sir," Amy said as she got up. "I'll have all the records pulled and have our entire staff looking for anything that may help. I'll also get the records from all the psychology evaluations. I'll let you know as soon as I have anything."

Mike got up from his desk and walked around to where Amy was standing. As he led her to the door, he said, "Thanks, Amy. Get with Colonel Erickson when you leave. I want you to provide him with all the information. I'm pretty sure I will be spending the next few hours on the phone with Washington. Be sure no one in your section knows why we need this information. Too many people already know about this project, for my liking. I sure don't want anyone else knowing we've lost Gene, and he's out in public view."

"No problem, sir," Amy said. "No one in the lab knows exactly where the embryos went or where the genetic material they used came from. I've heard the speculations, but that is all it is. Speculation and most of it is so far off that they would never believe the truth if they found out."

CHAPTER 20

"OK, let's get to work," Steve said as he led Gene down the aisle to the covered horse walker. "In here with the walker, we keep all the feed stacked on a pallet and the alfalfa and hay in the mesh cage on the other side. With the price of hay today, we keep it locked when we aren't down here."

Gene looked at the huge six-armed walker in the center of the area and asked, "What do you use that for?" pointing to the arms with ropes hanging from each arm.

"When the weather is bad outside, and we can't turn the horses loose in the pasture, we put them on the walker to give them some exercise. It's run by an electric motor and transmission that goes from a slow walk to a gallop. When we are cleaning the stalls, and the horses have to be left inside, we put them on the walker while we are cleaning their stall," Steve answered.

"There are a couple of stalls over by the arena we used last weekend for some overnight boarders. I didn't get a chance to clean them after the horses left, so that will be a good place to show you how Butch likes it done," Steve remarked as he turned left into the covered arena. "There is a wheelbarrow over there and a couple of stall forks. Bring those with you, and we'll get started."

Gene saw the large wheelbarrows and went to get one and the stall forks leaning against the wall beside it. He loaded the forks in the wheelbarrow and pushed it, following Steve into the adjacent area.

As he entered the arena, he was surprised at the size of the covered area. In addition to the arena, he saw a row of stalls along the wall, separated from the arena by a wide dirt aisle. The row of overhead fluorescent lights showed down on the stalls, and he could see fans over each one.

"Let's start on this one," Steve said. "The manure is pretty dry now, but that only makes it easier to pick up. Like Butch says, 'Women and horseshit— they are both easier to pick up when they got a little age to them.' Let me have one of the forks and push the wheelbarrow up so the front is just inside the stall door."

Gene handed Steve a fork and pushed the wheelbarrow up to the stall door. As he watched, Steve began picking the dry manure up with the fork, gently shaking it as he lifted it. "Try not to remove too much of the shavings as you are cleaning. We will strip these when we are done, but this is the way to clean it without having to waste the shavings.

It also means less to haul out to the area where we dump and less we have to haul in from the shavings container. Not to mention, the shavings aren't cheap," Steve explained.

"Now," he said, "once all the manure you can see is removed, take the fork and move all the shavings to the sides of the stall. Then, you will find a wet spot where the horse pees. The hard part is getting all the wet shavings up all the way down to the clay floor. These horses will pee in the same spot most of the time and then tromp the wet shavings down. If you don't get the wet shavings up every day, it smells horrible and is a lot harder to clean.

Actually, the manure is just processed grass and grain. Once it dries, it's not a big deal to have a little left in the stall, kinda looks like dust. But the piss will cause problems if left.

It stinks and is bad for the horse's feet. Make sure you get any wet shavings up and sprinkle a little stall freshener on the area before you put any new shavings in.

Now, after you get the wet crap out, use the fork to spread the shavings back over the stall from against the wall. If you see any more manure while you do it, pick it up," Steve said as he picked up a couple of clumps of manure and spread the shavings back over the floor of the stall. "Any questions?"

"No, I don't think so," Gene answered.

"Good. You can clean the next one down while I start the sprinkler on the arena. Just call me if you need me."

Steve pushed the wheelbarrow down to the next stall and walked to a coiled hose down the aisle as Gene took a fork and entered the stall. Taking a sprinkler attached to a five-foot stand, he carried it into the arena and placed it in the center of one end. Coming back out of the arena, he turned the water on and watched to make sure the spray was reaching the end and both sides.

He walked back to where Gene was tossing the manure into the wheelbarrow and watched for a minute. "When you get down to the wet shavings, don't spread the other shavings out until I get back," he said.

"OK," Gene replied. "What do you want to do with all this when we are done?"

"I'll show you where to dump it after we finish these stalls. I'll go get some more *Stall Fresh* and be right back," Steve said as he walked back toward the aisle into the walker area.

Gene continued cleaning the stall and decided that this would be a good place to stay for a day or so. Something told him that he needed to be here. He couldn't exactly put his finger on it, but the feeling was getting stronger as he worked. At least he wasn't out in public. The few people he had met did not seem to notice anything different about him.

The fewer people he met and the farther he was from any city, the better he would be able to evade the people who were frantically searching for him. Maybe after another couple of days hiding here, he would know which way he needed to go to disappear forever.

CHAPTER 21

General Nelson was on the phone with Washington when his secretary, Kathy Blevins, notified him that Colonel Moore was requesting an audience. "Have her wait. I'll call you as soon as I finish this. You can show her in then," he said.

"Yes, sir," she replied as she closed the door and walked back to her desk in the outer office. Sitting down and looking at Amy, she said, "He says to wait, please. It shouldn't be too long. Would you like something to drink?"

"No, thanks," Amy said as she continued to read through a file sitting on her lap. Her briefcase was sitting on the chair next to her, open and stuffed with folders she had retrieved from her office.

After a couple of minutes, Mike opened his office door. "Please, come in," he said, holding the door open. "Kathy, call Colonel Erickson for me, please. Tell him I'm on my way. Be there in ten minutes." Mike waited until Amy had entered his office and his secretary was on the phone before he shut the door behind him.

"Have a seat, please," he said as he returned to his chair behind the desk. "Have you found anything that can help us?"

"I think so—at least, I believe we can narrow our search to two possibilities. If I'm wrong, we may have spent precious time looking in the wrong direction, but we need to cover these possibilities anyway," Amy said as she placed two files on Mike's desk.

"The two possibilities are probably obvious—he will either go toward Roswell, New Mexico, or he will head north toward Aurora. The genetic material used was taken from specimens brought from both locations. If there is any conveyed information from the nucleotide base pairs, these two places would be most likely."

"What if there is no transferred information? Have you looked at the psychologist reports to determine if there are any other possibilities?"

"Yes, but the best information would be from Vicki when you get her statements. Even if I am wrong regarding Roswell and Aurora, these areas need to be eliminated anyway. I do believe that there is a better chance of him heading west on I-30 or north on either 287 or I-35 than any other direction."

"OK, take your material to the conference room. Rick will be there shortly. Right now, he is taking Vicki's statements, and I'm going down there to listen in and get Rick's input on how to conduct our search. Please ask my secretary to notify Colonel Lynch to also meet us in fifteen minutes."

"Yes, sir," Amy said as she stood and gathered her files from Mike's desk. Placing her files in her briefcase, she walked to the door and opened it as Mike picked up his phone. Shutting the door, she made Mike's request to the secretary and started toward the conference room down the hall.

Mike waited as his call to Washington was being answered. The current head of MJ 12 was requesting an update every hour, and Mike needed to let him know in what direction the search was to begin. Washington was also working feverishly with the FAA to get General Modelle and his team back in the air. They were going to need every piece of their search team working as soon as possible if they were going to avoid detection and public disclosure.

It was now evident that four aircraft had been hijacked and crashed. The news, both local and national, carried nothing except updates and videos of each of the sites. Mike had more on his mind than the country's tragedy and could spend a few precious minutes watching. "Radical Muslims, Koran thumpers, Shiites, Sunnis, Al Qaeda, a bunch of worthless camel-shit-eating ragheads. We ought to flatten their worthless countries and send a pack of coyotes to pick the bones, then bury what's left in a hog farm," he said as he thought of the thousands of Americans affected by the heinous acts. "Hope George W. sends them a '*Get War*" card real soon. I just wish I could hand deliver it myself."

"Yes, sir," he said into the phone, "We've looked into the issue, and Colonel Moore has a couple of suggestions that hold some promise. Colonel Erickson is currently 'interviewing' Vicki Grubbs, and we will all meet after I talk to Rick. Our initial search will be primarily west toward Roswell and north toward Aurora. I'll call back after our meeting. It should be in about a half hour or so. No, sir, not yet, but I will let you know before any of the local stations are provided any material. It should definitely be provided to the national news programs first, and we will follow up with the locals and nationals as they contact our local FBI officials.

Yes, sir," Mike answered and placed the phone back on its stand. Taking a moment to gather his thoughts, he slowly placed all his files regarding the escape and tentative plans of recapture in his briefcase and walked to his door. It was going to be a long day. He planned to call his wife after the meeting and warn her that he would probably not be home that night. Quite possibly not even until the week was over. It wouldn't be the first time he had remained at the facility for a prolonged time, but this had to be the worst.

CHAPTER 22

Butch came walking back into the barn, carrying a yellow five-gallon bucket. "Well," he said, setting the bucket down in the aisle, "looks like another trip to town. I've found every piece I need to fix that leak except one one-half-inch coupling. Another $2.00 in gas for a seven-cent piece. Reminds me of being married, except it costs more than $2.00 and sure wasn't worth seven cents."

"How's Gene doing?" he asked.

"OK, I guess. I've shown him how you wanted it done, and he seems to be doing all right. I've got him cleaning the stalls by the arena. The horses were only in there for two nights, so they aren't too bad. I'm going to take some *Stall Fresh*, and we'll cover all of the wet spots. We also need to bring in a little clay to fill in where we've dug out the wet areas. They are getting some pretty low spots in them," Steve answered as he picked up the sack of zeolite.

"We need anything else from town?" Butch asked as he started to walk down the aisle to where his truck was parked.

"Not that I know of," Steve answered as he walked toward the arena side. "See you when you get back. Anything else you want me to show Gene?"

"Just make sure he does those stalls right. If he knows nothing else, I can take care of the rest of it by myself."

Steve continued into the arena and walked down the aisle toward the stall Gene was cleaning. "How's it going?" he asked.

"OK, I think. I've got all the manure and shavings out and dug down to where the dirt is. Are we going to put more shavings in?"

"No, we only put fresh shavings down when there is going to be a new horse in these stalls. Sprinkle a little of this stall freshener on the area that was wet, then take the water bucket out. We'll clean it with soap and bleach, so it'll be ready when we need it next time. Let's take this wheelbarrow around to the dump area now," Steve said as he picked up the water bucket and the two stall forks. "Just follow me around back. We'll dump that load and get this bucket cleaned. After you dump, go back to the other stall and bring that water bucket."

They walked through the barn and out to the side of the main stall area. Gene could see several small piles of dirty shavings and manure about fifty feet from the barn. He pushed the wheelbarrow over to the area and asked, "Anywhere in here?"

"Yeah, then put the wheelbarrow back in the walker area before you go get the other bucket. Bring it to the horse washing area in the main barn."

Gene lifted the handles of the wheelbarrow, surprised at how heavy it was. As the shavings and manure poured out on the ground, he looked around at the series of stalls located outside of the barn. He could see at least enough stalls for seventeen more horses. He also looked to see if any of the area was visible to neighbors or the road. It appeared that no one could see him unless they happened to be on the property. It was fairly well isolated, and the buildings and trees kept it almost invisible from the road. He felt fairly secure here. Other than Steve and Butch, he thought he could remain clear of most of the people living out in this fairly remote area.

He was still having strange feelings that worried him a little. He did not know why his interest was increasing in this particular part of the country, but he knew something was definitely different about the way he felt here. It was different from when he had seen the material at that other location where he had been taken several times.

Walking back into the barn, he hurried over to the stall where he had been working. Removing the water bucket from its hanger, he went back through the main barn to where Steve was running water into the other water bucket. "Waiting for the water to get hot," he said. "You need to clean all the buckets in each stall at least once a week. Helps keep any of the horses from getting sick or spreading whatever they have. Be sure to put the same bucket back in each stall after you're done cleaning them. Now the water is hot. Start with this soap. It will kill any bacteria, and then rinse it out; then, pour a little bleach in and wipe the bucket down with a wet rag. Rinse it and put it back in the stall. Got it?"

"Sure. Where do you put the bleach and soap when you are done?" Gene asked as he watched Steve finish rinsing out the first bucket.

"Just leave it sitting in here by the wall. Some of the horse owners use this soap when they wash their horses, especially those that use the pool."

"You have a pool for the horses?" Gene asked.

"Yeah, I'll show it to you when we're done here. There are several people who come out two or three times a week to swim their horses. Mostly guys that race quarter horses, some barrel racers, but some just to keep their horses in shape without having to run them all the time," Steve answered.

"Do many people come out here for that?" Gene asked, wondering how many more people would see him out here and remember him.

"Yeah, but they all know where to put their money for swimming their horses, and you don't really need to be down here. Most of the time it is in the afternoon, after five, so you won't have to deal with them. You should be finished with all the cleaning and feeding before they show up, and Butch is normally around in case they need help. Most of them know to bring an extra beer when they come. Old Butch does like a cold beer every now and then. Budweiser is his favorite, but he always says free beer is a good beer."

Gene felt a wave of relief. He had only met six people since leaving the facility, and none of them had paid any particular attention to him. Everyone he had met had been extremely nice, but he had no doubt that when the search came this way, they would remember him.

CHAPTER 23

General Nelson walked down the hall after leaving his office. He had told his secretary to notify Rick that he was on his way to interview Vicki about her actions regarding Gene. Rick had taken her to one of the secure cells one floor below the administration area. Each cell was furnished with a complete monitoring system, and everything within the cell was recorded both on camera and audio systems.

Mike entered the appropriate code for the door and entered. It was evident that Vicki had been rushed from her home. She wore a simple jogging suit with sneakers, her hair looked as if she had been pulled from the bed, and the lack of makeup was evidence of a hasty departure.

"Well, Rick," Mike said as he walked to the table and looked at Vicki, "what has she told you regarding Gene's disappearance and location?"

"Nothing, so far, only that she admits to taking him from the facility and dropping him off base."

"You've got to do better than that," Mike said as he sat down directly across the table from Vicki. "You know we have to get Gene back. You are fully aware of what we will do to keep this project from becoming public. I understand why you thought you had to do this, but what you did has repercussions far beyond your feelings for Gene."

Rick sat quietly beside Mike as he watched Vicki. Her head was hanging almost to her chest as she started to speak. The tears were running down her face, dripping on the table. "I only did what I had to do," she sobbed. "I know what you were going to do with him when you had what you wanted. He was more than a piece of material to me. He was like a son to me. I could not let you destroy him like you did all the other creations you produced here. He is a person. You can't just throw him away as if he never existed. I don't care what you do to me, but Gene has to have a life of his own.

You have no right to dispose of a life, even if it is created by you. Gene is part human, too. You have no right!"

"We determine what is right regarding this program," Mike said. "You knew when you started working here what we were doing and why each 'product' was to be handled as they were. What you have done is treason. Now, you can do what is right and help us minimize the damage. Your mistake in releasing Gene can't be undone, and you will face the consequences. However, you can help us prevent the obvious larger situation. Your ultimate fate is in your hands, and so are those of millions of people who cannot understand or accept this truth. Can't you see the ultimate result of your actions?"

"I know. But Gene's life is more precious to me than what you believe will happen if he is known to exist. The world has to accept other life off this planet at some time. The evidence keeps mounting up. Sooner or later, it has to be told. Protecting Gene will only speed up this understanding. Let him be your example of the good that can come from accepting the truth."

"That will never happen," Mike said. Rising from the table, Mike looked down at Vicki and shook his head slowly. "I'm sorry you feel that way, Vicki. I had hoped you would realize your mistake and assist us. Now, I must do whatever I possibly can to find Gene. That includes putting you through every means of interrogation at our disposal. We will have any information you possess. You do know that, so the rest is up to you."

Turning to Rick, he said, "Have her taken to the lab. I want her information within one hour. Do whatever is necessary. Meet me in the conference room in fifteen minutes. Leave the work to the technicians. Have them send the results to you as soon as they have any answers."

"Yes, sir. I'll take care of it and see you in the conference room. I've got to stop by and see what Lieutenant Colonel Pratka has told us. I don't think he knows anything that would help us find Gene, but I'll know for sure before I see you again." Standing up, Rick looked at Vicki and continued, "You can make this a lot easier on your friend Don, you know. Tell them what you know, and you just might save Don's career and keep him from being sent away. Think about it."

Rick followed Mike from the cell and turned down the corridor opposite Mike. His destination was located a few cells down from where Vicki was left. Lieutenant Colonel Pratka had already been subjected to intense questioning and had admitted to only knowing Vicki had planned the escape. His part of the plan had only to do with bypassing the security systems that allowed her to get Gene out of the facility. Maybe knowing Vicki's fate would prompt his memory if there was anything else he knew.

"This is one side of this business I detest," thought Rick as he approached the cell door. "Both of them are good people. They just got caught up in the emotional side of doing this work. Now, their emotions have started a crisis that will end in their own destruction."

CHAPTER 24

Butch just drove in and parked as Gene and Steve were coming out of the barn. "Done in there?" he asked as he shut the pickup door. "How about giving me a hand with this broken water line."

"Sure. You got the water shut off?" Steve asked as he joined Butch walking toward one of the outside stalls.

"Yep, but it's plenty muddy where the line broke, and water's been running for a couple of hours. I've got the PVC primer and glue already down there. Maybe Gene can learn to be a plumber. All you got to remember is, 'Shit runs downhill and payday's on Friday.' Hell, even my ex-wife knew that—at least all the shit ran down to me, and she damn sure knew when payday was," Butch said as he opened the ten-foot gate at the front of the pen.

"When we finish here, Gene wants to see the horse swimming pool," Steve said as he walked to the side of the water tank. "How did this one break?"

"Damned horses, they can sure tear shit up. Especially this one. That guy can open any gate that's not chained, untie any rope, and will let every other horse out he can get to. Should have named him Houdini," Butch replied. "Come here, Gene. You ever work with PVC pipe? Just knowing how to glue it together will come in handy one of these days."

Gene walked over to the hole Butch was working in and looked at the pipes running underground. "Never done it before," he said. "Why are there so many pipes in there?"

"Well, this is where the main pipe comes into these eight stalls. There is a shutoff right here before the other pipes lead to the other stalls. That way, I can shut down the entire side without shutting off the water to the main barn or the other outside stalls. Then, one pipe leads to this water trough's float, and one pipe runs the length of this area. Each stall has its own pipe, leading from one running along the fence, and each one of them has a shutoff before it reaches the float. That way, you can isolate any one stall or the entire area. This line also goes to the horse pool," Butch answered as he finished joining the pieces of pipe.

As he turned the water on, he watched for a minute to see if there were any leaks and, when satisfied there were none, shoveled the sand piled to the side back into the hole. "Gotta keep as much underground as possible. Keeps it from freezing and the horses from stomping on it. Except this idiot here—he can stick his nose under this rod and grab the pipe with his teeth. Glad I only have one like him here."

Butch picked up the bucket with the repair material and started back toward the barn. "Well, I was supposed to pick my kids up today, but with all the flights canceled, I don't know when they will get here. Damned ragheaded bastards are screwing up my life as well with what they did in New York. Bush ought to wipe those shit-eating assholes off the face of the earth. If they aren't fighting each other, they are causing problems everywhere else.

Steve, go get Blondie. We will swim her and let Gene see how it works. I'll be there as soon as I put this up," Butch said as he walked toward the barn.

"Come on, Gene, I'll show you where all the halters and lead ropes are. You ever halter a horse?" Steve said as they walked toward the tack room.

"No, just seen them on the horses," Gene replied.

"We keep a bunch of them hanging in here along with several lead ropes. Each stall in here has its own halter that is numbered to keep track of which stall the horse wearing it goes into. I know each horse's name and which stall it belongs to, but if anyone else is helping, all you got to do is put the horse with a *B-7* on its halter in stall B-7," said Steve as he picked up a halter and attached a lead rope to it.

"Blondie is out here in one of the back stalls. She is Butch's horse. He picked her up at the lion facility in Bridgeport. They take animals that need to be put down and feed them to the tigers and lions they keep up there. They called Butch about this one, and he went up to look at her.

She had tried to cut a hoof off. It looks like she got it caught in some barbed wire and sawed it until it was almost cut off. He doctored her twice a day for six months to save the foot. It took almost another year and a half of therapy to get her sound, but she's sure a pretty thing."

They walked down the aisle between the stalls and stopped in front of the gate where Blondie was standing. "She's a dappled gold palomino and sure is a good-looking thing. Has a great disposition, too. A real sweet horse. Butch doesn't like mares, says they're too moody, but I do think he's a little fond of this one."

As they entered the stall, the horse walked over to Steve and lowered her head. "Most of the horses here are trained to put their heads down when you walk up to them. Makes it a lot easier to put the halter or headstall on them," Steve said as he placed the halter over Blondie's nose. "Now, take the long strap on the right side over the head, behind the ears, and buckle it here where you hold it in your left hand. She will stand here as long as the lead rope is on the ground.

We can walk off, and when we come back, she will be standing right where you left her."

Steve picked up the lead rope that was attached to the halter and began walking to the gate. After opening the gate, he turned down between two stalls and headed toward the pool. "This horse won't kick, but be careful around them. Don't walk too close behind them," he said as he noticed Gene following right behind Blondie.

Butch was standing by the ramp leading down into the pool with a long lead rope in his hand. "How's my little lady?" he asked as he snapped the long lead to the halter and removed the rope Steve had been using. "Ready for a little swim?"

He walked along the left of the ramp as Blondie started walking down the cement ramp into the water. "It's twelve feet deep and sixty feet across," said Butch. "The ramp slopes down, so the horse is actually swimming before it gets into the actual pool. The ramps are concrete to provide stable footing as they go in or out, but the rest of the pool is clay. Nothing to brush against and get hurt on."

He continued out onto a bridge elevated about six inches off a metal tank in the center of the pool. As he walked further onto the bridge, it began to lower until it rested on the tank. Blondie was swimming alongside him as he stepped onto the tank. The bridge raised back up as he stepped onto the tank, leaving a gap between the bridge and the tank. "The springs raise the bridge so the lead rope can pass under it as the horse swims around the tank. All you have to do is stand here in the center and let the horse swim around you. When you are ready to come out, let the horse swim up the other ramp leading out and step up on the bridge. Your weight will bring it back down to the tank, and you just walk out.

I spent several days designing this system. It took several bottles of Jack Daniel's and a few beers to come up with this idea. I sure enjoyed that part. Digging this pool was a real pain, though. Ol' Mad Mike Jackson did the concrete work for me. You remember him, don't you, Gene? You met him at lunch today. Grouchiest man in the county but a better man you couldn't meet. When he gives you his word, it is rock solid. That's the way it used to be out here. Now, with the damned Yankees and city folks coming out, you gotta get a dozen lawyers and a notarized contract. Even that isn't worth the paper it's written on. Give me a man like Jackson, whose word and handshake mean something.

OK," Butch said as they walked back to the barn, "How about washing her down and putting her up for me, Steve. I gotta run home for a minute. I'll be back to take Gene to get something to eat after you bring in the other horses and get them fed."

"Sure thing, Butch," Steve said, taking the lead rope. "I'll show Gene how it's done."

CHAPTER 25

The conference room was still empty when General Nelson entered. Mike liked to be early whenever possible. It gave him a few minutes to think without a bunch of people around and to plan how he wanted to use the people coming in. He laid his briefcase on the table and opened it. Withdrawing several folders, he considered what had to be done with Vicki Grubbs and Don Pratka.

Vicki for sure had to disappear, but considering her medical condition, he debated keeping her here in the facility until she died. That would also allow her to work with Gene when they finally got him back. She could never be permitted to leave the facility again, and that would lead to several issues, but all in all, that would probably be the best solution. Mike felt sorry for the situation Vicki had gotten herself into, but the program could not stand public knowledge. His first obligation was to complete their mission and safeguard the program.

Lt Col. Don Pratka was a different issue. He did have some emotional attachment to Vicki, dating back to his friendship with her husband, James, before his death. He obviously had some empathy with Vicki's feelings toward Gene, but he was a military man and had sworn an oath to follow all lawful orders. Mike certainly wasn't about to court martial Don. That never happened in this program. MJ 12 had its own system of dealing with military members regarding the security surrounding the program. As much as he disliked it, he would have to send Don with the gentlemen coming down from Washington. They would provide the final solution to Don Pratka.

The door swung open, and Karyn walked in carrying her briefcase. "Well," she said, sitting it on the table, "as I told you earlier, I think the solution to our problem is in using the terrorist angle. It doesn't require any knowledge of where Gene went when he left, and it will ensure we get the support of the entire community, even the state and the rest of the country.

I'm sure you already know," Karyn continued, "there have been four crashes. What I propose is to inform the country that there were to be five. The members of that particular team did not get the chance to hijack their airplane because one of the key members did not make it to Boston."

"Sounds reasonable," Mike said. "Let's wait until the rest of the staff are here to fill in the details. After they hear about it, maybe they will have some ideas that might help implement it."

"Sure," Karyn said as she took a stack of folders from her briefcase and placed them around the table. "I have a brief scenario outlined here for everyone and a series of photos. I also have a CD with all the photos to show. The photo lab can make any changes to them we think necessary."

Colonel Erickson walked in and held the door as Amy followed him. "Not much new," Rick said as he walked around the table to take a seat on Mike's right. "Vicki's told us all she knows, I think. And Don doesn't really know what she did after she left. I'll fill you in when everyone's here." He took his seat and placed his briefcase on the floor by his side.

Amy took a seat opposite Rick at the table and placed her briefcase on the table. As she opened it and took out a folder stuffed with computer runs, she said, "Not much hard data, but some pretty good guesses as to what might be running through Gene's head."

Lt Col. Mark Mallory entered and took his seat beside Amy, laying a single folder on the table in front of him. General Nelson looked around the table and said, "All right, let's get started. First, Mark, what have you accomplished regarding tightening security?"

Mark stood up and passed a single sheet of paper from his folder to everyone. "As of right now, every single code for entry or exit has been changed. The paper in front of you has the codes necessary for your specific area. I would like for you to change those codes to something you want for your personnel and come to my office this afternoon to make the changes. That way, only you and your people will know your codes. Once everyone has made the changes, General Nelson can decide who gets access to each area outside his own.

I have also directed Major Cory Romine to design and implement the changes to our electrical grids. They will receive power from three independent sources, one of which will be its individual battery. Should any one source of electrical power drop, either one of the others will immediately pick up the load.

They are also being isolated from each other so that no two systems share a common line. Additionally, their fail-safe mode will be to lock any door that is closed. After the problem is resolved, each lock must be recoded by an individual authorized in that area.

Finally, the main exits have been fitted with a deadbolt that operates by mechanical means. The keys are to be kept by those individuals authorized by General Nelson. Even should we have a complete electrical failure, the batteries will power the electronic locks in each area for up to twelve hours."

"If the power cannot be restored within twelve hours, the locks remain in their locked position until another source of power can be provided," Cory said as he looked at General Nelson for his approval.

"OK, Cory. Thanks for rushing this through. I realize it's like locking the henhouse after the fox is inside, but at least we can be assured it won't happen again. That will be all for now. Come see me in the morning, and we'll go over access authorization for everyone," Mike told him.

As Cory rose and left the room, Mike said, "Rick, fill us in on what you have learned from Vicki and Don."

"Vicki admits to taking Gene out of the facility. I won't go into the reasons, but she fully intended for him to escape and hopefully never be caught. She did a pretty good job of planning, and truthfully, I don't think she knows exactly which way Gene went after she dropped him off this morning.

She said she did provide him with some clothes, a T-shirt, jeans, and a pair of sneakers. She also gave him a couple of thousand dollars, all in twenties. She said she drove him west and let him out in White Settlement. That would be the quickest way to get him out of town. The intersection of I-30 and 820 is right there, and he could probably get a ride at one of the truck stops in that area.

As I said when I came in, Don doesn't appear to know anything else regarding Vicki's plan. I think Vicki intentionally did not tell him for two reasons. Number 1, if he didn't know, he couldn't tell anyone. Number 2, I think Vicki actually believed that not knowing the full plan would prevent Don from being punished to any great extent.

Now, having said that we really do not know for sure which direction Gene took after being dropped off. I don't want to commit our search to any single direction until we have more information."

"I agree," Mike said. "Amy, what have you learned from your lab people?"

Amy opened the folder in front of her and said, "There is no absolute guarantee of this, but the genetic material primarily used came from the Roswell donors. Now, this is going to get a little scientific but bear with me, and I think you will know where I'm heading.

A single nucleotide polymorphism, or SNP, can be mapped within a gene. Some SNPs are linked to specific genes that are passed from generation to generation. Once thought to only be linked to mutated genes, we have discovered that other SNPs are linked to normal, healthy genetic material. By following the specific SNP, we can trace what genetic information should have been passed. Now, this only applies between generations as far as we know. But it may show areas within Gene that were derived from the genetic material we used when we engineered his embryo. Our research into the genes we used shows that almost 90% of the genetic material came from the Roswell donors, as I've already said. The remaining 10% came almost exclusively from the Aurora remains.

This would lead me to favor any instinctive behavior that would be based on Roswell's donors. There was very little from the physiologists that was useful. If I had to make a bet, I would favor Gene being drawn to Roswell if there is any 'homing' instinct."

"OK," Mike said, "there are two reasons for concentrating our search westward. Karyn, go ahead and tell us your plan and whether or not this information has any bearing on it."

Karyn rose from her seat and walked toward the television and disc player. "In front of you is a folder that outlines my plan." She turned the television on and placed a CD in the player. As the television came on, a series of pictures showed brightly on the screen.

"As you see, I have placed photos of six individuals on the screen. All six appear to be of Middle Eastern descent. A copy of each photo is in the folder you have. One of these photos is of Gene, digitally enhanced to make him appear of the same origin as the others. The beard and attire have been altered to look identical to the other pictures.

I have made tentative plans, coordinated with both the FBI and CIA, to release information regarding the 'fifth' team of hijackers. They will supply these photos to the national media, and it will be released that one of these teams failed to arrive in Boston. The reason he failed to arrive is because he was denied boarding here at DFW airport."

Karyn paused a minute as everyone looked at the photos in their folders and then at the pictures on the television screen. "Now," she said, "we can use this information to enlist the entire state's population as well as police forces to concentrate on the DFW area. We can also request assistance from the military here at the JRB.

Local news will certainly play this up as a nationwide search for these 'members' is mounted. We don't need to have any mention of our facility involved. As far as the general public knows, Gene is a part of a terrorist organization tied to the Al Qaeda group. The only problem I see is if he is captured by either civilians around here or the local police, he may not live to be returned.

These folks around here might not see any reason for him to ever be seen again if they find him. I know what a backhoe and a sack of lime will do as far as removing any evidence of an animal or human. I've heard enough stories from some of the old-timers around here to know it wouldn't be the first time someone disappeared."

"I think you have a good plan, Karyn," Mike said. "Does anyone have anything to add or see any flaws? If not, let's see what we need to do to get it implemented. Major Fleenor, get your Washington folks on the horn and brief them on this. If you need a little horsepower, have them call General Modelle or me."

"One other thing," Karyn said as she turned the television off and removed her disc. "In the folder, you also have a picture of Gene, dressed as described by Colonel Erickson following his initial interview with Vicki. I have additional photos of the other members of this 'team' without beards and wearing similar clothes. These pictures will be shown beside their 'native attire' pictures. That should help locate Gene. Of course, I doubt if any of the others are ever found since they don't really exist. The only drawback is if someone is misidentified as one of them."

"Well, if there aren't any suggestions at this time, let's get busy implementing this plan. Everyone, be sure to coordinate through Rick with any changes you think would improve our current strategy," Mike said, rising from his chair. "That issue of misidentifying someone doesn't bother me in the least—maybe a few 7-11 owners or taxi drivers end up in those lime baths Karyn mentioned. I just hope there are enough backhoes around and enough lime to get the job done right. I'll notify you when I think we need to get back together."

CHAPTER 26

Gene and Steve were coming out of the barn when Butch drove up. Steve was carrying a lead rope and walked to a series of holding pens located just outside the main barn. All the horses were standing in the pasture just outside the gate, leading to the stalls and holding pens. "Looks like they are ready for dinner," Butch said as he joined them. "I'll give you a hand getting them in. Gene, you can stand over here in this empty pen for now. It goes real fast if you work together.

Most of the horses know which stall they belong in and will stand in front of it if their gate is closed. Those going into the barn will stand in the aisle, waiting to be taken in. You just can't let them all in at once. They will bunch up like fat women at an all-you-can-eat buffet," he said as he opened the gate and let two horses in.

The horses came running into the alleyway as Butch shut the gate before the next horse could come in. Steve opened the gate to one of the holding pens to let the first horse run in. Butch opened the gate to one of the stalls as the horse stood in front of it, pawing the ground.

Steve looped the lead rope around the horse's neck in the holding pen and led it out a gate on the side toward the barn. "About half the horses go inside the barn. The rest of them go in these stalls. Some people want their horses inside where it's always dry and out of the weather. It costs more for that, but we always try to provide whatever service the owners want," Butch said as he shut the gate on the other horse after it entered its stall.

He walked back down the aisle and reopened the gate to let a couple of more horses into the alleyway. Steve had just returned and was coming back through the holding pens. Both of the next two horses were run into the holding pens, and the gates closed as Steve put the lead rope on another horse and led it toward the barn.

"OK," Butch said as he opened the gate to the pasture again, letting two more horses in, "Come on in here and open the gate to the stall at the end. These two go in the stalls beside each other down there. They'll follow you to their stalls and wait for you to open their gates. As soon as you get them in, I'll let two more in here."

Gene was a little apprehensive as he walked down the alleyway behind the horses. He wasn't entirely comfortable being this close to a thousand-pound animal that could kick him across the fence if it decided to. The horses stood beside the gates at the end and watched as he walked up. As he opened the gates, the horses ran in and went straight to the feed troughs under the three-sided shed.

He shut the gates and started back toward Butch as Steve came back from taking another horse into the barn. "Not too tough. The horses do most of the work. You could probably open every stall and just let them find their own way in, but sure as hell, one of the idiots would take off and find its way out to the highway. The owners really don't want to have to scoop their horses up off the road with a shovel," Butch said as he opened the gates again.

After they finished putting all the horses in their stalls, Steve took Gene to get a wheelbarrow full of feed pellets. As they walked through the barn, he showed Gene how much each horse got and which horses had special feed placed in front of their stalls.

"There are a few horses that the owners want to have a different feed. There are signs in front of those stalls showing what feed to give them. Their feed is normally sitting beside the stall, but sometimes you have to get another sack from the storage area.

Also, some of the horses get coastal hay, and others get alfalfa. The signs show which hay to use. Once we have fed each horse in here, we will feed the horses in the outside stalls. There is a wheelbarrow in an empty stall out there with their feed."

They walked out of the barn and pushed the wheelbarrow down the alleyway, feeding each horse as they came to its stall. "Make sure you look at their water while you are in here putting their feed in the troughs. They all have an automatic watering system, but sometimes something goes wrong, and they either don't put out enough water or stick open and let it run over. If it's getting dirty, just slosh some of the water out and let it refill."

After finishing the outside horses, they returned to the barn as Butch was finishing refilling the water buckets for each horse. "That's it for now," Butch said. "Gene and I are going into town for something to eat. I'll bring him back in an hour or so. You can show him the routine for the shutdown when we get back."

Gene and Butch went out to the truck as Steve started walking to his house. "We'll stop by my house for a minute before we go into town. I'll get some sheets, a pillow, and a couple of blankets for you. There's a coffeemaker and some cups already here," Butch said as he got into the truck.

After Gene got in, they drove back out onto Old Base Road. "I'll take you through Aurora Vista," he said as he turned off the road. "They started building this subdivision about six years ago. A lot of nice homes, but I wish these folks had stayed back in town. I liked it much better before I had 150 houses just across my fence.

All this construction out here has caused a few problems. The roads can't handle all the new traffic, and it's hard to even get on 114 in the mornings or evenings when these folks are going to work or coming home. They've already put in one stop light, and I think there will be more as people continue to move out here.

Of course, there's the problem of their dogs. I've had a few problems with loose dogs chasing the horses in the pasture. I've told the owners to keep their dogs off my property because they can cause the horses to get hurt. The animal control people have told them also, but the bottom line is if I keep seeing the same dogs running after the horses, I'll shoot them. This isn't a town, and people have to understand that. The dogcatcher out here is the landowner's gun."

As they came out of the residential area, Butch turned right on Farm to Market 718. "My place starts here on the right where the white pipe fence is. The first gate leads down to my arena and barn. The symbol across the top of the gate is my brand. It is read Check 6. That's a term used by pilots to tell another one to look behind him. Basically means to watch your ass. It applies as much out here as it did when I was in the Air Force. Some of these 'good old boys' will take you to the cleaners if given a chance.

That's especially true of horse trainers or traders. I'd trust a used-car salesman before I'd trust them. There are a few good ones, but they are as rare as hen's teeth," he said as he pulled into the driveway leading to his house.

"Come on in. I'll get the sheets and stuff. There are also a couple of my old hats here that might fit you. Can't have you running around bareheaded. Might even make you look like a cowboy," he said as he opened the door to the house.

CHAPTER 27

Mike returned to his office. As he sat at his desk, he noticed how late it was getting. In addition to his clock telling him it was almost five in the afternoon, his stomach was letting him know it had been too long since he had eaten.

"Kathy, can you please come in for a second?" he spoke into the intercom, sitting on his desk. He had noticed that his secretary of more than five years never left until he was gone. Kathy had also been every facility commander's personal secretary for over twenty-five years. If one person in this facility knew its history, she would be the one.

"Yes, sir?" she said as she opened the office door carrying her notepad. "What can I do for you?"

"It's been a long day. I know I haven't eaten, and I'm pretty sure the rest of the staff is getting to be as hungry as I am. Would you please give them all a call, and let's see who would like to have something brought in? Take a quick poll and see what they want. Something we can go pick up pretty quickly."

"Yes, sir," she answered. "Who do you want me to call?"

"Let's get Rick, Karyn, Amy, and Jerry. And you, of course. We'll eat in the conference room, say, in about thirty minutes."

"Yes, sir," she replied as she started back toward the office door. "What would you like to have? I think the closest places with carryout are Chinese, Mexican, burgers, and pizza."

"I really don't care," he said as he picked up his telephone. "If there isn't any general consensus, limit it to a couple of choices that are located close enough to get without too much trouble, and I'll send Major Romine to get it. I'll be happy with whatever the majority wants."

Karyn closed the door behind her, and Mike began dialing the phone. As he waited for it to be answered, he opened the folder Karyn had provided him at their last meeting.

"General Modelle," he said into the phone, "Mike Nelson. I wanted to give you a quick update in case information is getting to you too slowly following your diversion to Memphis."

Mike sat listening for a couple of minutes as he spread the photos of Gene and the other 'terrorists' across his desk. "Yes, Sir. I'll notify General Brown and make sure the tower is expecting your arrival. I'll have the hangar here ready and the vehicles you've requested. No 'code' as always, I assume.

Got it. A couple of things before I hang up. Colonel Lynch's plan seems to be the best choice to proceed with, and you'll get the full briefing when you get here. Major Fleenor is coordinating with the White House, and I'm sure it's going smoothly. But with you and your people caught out of place, I'm not completely comfortable with the locations and secure communications with other players. Some of the information isn't getting out as fast to those who need to know as I would like.

The other thing we need to cover—and you'll have time to make your decision before you arrive—is the disposition of Vicki Grubbs and Lt. Col. Don Pratka. By the time you get here, we will have any further useful information available from them. I believe we can still use Vicki for our purpose, and considering her medical situation, I propose leaving her in the facility for now. Don—that's another matter entirely. I favor immediate disposal.

Yes, sir. I understand. No, sir, I plan on sending the entire staff home for the night. We can't really accomplish much more today, and it will take some time for our plan to be implemented after I give my final review and approval. Yes, sir. I'll have a briefing set up for one hour after you arrive."

Mike listened for another minute and said, "Yes, sir," and replaced the phone. He sat back in his chair and closed his eyes for a while. "Gonna be a short night, and if any of us really gets any sleep, it will be a miracle," he thought as he rubbed his eyes and arched his back. "This has got to be the worst nightmare in my life. No sense in worrying about it now. Just get the plan going and take care of it as we can. I'll have to make sure General Modelle knows this was more my fault than anyone else's. I sure don't want them taking any blame. Except, of course, Don Pratka. His actions are inexcusable."

"General, I've taken everyone's requests, and it's pizza for all of them. Major Romine just left to pick them up. I ordered five, all different. I hope that's OK," Kathy said as she leaned through the open door. "Cory should be back in about fifteen to twenty minutes. Will there be anything else?"

"Yeah, would you please have Rick, Karyn, Amy, and Jerry meet me in the conference room in five minutes? Also, make sure the VIP suite is ready; General Modelle will be arriving early in the morning. He finally got special clearance to leave Memphis and fly in. I think we need to find a motel somewhere on the west side, around where 820 and I-30 meet, that has enough rooms for twelve people.

When you pick one, see if you can get all the rooms together. Make the reservations under the Immigration and Naturalization Service. We still have an account with them, don't we?"

"Yes, sir. It is still an active account. I know we used it last year when we had the team back at Roswell. I'll have the reservations ready before the pizza gets here. Shall I call you when Cory gets here?"

"Yes, please. I'll let you know then when to come into the conference room. Also, please get some Dr Peppers from the lounge. If anybody wants anything else, they can get it when we start eating. You live in Texas, by god, you ought to drink Dr Pepper," Mike said as he stood up. "I'll be in the conference room. Send the rest in as soon as you get ahold of them. Thanks, Kathy.

You know, Kathy, if we could get those damned Muslims to drink Dr Pepper, I think we might even make decent people out of them. Look what it's done for the Yankees that have lived here for a while. Some of them have turned out just fine," Mike said, smiling as he gathered his notes and started for the door.

"The only ones that don't seem to come around to civil behavior are those damned Okies. I'd rather have a sister in a whorehouse than a cousin living in Oklahoma."

"Now, sir," Kathy smiled, "you know I'm an Okie."

"Yeah, but at least you married a Texan. I think most of the Okie has been rubbed off, and a lot of *Texan* poked in," Mike remarked, barely able to keep from laughing. "You got here as quick as you could."

CHAPTER 28

As Butch led the way into the house, Gene noticed several old hats hanging on racks made of old horseshoes. Butch told him, "Take one of those hats there and see if it fits. Get a felt one, though. Only Yankees and city dudes wear straw hats after Labor Day. That's one way to tell a real cowboy—look at the hat. Those have a little character and will make you look like you've been wearing it awhile."

Butch continued through the house as Gene picked an old black hat off the rack. Placing it on his head, he looked around for a mirror. Walking down the hall toward where Butch had gone, he came into the kitchen.

Butch was listening to a message on his phone recorder as he entered. "Well, that's good news," he said as the recording ended. "My girls were stuck down in San Antonio visiting some friends when those Muslim shitheads ran our airplanes into the Trade Center in New York. Their flight up here was canceled, but they are renting a car and driving up. They should be here in a couple of hours."

Looking at Gene as he was trying the hat on, he remarked, "You've got it tilted like an old Chevy with a fat lady in the seat. Put it on your head straight so it sits square on your head. Only queers tilt their hats. Can't have folks thinking I'd have one of those cocksuckers hanging around out here. That would start more fights than five bulls in a one-cow pasture trying to figure out who got to run his fruity little ass back to San Fag-cisco.”

As he helped Gene adjust the hat, he asked him, “Where are you from, anyway? Looks like you may have a little of the Orient in you.”

“Well,” Gene answered, “I’m mainly from out around Roswell, New Mexico. Not really sure where all my family’s from. Guess there could have been someone besides Mexican back there somewhere.”

“Yeah, I’ve seen lots of servicemen bring a wife home from overseas. Guess one of your grandpappys got a little lonely overseas or married up with one of the ones born over here,” Butch said as he stepped back and checked the way the hat looked.

“Step into the bathroom there and look in the mirror. The way a man wears his hat says a lot about him. I’ll go get a pair of boots my youngest daughter left. I think they’ll fit you.”

Gene stepped into the bathroom and looked in the mirror. The hat changed his appearance drastically. It would probably help disguise him and delay anyone from recognizing him when they were shown his picture. He knew that was inevitable. Even now, he was afraid that the search was well underway and the noose tightening every minute. He didn’t really understand why it seemed so important now for him to be in this area.

Butch came back carrying a pair of well-scuffed black ropers. “Here, try these on. It’s time for my poor little orphan girl to get a new pair anyway. She’s not really country, but she makes a good hand for me when she’s around. Just wish I could find her a new mama. Need one young enough to be around after I’m gone. Just breaks my heart to think of my little girls being orphaned like that.”

Gene followed Butch into the living room and sat down on the couch. As he took his sneakers off, he looked around the room. A lot of Southwest art, statues of Indians, paintings of them, and sand paintings adorned the walls and tables.

"Are you Native American?" he asked as he tried on one of the boots.

"Not really. My grandmother was Cherokee, so I'm only about one-quarter. I don't claim to be or do any of the 'Indian' stuff, like live on a reservation or follow their old ways. I'm just another mixed-blood American. I believe if you are going to live in this country, you better be an American. Speak our language, obey our laws, and forget about what happened way back before you or I were born.

It doesn't matter who or where your great-great-great whatever was or came from. You are an American now. Stand up for yourself and become a part of the country where you live, or go home," he said. "That's just the way I feel."

After getting both boots on, Gene stood up and walked around the room. "How do they feel?" Butch asked. "Not too tight?"

"No, feels all right. Sure feels different than regular shoes," he answered.

"Well, everything a cowboy wears is for a purpose. Hats are for keeping the sun, rain, or snow off. Boots are tall to keep from rubbing your ankles and legs on the stirrups and help stop snakebites. Long-sleeved shirts protect your arms, and good-quality jeans protect your legs.

If you stick around for long, we gotta get you some longer jeans too. Those are about four inches too short for wearing boots. They need to kind of drag the ground in the back and crease a couple of times in the front. That way, when you are sitting in a saddle, they cover your boot top.

Short ones end up looking like Andy Griffith playing Sheriff Taylor or Barney Fife. Kind of doofus looking. But this will do for now.

I'm gonna get some sheets and stuff. If you want a Dr Pepper, there's some in the refrigerator. Help yourself," Butch said as he walked down the hall toward the bedrooms.

"I'll get a couple of blankets in case it turns cold. The heater in the office works all right, but it's better to have these and not need them than to need them and not have them."

While he was waiting, Gene wandered out of the living room, looking at the rest of the house. He had never been to another person's house and was surprised at the decoration. Old saddles were displayed on racks made from old horseshoes and baskets made from old ropes. Pictures of cowboys roping cattle were hung along one wall as he walked into a large room with a pool table. On the opposite wall were several pictures of airplanes and a stand holding an old pilot's helmet, and several medals were resting on a bronze bust of a fighter pilot.

"You fly these?" Gene asked as Butch came back carrying an armload of bedding.

"Yep, in a former life. Flew for the airlines, too. Spent almost forty years of my life making a living pushing iron through the sky. Now, I'm just another dumb-ass country boy trying to earn a living.

Let's go grab something to eat. I'm sure you're hungry, and I need to get some food in my belly before those two alcoholics I call daughters get here and make me stay up all night drinking Jack Daniel's. I think they're trying to kill me. That's why I've got to hurry up and find them a sweet lil' mama," Butch said as he walked toward the door. "You eat 'yard bird'?"

"Eat what?" Gene asked as he followed him out of the house to the truck.

"Yard bird, chicken, the original white meat."

"Yes," he replied, wondering how anyone could ever learn this strange brand of English called Texan. "Are we going back to where we ate lunch?"

"Nope, we're going to a little place called Southern Delight," Butch said. "The old gal that runs it is Nanette Bost. She's a good ol' gal, cooks some pretty good chicken; good burgers too," he said, climbing into the truck.

CHAPTER 29

Mike entered the conference room and laid his folders on the table. He had begun to feel a little better now that there was a promising plan being developed. He had surely dreaded having to use the escaped prisoner story. It would have led to too many questions, and since it involved other agencies, he never felt entirely comfortable depending on their ability to keep the story straight. All it might take was one nosey reporter asking the wrong person the wrong question, and it would fall apart.

As unfortunate as it was, the current situation provided a much better solution regarding the search. He knew they could limit the number of people knowing the truth, and control over those organizations was never in doubt. MJ 12 had been using them for years to channel information where it suited their purpose.

Colonel Lynch came into the room carrying several folders. As she sat them on the table, she told Mike, "I've completed the package for the 'fifth airplane' group. Jerry has been in contact with the White House, and they are ready to implement the plan as soon as it arrives. What are we using for the transmission system?"

"General Modelle will be here in the morning and will use one of his dedicated sat-com links," Mike answered as

Amy and Rick came into the room. "Have a seat, folks. As soon as Jerry gets here, we have a couple of items to firm up, and Kathy's got Cory bringing pizza. We just need to have this discussion together before we let them in."

Major Fleenor came in and set his briefcase on the table. As he sat down, he opened it and pulled several sheets of paper out. Passing one to each of the people sitting around the table, he said, "Here are the names of the principal players we will work with within the CIA and FBI. They have been told that the information they are receiving was gathered by various organizations. And since it is being provided by one of their own agencies, it will never be questioned."

"Good. As I've just told Karyn, General Modelle will be here early tomorrow morning. He received permission from the FAA—with a little assistance from President Bush, I'm sure—to continue his flight from Memphis to here. He will be staying with us in the VIP suite, and his team will be put in a motel on the west side of Fort Worth. Kathy has made the reservations.

We will provide Paul with a briefing as soon as he is settled. I want everything ready to roll as soon as he gives us his approval. I don't see any reason for him to delay implementation. I want each of you to brief him on your specific actions and be sure to be completely honest when you answer any questions. Tell him of any problem issues that may arise and how you can handle them if they do.

Amy, your area is probably the only one that relies mostly on guesswork since there is no hard data supporting your theories. Be sure you let him know that. I'm sure he will surmise that anyway, but I want him to know we are being as up-front as possible.

Along with that, don't fail to mention that even if Gene isn't headed west, we still need to cover that possibility. Worst case, we may lose a little time going in the wrong direction.

Karyn," he continued, "I want you to follow Amy in the briefing. Have your slideshow ready and a copy of the news release you've prepared. Have a list of all the news agencies that will receive our release, especially the local ones. Be as specific as possible when you discuss the coverage in this area. Let him know that Fort Worth, Denton, Abilene, Dallas, and other stations will replay these tapes repeatedly throughout the day. Stress the rural areas that will see it.

Jerry, I want you next. Give General Modelle a list of the people we are using to get the 'fifth airplane' story generated. I'm sure he will want to see exactly who holds our fate in their hands. If I know Paul, he will be placing several calls before he transmits the information to get this started. It's not because of your rank—he'd do the same if I'd set it up, and as a matter of fact, so would I.

This whole plan depends on making damn sure the world believes there was another group of terrorists ready to hijack another airplane. I trust each and every one of you to do this right. You have all been involved with this project long enough to know its significance and what would happen if word ever leaked out.

Rick, I want you to brief Paul last. I'm sure I will be busy with him for the first few hours, and I want him to know you are fully up to speed with the plan. Additionally, I want you to set up a communications center dedicated to the search team. Karyn can help you wherever you need. You will more than likely be the one who will manage the operation once underway. I don't know yet exactly what equipment the team is bringing, but get the specifics so Karyn can make sure it is compatible with our equipment.

Finally, I plan to take full responsibility for this problem. Of all the people involved, I alone should have seen the problem growing. Following James's death, and especially after Vicki was diagnosed with cancer, I should have had her replaced. At the least, I should have taken measures to safeguard our product.

As much as we try to approach our work scientifically, there are times our emotions get in the way of what we know needs to be done. To Vicki, Gene was her son. She spent too much time mothering him. It is for that reason I am recommending to General Modelle that she be kept here for her remaining time. I think she can still be useful in the time she has left to complete Gene's education and encourage him to develop any mental progress that we have hoped for since the inception of this program.

However, I intend to recommend that Lieutenant Colonel Pratka be disposed of. I want you to know that these decisions are mine and mine alone. Regardless of his feelings, Don had the responsibility to notify either Rick or myself of Vicki's plan. Had we been notified, we may have been able to convince Vicki that keeping Gene here would have been in his best interest.

Well, that's about it for now. After we eat, if any of you have any questions or suggestions, I will be in my office for an hour or so. Please stop by, and we'll talk. Rick, do you have anything to add?"

"No, sir, I think we have a good chance of success. Everyone has done a great job of planning this, and I especially want to thank Karyn for coming up with the idea. I would like everyone to stop by my office tomorrow morning before we brief General Modelle just to let me know of any changes or if there have been any last-minute problems. Any issues brought up will be brought directly to you, sir," Rick said as he looked at each of the staff members.

"All right then," Mike said. "Jerry, would you please see if Kathy and Cory are out there? I think it's time to eat and wrap this day up."

CHAPTER 30

As they drove out from Butch's house, the sun was getting low in the west. "Pretty this time of day," Butch said. "My dad always said that sunrise was the best time of the day. I'm pretty happy watching the sunset. Looks just as pretty, and you don't have to get up near as early to see it."

They turned left on 114 and headed toward Boyd. Traffic was fairly heavy as they drove, and Butch remarked, "When I moved out here, there weren't five cars in line from Rhome to Boyd at any one time. Now, it's damn near bumper-to-bumper. This area is building up so fast. It's almost a solid town from Fort Worth to Decatur. Pretty soon, it will be a solid town from Boyd back into Grapevine.

It was a two-lane road out here until they built the Texas Motor Speedway and Alliance Airport. Now, people are building subdivisions all along the road. Just like Aurora Vista between my house and the stables. Used to be two hundred acres of open land where you could ride. Had lots of deer and turkeys. They would be all over my back pasture in the mornings and evenings. Used to listen to the coyote pups at night calling for their mamas.

Guess that's what some call progress," he said, shaking his head. "I kind of liked it the way it was, but you gotta accept what you can't change. There are some nice folks coming out. Been a real pleasure getting to know them."

As they crossed the railroad tracks going into Boyd, Gene noticed several small businesses on both sides of the road. The little he had seen of Fort Worth during his drive with Vicki from the base had been much more congested. Most of that area had been houses, but a lot of businesses also. Stopping at the one light, he saw the road leading back toward Azle. It had only been a few hours ago that he had been walking up 730 and away from his former life.

Out here, people were very different from those he had met at the facility. A lot of it was because those had been scientific or military professionals, but he also knew that these people took care of each other and were closer even though they came from different walks of life. Here, the richest man would sit down to coffee with the poorest. Wealth or power seemed to make no difference.

"Right here is our only grocery store," Butch said as they passed the traffic light. "It's called IGA, pronounced the same way, not like the big stores in Fort Worth or larger towns. They carry most of the basics, but since the Super Wal-Mart went up in Decatur, I think a lot of folks drive up there to do their shopping.

I stopped in the other day for some Slim-Fast. Makes a quick meal if I don't have time to come to town or cook lunch at home. They didn't have any. 'Course, from the looks of most of the gals around here, they didn't sell much of it anyway."

As they pulled into the Southern Delight Restaurant, another pickup was stopping right beside them. "Hello, Bing," Butch said as he shut his door. "Coming in for the gourmet bachelor dinner?"

"You bet," Bing said, "Best breasts in town, or so they say. What you been up to? Still working with those knot-headed horses out there?"

"Yeah, guess I'll do that till I die. I swear, if I won the lottery, I'd keep at it till all that money was gone, too. Sure, can't make a living working horses. If it weren't for the money I make modeling for the *American Paint Horse Magazine*, I'd be too poor to pay attention," he said as he opened the door to the restaurant and waited for Gene and Bing to enter.

"Bing, this is Gene. Gene, this is Bing Knox. Wanna sit with us, Bing?"

"Sure thing. Nice to meet you, Gene," Bing said as he pulled out a chair. "How'd you get so unlucky, having to hang around this sorry ol' cuss?"

"Nice to meet you, too," Gene said as he sat down at the table across from Bing.

"Bing here is a newly divorcee. He decided to give all his money to his ex-wife and her lawyer—didn't you, Bing?"

"Well, I think that wasn't me that decided it. I seem to recall some judge telling me that it would be the neighborly thing to do. The way he said it, I didn't see much room to wiggle out of it," Bing answered as he picked up the menu.

Nanette walked over with a notepad and asked, "Evening, gentlemen. May I take your orders, please?" she asked.

"How'd you get so formal, Nanette? You normally just stand back there and yell, 'What the hell you want this time?' when we come in," Bing said, smiling up at her.

"I've decided to add class to the place. My only problem is that I keep getting the same old no-class bunch of cowboys coming in. Guess it's no use trying to impress you, is it?"

"Nope, sure ain't. Like Bing says, 'You can put lipstick on a pig, but you still got a pig when you wake up," Butch said, winking at Nanette.

"Now, he's one to talk," she said. "Y'all ready to order, or do I need to get the cook to read you the menu?"

"Cheeseburger and fries for me," Butch said as he laid the menu back on the table. "A fresh jalapeno on the side if you got one. And a Dr Pepper."

"Medium rare on the burger, I bet. And I know— don't overcook the fries," she answered. "How 'bout you, Bing?"

"Same for me but burn the burger. Dr Pepper too."

"How about you, son?" she asked Gene.

"That will be fine, too," Gene answered. "Make my burger medium and a Dr Pepper."

"You got it, boys," she said, walking away. "I'll have your drinks right out."

"You gotta hear this story, Gene," Butch said. "Tell him about your ex's lipo, Bing."

"Well, sir," Bing said, smiling at Gene. "Now, my ex was a big ol' gal. Didn't start that way, just grew into it. Anyhow, after the divorce, she figured she needed to slim down a bit. So she goes to this clinic somewhere down in Dallas and has them try to suck all the fat outta her.

After they got all the excess insides pulled out, she had lost almost one hundred pounds. Since her body had lost all that inside, the outside was a few sizes too large. To fix that, they had to cut off a lot of excess skin.

Well, the doctor was a friend of mine, so he sent it to me. Kind of a remembrance, you know. After I get this 'package,' I get this great idea. I take all that skin to a buddy of mine that does tanning and leatherwork.

I got two pairs of chaps and a new set of saddlebags!" Bing said as he and Butch started laughing. "She shore was a biggun!"

Nanette was bringing their food as Bing was finishing the story. "I heard that, Bing. You ought to be ashamed of yourself. I know for a fact that you just made that story up. I don't know why you boys are so hateful to your exes. Hell, you're lucky just to get a woman to put up with your bullshit. Now, you just quit telling this poor boy all those lies and eat!"

"Yes, ma'am," Butch and Bing replied, grinning at her as she set the burgers down and walked away.

"Listen, Gene," Butch said as he picked up the bottle of catsup, "you can't really believe everything you hear around here. Folks out here like to spin a good tale. Whether or not it's true, that doesn't stand in the way of a good story.

Now, let's eat up and get you back to the stables; I gotta be home when the kids get there. If I'm not, they'll drink all my Jack Daniel's before I get even a taste."

"Girls coming in?" Bing asked as he took a bite of his hamburger.

"Yep, driving up from San Antonio. The flight was grounded because of those assholes from Iran or wherever."

"Hell of a deal," Bing said as he dipped his fries in the catsup. "Glad the girls are going to make it in. Tell Mischelle and Jeannie I said howdy. Maybe I can get a chance to see them before they leave."

"They'd like that. I think we are going out to Red's Take 5 Sports Bar in Bridgeport tomorrow night. Karaoke night, and the girls just love to hear me sing. 'Course they got to, if they want me to buy their drinks."

"Sounds good. I'll try to make it. You gonna take Gene, here? He needs to hear what a coonhound sounds like when it's got its balls in a vise."

"We'll see," Butch said as he finished his burger. "You ready, Gene?"

"Yes, that was pretty good. Thanks," Gene replied as he wiped his face with a napkin.

"See ya," Bing said as they walked to the cash register to pay.

CHAPTER 31

The day started early for General Nelson. Notice of General Modelle's inbound flight came just thirty minutes before it was scheduled to land at 0545 on September 12. General Gary Brown had personally made the call. Gary was well aware of the importance of ensuring the secrecy of the 'facility' and had instructed the airmen in the tower and radar approach control to notify him as soon as they had control of the approaching jet.

Fort Worth Approach Control had taken the jet, using an Air Force call sign, from Fort Worth Center when it was still about forty miles east of Dallas. Once it was routed north over Denton, they notified the tower of its arrival and requested the landing runway to set up the handoff to the tower personnel.

As directed by General Brown, the tower called his private home number and advised him of the impending arrival. Gary immediately directed the tower to have ground control taxi the plane to the only hangar off-limits to any other aircraft. It had been so long since that particular hangar had been used that the tower personnel had to look at their airport diagram to issue the correct taxi instructions.

As soon as Mike answered the phone, Gary said, "Sir, your aircraft is over Denton, and ETA is thirty minutes. Will there be anything else?"

"No," replied General Nelson. "That will be all. Thank you." Gary knew the matter was best forgotten. He had not told the tower anything other than that this aircraft was a VIP flight, on official business of the FBI, which was his direction from Mike when he had notified him of the incoming flight once FAA approval had been received.

Mike sat up on the edge of the bed and stretched. It had been a very short night indeed. His wife of almost forty years was used to middle-of-the-night phone calls and quick departures. "You want me to make breakfast for you, honey?" she asked, still half-asleep and hoping he would say no.

"No, you go back to sleep. I'll just take a quick shower and go. I'll try to let you know when I'm coming home but don't expect me until late tonight. I may have to stay on base for the next day or two, so don't plan any meals. I'll either eat out or bring something home if I get the chance."

Mike slowly got up and walked to the bathroom. His wife closed her eyes and was asleep again before he closed the door. As he used the toilet and started the water in the shower, he prayed that this would not last too long and that Gene could be brought in with no one ever knowing of his origin.

After taking a shower and shaving, he took his uniform from the closet, got a clean shirt and socks, and carried them along with his black boots into the kitchen to dress. He had taken to wearing black ropers with his uniform years ago and couldn't stand wearing normal shoes anymore. As he was dressing, he dialed Rick's number. After listening to the sleepy hello from Rick's wife, he asked if he was awake. "Yes, but he left almost an hour ago," was the groggy reply.

"Sorry to disturb you," he said as he hung up the phone. "Should have known," he thought. "He's always been there when I've needed him. Sometimes, he's there before I even know I'll need him."

Mike left the house and started his staff car. It always expedited getting on or off base when in the car with its two stars mounted on the plate where a license plate should be. It also had reserved parking at any of the facilities on base and usually was respected by the local police.

As he drove on base, he returned the salute of the gate guard and proceeded straight to the facility. Seeing Rick's car in its usual spot and the other reserved spots open, he decided to tell Rick to start the recall of his staff as soon as he saw him. He would take care of General Modelle and give him a quick synopsis of the plan before the staff meeting.

After keying in his entry code, he noticed one of their security guards approaching the door. Waiting until the guard used his key to unlock the outer door, he smiled, thinking that Rick had sure lighted a fire under security and maintenance to get these locks in this fast.

"Morning, sir," the guard said. "Colonel Erickson said that I should notify him when you arrived."

"Don't bother," Mike replied. "I'll give him a call when I get to my office."

"Yes, sir," he acknowledged as he locked the outer door and turned to open the next door just ten feet away.

Mike walked through the second security door and down the hall to his office. Turning on the lights in his secretary's office, he proceeded to his closed door. As he opened it, he heard his phone ring. "Yes," he answered. "Thanks, Rick. I'll meet you in the conference room in a minute." He hung up and wondered how that guy knew he had arrived. "Bet that guard called him anyway. Don't know whether to be pissed or glad."

He opened his briefcase and put all the folders from yesterday's meetings inside. Snapping it closed, he walked down the hall to where he knew Rick had a fresh pot of coffee brewing.

"Morning, sir," Rick said as Mike entered the room. "Get enough sleep?"

"Looks like more than you did. You make this mud?" he asked as he poured a cup of coffee.

"You bet. Just like you like it. Just boil the water, throw a handful of grounds in, and wait till they sink to the bottom. Good old cowboy coffee," Rick said as he took his seat.

Mike placed his briefcase on the table and sat down to sip his coffee. "General Modelle should be out front in five or ten minutes. I'll take him to my office for a quick word. Please call the staff and have them ready to start the brief in an hour or so. I'll let you know exactly when after I talk to Paul."

"I've already called them," Rick said. "They should be here within the next five minutes. I wanted to go over each section before the general was briefed. I still don't know if General Brown got the transportation ready for the teams."

"That's been covered," Mike answered. "Kathy confirmed it last night before she left. They have been taken to the motel, and the keys are in the rooms reserved for Paul's teams. I didn't want those people over at the motor pool seeing the teams or their equipment. I've got a van that will take them to the motel as soon as General Modelle gives the word."

The door to the conference room opened, and Karyn came in carrying a box filled with folders. As she set the box on the table, she smiled and said, "Good morning, gentlemen. I guess the hunt is about to start. Is this some of your 'cowboy' coffee, sir?"

"Yep, never been hunting without it. You ready for the brief?"

"Yes, sir. I've made copies of all the photo arrays and blowups of each individual for the teams. The tapes are encoded and ready for transmission to Washington."

"Great," Rick said as Jerry and Amy came in. "Morning, folks, coffee's ready."

"No thanks," Amy said. "I've seen that stuff you make burn holes in the sink just washing out the cup it came in. I've got some good stuff in the lab. I'll just run down there and get my notes from the safe and bring a pot back. Let's try not to kill General Modelle while he's here."

"Rick, I'm going out to meet the General. I'll have my pager on if you need me, but I will be back in my office with Paul in a few minutes. I'd appreciate it if you would call Kathy and tell her we are ready to get to work. I'd like to have her here in case we need anything coordinated with the base."

"I'll call right now," Rick said as Mike set his empty cup down and started for the door. "As soon as Amy gets back, we will do a quick run-through of the plan. Just to make sure we remember what we had in mind when we left last night."

CHAPTER 32

The sun wasn't even peeking above the horizon when the noise of a door opening woke Gene. Adrenaline ran through his system as he envisioned a team of black-clad men running into the barn to get him. Immediately awake, he glanced out the window of the office into the interior of the barn. Lights came on, and he heard the horses neighing.

Quickly, he sat up, throwing the sheets and blankets off. Jumping off the sofa where he had been in the deepest sleep he could remember, he grabbed his jeans and pulled them up. As he was reaching for the boots Butch had given him, he heard someone saying, "OK, boys and girls, breakfast is coming."

Realizing Steve was the one walking down the aisle in the barn, he sat back down. Relief flooded over him. Suddenly relaxing, he had not realized until now how scared he really was. He couldn't stay here for too many more days. He had to make plans to get farther from Fort Worth if he was to survive.

Steve knocked on the door and turned on the office lights from the switch outside the office. "Rise and shine. Work to be done. Horses are hungry, shit's piled up, and the boss will beat us with a wet rope if we don't have our asses moving when he gets here!"

Opening the office door, Steve stepped inside. "Morning, Gene, you get enough sleep? Not the greatest bed, but it's better than one of those stalls.

I've heard that some of the hands working over at the track sleep in the empty stalls. Throw down a bed of shavings and pull a saddle blanket over themselves. It's not like the plush conditions you got here.

Speaking of plush conditions, I talked to my wife, Sheril, and she said it would be OK for you to sleep up in our house while we're gone. When we get the horses fed and turned out, we'll clean the stalls, and you can go up there to take a shower."

"Thanks," Gene replied as he finished dressing. "What do we do first?"

"Let's get the feed in each stall and refill all the water buckets. I've brought you a long-sleeve shirt; kind of cool this morning."

Gene took the shirt and put it on over the T-shirt Vicki had given him. Picking up his hat, he followed Steve out into the barn. He could hear the horses stomping and jerking their buckets with their teeth as they walked down the aisle. Each one of them was pacing back and forth at the front of their stalls.

"You'd think they hadn't eaten all year. Guess that's where the saying 'eats like a horse' comes from. We pour it in the front end, and they shove it out the back end. Then we have to clean it up afterward. It seems like a waste of time, doesn't it? Maybe one of these days, somebody will come up with a feed that just disappears after they eat it.

Course, Butch had this great idea. Diapers for horses. You can bet he wouldn't be the one changing them, though. Wonder what a horse diaper would look like. I know what he'd say: 'Looks like a Depend for a fat lady.' He sure does go on about fat women."

As they came to the stacks of feed sacks, Steve picked one up and dumped it into the wheelbarrow. "Get another one and pour it in here. It takes about one hundred pounds each morning and another hundred pounds each night."

Gene picked up the fifty-pound sack. "How do you open it?" he asked.

Steve reached over and showed him the top stitching on the sack. "Just grab this side, where the white strip is on the right side, and pull. The stitches will pull right out."

Gene pulled the strip, and the top of the sack opened. Picking it up, he almost spilled the feed, and Steve said, "Careful, this is about $10 a bag. Spilled feed also attracts mice. And mice attract snakes. And I hate snakes."

He finally got the sack up and dumped the feed into the wheelbarrow. "Now," Steve said, "just push it into the barn. You're too short to pour it over the top of the stall, so you'll have to go in each one. Give each one a full scoop. I'll go in with you for the first couple. These horses will make way for you to come in. They know where you're heading, and all that's on their minds right now is eating."

They came to the first stall, and Steve opened the door. Gene filled the scoop and walked into the stall with the horse. As he started pouring the feed into the bucket mounted on the front wall of the stall, the horse stepped to the side and waited until he was finished before sticking his head into the bucket.

As Gene moved back to the door, Steve swung it open and said, "Pretty easy, huh?"

"So far," Gene replied. "Are they all like that, moving over and waiting?"

"Most of them, but one or two will try to shove their noses into the bucket while you're pouring the feed in. Just put your shoulder against their heads and shove them over a little.

I'll get the ones with special feed as we go and show you how to do them. You don't need to latch the door when you go in, but just pull it closed behind you. These horses won't leave the stall with feed in their buckets," Steve said as he latched the first stall.

Gene pushed the wheelbarrow to the next stall and filled the scoop. Opening the door, he stepped inside and walked to the feed bucket. Just as before, the horse stepped to the side and waited. "You've got that down," Steve said as Gene walked back out and latched the door. "Let's get this finished, and we'll bring some hay in."

It only took about fifteen minutes to complete feeding the horses in the barn, and they put the wheelbarrow back by the stack of feed sacks. Opening the hay cage, Steve said, "You can keep this key with you for now. Butch has another one, but don't lose it. He doesn't like to have to come over here just to unlock the hay or tack room. Both use the same key."

Steve lifted a bale of hay and sat it in another large wheelbarrow. "These weigh about 115 pounds each. It takes one for each feeding. We also need a flake of alfalfa. There is one horse that the owner doesn't want getting this coastal Bermuda."

Gene pushed the wheelbarrow back into the aisle of the barn. Steve cut the three nylon strands holding the hay with his pocketknife. "You got a knife?" he asked.

"No. Never had one," Gene replied.

"Well, I'll let Butch give you your first one. Kind of a tradition. Your first knife should come from your father, but since you're gonna need one, I'll let him have the honor. Also, any time a man hands you his knife, give it back the way it was given. If it was open, give it back open. If it was closed, close it before you give it back. Some of these old rules go way back, and some of these old cowboys are pretty particular about them."

Finishing putting the hay in each stall, Steve started unrolling a hose by the wall. As he turned on the faucet, he started down the aisle, stopping at each stall. "Just open the door and turn on the shutoff when you step inside. Fill the bucket to about two inches from the top. If you get it too full, they tend to slop it over, and that gets the shavings wet," he said as he filled the bucket in the first stall.

"Go down this side to the end and back up the other side. I'm going to check how much feed is in the storage area outside," he said as he handed Gene the hose.

Gene walked from stall to stall, filling the buckets and being careful to make sure the doors were firmly latched before going to the next one.

Steve returned just as he was finishing and said, "Roll the hose up and turn off the faucet. We'll feed the outside horses now and take a short break while they finish eating."

Gene replaced the hose where Steve had picked it up and followed him out of the barn. "We'll do the same thing out here, but some of the stalls can be done two at a time."

He pushed the wheelbarrow full of feed into the aisle between the stalls and walked toward the end of the row. "It's a little harder to push this in the sand than on the concrete in the barn," he said as he came to the first set of stalls. Taking a small bucket, he filled it with a scoop of feed and refilled the scoop. As he entered one of the stalls, Gene could see a long trough running beneath the iron-rod fence separating the stalls.

Steve poured the bucket of feed in one end, reached through the fence, and put the scoopful in the other. "These eight stalls are called loafing sheds, and there are two horses in each shed. You can feed them from either side. While you are in here, check the automatic water; it should be almost full, and there should be no grass or moss inside. If it's dirty, just use your hand and scoop out the crap. If it isn't full, tell Butch, and he'll figure out what's wrong and fix it."

They finished putting feed in each stall and returned the wheelbarrow. "All right," Steve said. "Pick up that bale of hay and put it in. We'll give them each some hay and head to the house."

Gene struggled to lift the heavy bale but finally got it in. "Looks like you could use a little more muscle. You can cut the strings and take only a half bale at a time. You gotta break it into three- or four-inch flakes anyway," Steve said as he cut the strands of nylon holding the hay.

"Go ahead and put the hay in the troughs, just like you did the feed," he said. "Try to keep it as far from the center fence as possible so they won't steal each other's feed."

As Gene finished putting the hay into each stall, Steve said, "Pretty work, pretty work. Let's go get some coffee. Butch will probably be here soon, and we'll figure out which horses need to stay in. Some of the boarders leave a note for us, but Butch usually wants one or two left up for him to work."

CHAPTER 33

It was still dark out as Mike exited the facility. He knew General Modelle's aircraft had landed and was taxiing toward the hanger. His handheld receiver had been tuned to the FAA frequencies since he had arrived at his office. He had preset channels for the tower, ground control, base security, and scanners for the local police departments.

He could see a 'follow me' truck leading the jet down the parallel taxiway as they taxied back from the landing runway. As the 'follow me' truck made the turn off the taxiway and headed for the hanger, he saw it flash its lights and turn back toward Base Operations. The drivers had been directed to release the aircraft once clear of the active taxiway, and the pilots would continue to the hangar on their own.

Three of his security men came out of the hangar wearing orange jumpsuits with silver reflective tape in two rows across the chest. One of them walked out directly in front of the inbound plane and raised two lighted wands above his head. As he moved the wands from front to back, the pilot turned his nose light off to prevent blinding the guide man with his lights. As the plane drew closer, the guide man stopped waving and slowly brought his arms together over his head.

Once stopped, one of the security men placed chocks on both sides of the main wheels, and the other one went to the exterior door, turned the release handle, and lowered the door. As the engines began to wind down, General Modelle appeared at the top of the stairs formed by the lowered door.

"Good morning, sir," Mike said as he rendered a crisp salute. "Welcome to Texas." He snapped his salute down after receiving a salute from Paul. "How was the flight?"

"Skies are pretty empty right now," Paul replied. "How's the operation coming?"

"Just waiting for your final approval. The staff has a briefing prepared, and it can be implemented immediately," Mike answered.

General Modelle stepped off the bottom step and took his suitcase from the security guard standing beside the stairs. "Let's get started. Where can I get a good cup of coffee? That weak brew on the airplane didn't cut it. Is Rick still making that cowboy coffee of his?"

"Yes, sir," Mike said. "Not too many of the folks working here can stomach it, though. Colonel Moore is making a regular batch to bring to the briefing. I didn't know you liked Rick's coffee."

"I really don't, but you gotta humor him. Guess the worst thing about it is getting the grounds in your mouth as you drink it. He says you gotta keep your teeth together and strain it. Never knew where to spit the grounds after that, though," Paul said, smiling. "He's a hell of a great guy. Never hurts to play along and let him think you enjoy it."

As they approached the entry, a security guard met them at the door and stepped aside as they walked through the first door.

"Looks like you've changed your security system. Was that one of the problems you found?"

"Yes, sir," Mike answered. "Rick made Lieutenant Colonel Mallory install keyed locks on all the outer doors.

He'll brief you on the new systems after we get the operation started."

As they approached Mike's office, he said, "You can set your suitcase here by Kathy's desk. She'll have it taken to your room when she gets back. I'd like a minute of your time before the briefing. I need to discuss a couple of items. Shouldn't take five minutes, and then you can get that cup of Rick's brew."

They continued into the office, and Mike shut the door. "Please have a seat," he said as he walked around his desk to his chair.

Sitting down, he continued, "First and most importantly, I want you to know that all the blame for this is mine. I should have foreseen Vicki's actions. This is entirely my fault.

Next, you need to know that the staff and heads of all the departments have done outstanding work on this project and have been instrumental in developing the plans to keep it under control and devise a plan to recover our product, Gene."

"I appreciate your taking the responsibility, Mike," Paul acknowledged. "I've never known you to try to cover any of your mistakes, and you have always been completely honest in all your dealings with me. And everyone else. I also know that I might have done things the same way had I been here seeing things day to day.

You aren't to blame for having made an error in judgment relating to Vicki. You are just as human as the next man, and your compassion isn't a fault. It's what makes you a great Commander. You've always tempered your actions with extra regard for your subordinates. That's only one of the reasons that you were put in command of this operation.

I've seen too many Commanders try to pass the blame or make lame excuses for mistakes. Too many of them think the way to promotion is to disregard their troops and screw over anyone they can to get to the top. They nearly all fail at some point. I've seen passed-over officers I'd rather have in command.

Some of our best officers get left behind because they won't be a 'yes man' to every dumb-ass idea that comes from a Squadron Commander whose method of leadership is fear and intimidation. I'm sure you've seen it a hundred times yourself. No, you don't need to concern yourself about your future or that of your people. I've already had a discussion with the President. Let's forget the past and get this little incident taken care of."

Mike relaxed a bit and said, "Thanks, sir. I appreciate you standing up for us, and I mean all of us. With one exception, that is. I have placed Lieutenant Colonel Pratka in a cell on the third floor. He was repeatedly debriefed, and I'm sure we have all the useful information from him. I can find no excuse for his actions, and I have arranged for his 'departure.' He will have an accident coming to work this morning if you agree."

"Go ahead. He knew the consequences when he elected to put this operation in jeopardy," Paul said as he stood up. "Now, how about we get that coffee and hear what you have in mind for regaining our little man."

As they left his office, Mike nodded to Kathy and asked, "Has General Modelle's team been taken care of?"

"Yes, sir. They are already headed to the motel. One of them, the communications man, stayed behind. He's down in Colonel Lynch's office checking our electronic gear. Colonel Erickson is going to join him after the briefing. Morning, General Modelle. I've put your suitcase in your room, and your briefcase was brought in to me," Kathy said as she stood and handed it to Paul.

"Thanks, Kathy. You look lovely as always. You just let me know if Mike ever mistreats you. I'd love to have a first-class secretary like you in my office. Mike certainly doesn't deserve you," he said, smiling.

They left the office and walked to the conference room where everyone was waiting. "Good morning, General," Rick said as they all came to attention and raised a salute. "Welcome to Texas."

Paul returned the salute and said, "Thanks, Rick. Please, everyone have a seat. I'm ready to get this going. Is that coffee any good?" he asked, winking at Mike. "Best there is, sir," Rick said. "Would you like a cup?"

"I flew all the way here, diverted, spent the night in a crappy hotel in Memphis, and put up with your boss detaining me for hours. All of that just to have a cup of your coffee. Who's going first?" he said as Rick handed him a cup, and they found their seats at the table.

CHAPTER 34

Gene and Steve were walking toward the house as Butch turned into the driveway. He stopped his truck beside the house and waited for them to arrive. As he got out, he said, "You're not quitting already, are you? The sun's just now up, and it's time to start."

"Well," Steve replied, "we've been at it since six o'clock. It's after eight now. Gene fed all the horses, put out hay, filled the water buckets, and was waiting around for you to finally show up.

What happened?" he asked as he poked Gene and gave him a wink, "You stay out all night again Butch?"

"Nope. My darling daughters, that's what," Butch said. "Finally, drive in at nine o'clock. Takes them an hour to get their junk settled in their room—after I carry it all in, of course. Then, they decide that since it's been such a harrowing experience, driving all the way from San Antonio, they just might need a little 'relaxer.' I guess you know what that means.

Well, I'll tell you. It means they are going to keep their poor ol' pappy up half the night, drinking Jack Daniel's and giggling. I love those girls to death, but they are still lying in bed while I'm up. I know they are trying to kill me. They do this every time. One of these days, I'll make them get up and go when I do. Worthless little urchins."

"How about a cup of coffee? Maybe that will settle your nerves and get you to quit bitching. I know you probably made *them* stay up. And I know for a fact you were going to sip a little Jack when you got home anyway," Steve said as they got to the door to his house. "Sheril said she would have a fresh pot for us when we finished feeding. She might even make you a bite to eat if you're nice."

"I'll take some coffee, but I turned the television on real loud as I walked out. They are going to want a real breakfast. I just wanted to come by and make sure everything was going OK."

"Just fine," Steve answered. "Gene's got the hang of it. Those three-wire bales are a little heavy for him, but I told him to cut the strings and pick them up half at a time. That reminds me—he doesn't have a knife. Never had one, he says."

"That a fact?" Butch asked, looking at Gene. "You never had a knife?"

"No, sir, sure haven't," he replied. "Guess I've never needed one before now."

"Well, I'll just have to fix that. I'll get you one when I go into town for breakfast. Do you want to go with the girls and me?"

"Sheril's cooking us breakfast after we turn the horses out. You're welcome too, Butch. You can even bring those poor little orphans of yours," Steve said. "Sheril, get us some coffee, please. Y'all have a seat."

"Thanks, but those kids have to have a menu. I think they like seeing all the folks down at the Double K. Folks in this town seem to like those worthless kids of mine. I think half the reason my kids come to visit is to see all their friends out here," Butch said as he took a cup of coffee from Sheril.

"You need sugar or cream?" she asked Gene as she handed him a cup.

"No, ma'am," he replied. "Just black is fine, thanks."

"Butch," Sheril said, "you've never told me why you got divorced. How come a good-looking guy like you ain't married?"

"Guess it's because that marriage was doomed from the start. It was one of those mixed marriages. We came from different religions. I was Baptist, and she was slut. Just didn't work out," Butch said.

Steve almost spat his coffee out as he saw Sheril's face. "You sure do like to tell that one, don't you?" he said, laughing.

"Yea. Don't always have a great opening like that to work it in, though," he said as he finished his coffee. "Thanks for the coffee. I'll be back after I feed my kids.

How much hay is left down in the pasture, Steve?" he asked.

"I checked yesterday, and there are still a couple of piles left. The horses have picked it pretty clean. We'll need more either today or tomorrow."

"Go ahead and put the forks on the skid-steer. When we get here, I'll let the girls load it and take it out to the pasture. They like driving the equipment. They seldom ever run over anything now, and it keeps them busy. Then later, they can whine to everyone about how hard I make them work while they're here."

"OK, it'll be ready when you get back," Steve said as Butch set his empty cup on the counter and walked to the door.

"Be back in an hour or so. Thanks again for the coffee," he said as he left.

"What's a skid-steer?" Gene asked as the door shut.

"It's a loader, like a Bobcat, but made by John Deere. The one we have has a big bucket on the front and can be replaced by a set of forks. We use the bucket to move the manure piles you made when you dumped the wheelbarrows. After there is a bunch piled outside the barn, we use the skid-steer and haul it to a bigger pile out in the pasture.

Then, when there gets to be six or seven months' worth of that, Butch calls a fellow out in Weatherford to haul it away. That guy takes it to some place in Dallas, and they mix it with all the other stuff they pick up and make compost.

There are lots of attachments you can put on the skid-steer. There's a posthole digger, a mower, and a bunch more. All we ever use is the bucket and forks. Butch buys the feed a ton at a time, and it's loaded on his truck on a pallet. Then, when he gets here, we take the forks, take the pallet off the truck, and move it inside the barn. Those sacks you used this morning—that's what's left of the last pallet."

"That's that big yellow thing in the shed outside the barn," Gene said, nodding his head. "Guess it takes a lot of equipment to work this place."

"Either that or a lot of manual labor. It would take two or three times as long to clean the barn each day if you had to carry each wheelbarrow out to the big dump site. And unloading a ton of feed a couple of times a month wouldn't be fun.

I guess it could all be done by hand, but it would take so long. It would take more people working to get it done right every day. Guess Butch has figured out that the equipment is cheaper than another worker out here. Plus, it's harder than you think to find someone who's willing to do an honest day's work. Seems lots of people want a day's pay but sure as hell don't want to do a day's work.

Speaking of work, let's get going," Steve said as he sat his cup down. "The horses should be finished with their breakfast by now. I bet they're ready to go run in the pasture. You're going to like seeing this. They really cut loose after being locked up all night."

Gene stood up and put his cup on the counter as Steve opened the door. As he followed Steve back toward the barn, he saw a truck pull in and park. A slight feeling of panic came over him. He hoped the hat and boots he had started wearing would provide enough disguise to prevent anyone coming out here from recognizing him.

"Morning, folks," Steve said as the couple got out of their truck. "Gonna ride a little today?"

"Yep, we're gonna take a short ride around Aurora Vista, then when we get back, we'll give them the brushing of their lives," the man said as they walked to the barn. "Butch around?"

"Just left. His kids are in town, and he's taking them to breakfast before he brings them over here."

"Good. We need to get a vet to check out ol' Repo and get him and Skinner trimmed. If we don't see Butch, please ask him to schedule that for us."

"I'll tell him. I'm sure he'll be glad to take care of it for you."

CHAPTER 35

General Modelle was sitting at the head of the table as Rick stood beside his chair across from Mike. "General, Colonel Amy Moore will start us off with a quick rundown of what she believes may help narrow our search and why.

Colonel Karyn Lynch will then follow her with specifics of the program she has developed. This program will give us the best chance of success I believe possible. Last, Major Jerry Fleenor will update you on his contacts, who will be used to fully implement this plan. Amy, please go ahead."

Amy stood and passed a series of folders around the table and said, "I have been through all the data we have, both from psychological examinations and scientific facts known regarding Gene's mental development. I have also factored in what we could determine of Vicki's influence regarding moral values and abilities to interface with the civilian population and have considered his physical attributes.

The folders you have contain the specifics of each of these areas. I have broken each subsection down with known facts or professional observances and summarized them. Following this information, I have provided my theories and discussed how and why I came to these conclusions.

After my briefing, and when you have a chance to review the data, I will be glad to answer any questions or explain anything you need a deeper analysis of for complete understanding.

It is my belief that Gene does have the potential for genetic remembrances. That was one of the goals of this project when we developed him. The genetic material used in his case came exclusively from the Roswell and Aurora sites.

As the data covered in detail in your folder explains, specific strands of DNA are more capable of retaining an inherited trait. Combining these specific DNA strands, which we know carry certain information with normal human inherited traits, such as the need for human contact, will allow us to accurately predict certain behaviors.

Regarding his need for human contact, it has been observed, during his evaluations and his time spent alone with Vicki, that Gene is normal in all respects. I further believe that there is an inherent need for contact with like beings, those whose DNA is an integral part of their genetic makeup.

Now, logic leads me to two theories. First, Gene will initially be drawn to either Roswell or Aurora. If, as Vicki told us during her interrogation, Gene was dropped off west of Fort Worth, in the vicinity of White Settlement, I believe he would continue west. This would be the most logical because traffic in that area would primarily be headed either east or west. His natural inclination would be west toward Roswell.

I should also note, even if my theory on his traveling west is proven wrong, we must search in that direction anyway and primarily look into the truck stops, gas stations, or roadside diners where groups of people traveling could be approached for transportation.

At the same time we are concentrating on Gene's probability of westward direction, we must also bear in mind that 820 is also in the same area and could provide an avenue for traveling north, toward Aurora.

The majority of the genetic material comes from Roswell; the drop-off was in that direction, and numerous gas stations and truck stops are located where 820, I-30, and I-20 either cross or are relatively close. That is why I have come to the conclusion that the west toward Roswell should warrant our main effort. Do you or anyone else have any questions?" Amy said as she replaced her notes and prepared to take her seat.

"Not at this time, thank you, Amy," General Modelle answered. "I'll read through the material you have provided and get back with you if I need anything further."

Rick took a minute to look around the table to see if anyone had any comments. Seeing none, he said, "Karyn, would you please show the General your plan and the details necessary to implement it?"

Karyn rose from her chair, handed a thick manila folder to each of the members, and walked to the television. As she turned it and the DVD player on, she placed a disc into the player.

"What you have before you is a series of photos taken from FBI, CIA, and Israeli Intelligence files. These photos are of known or suspected Middle Eastern terrorists. All except the last photo. The top photo is an array of individual photos placed together to further entice the viewer to conclude that all six individuals are related through ethnic backgrounds."

As she talked and General Modelle opened the folders and took each photo as she described them, she would have the same photo on the television as it would appear to any viewer sitting at home.

"You will notice that the top three are true Middle Easterners; the same for the two on each side of Gene's photo. In these photos, Gene has been digitally enhanced to slightly darken his skin, his apparel is typical of that region, and his beard will lend authenticity to the image we want to project.

The next set of photos are the individual photos of each man I plan to be placed beside the group photos as they are shown on the news programs.

That will enhance our projection of the appearance that Gene is Middle Eastern.

Next in the news transmission, we will present the group again, with the photo previously presented, but one-half size, and below that, a picture of what the individual may look like without the clothing and beard. This photo will portray each man as you might see him dressed here in America at any restaurant or at the airport.

Following that presentation, an enlarged photo of each individual will be shown separately. As you can see, the photo of Gene is exactly as he would appear if he is indeed wearing the clothes Vicki described during her interrogation."

Karyn waited a couple of minutes as everyone looked, from the photos on the desk to those on the television. The picture of Gene on the screen was of him wearing a T-shirt, jeans, and a baseball cap.

"Now," Karyn said as she replaced the disc with another, "this is a news segment we prepared using a stand-in for the newscaster. This is how we think the actual broadcast will appear."

Everyone watched as a well-dressed man on the television began talking about new information just received from his Washington bureau. This information was attained during investigations into the terrorist hijackings and subsequent crashes. As they watched, the flow of information presented was identical to what Karyn had just shown.

As the newsclip ended, Karyn told them, "Now, we have produced another variation to demonstrate how the local news will augment this broadcast."

The scene on the screen changed from what appeared to be a national news media broadcast to one representing one of the local stations. Now, additional information regarding the specifics of Gene being refused boarding on an American Airlines flight on the evening of September 10 was presented.

"The information of Gene being refused boarding will be provided at the same time as the news of the fifth group of hijackers is released. This total news package is prepared in a multimedia format and is ready for dissemination immediately. Major Fleenor has the specifics on distribution and how documentation has been arranged.

Do you have any questions, sir?" Karyn said as she stopped the DVD player and turned off the television.

"I do, but I will wait until Major Fleenor completes his briefing. He may cover them at that time. Thank you, Karyn. It looks like a superb plan," Paul said as he replaced the photos in the folder and closed it.

"Before Jerry begins, would anyone like a short break? Kathy has arranged to have something for us to eat, and there is fresh coffee coming," Rick said, looking around the room.

"I think a quick break would be appropriate," Paul said as he rose from his chair. "I know I need to dispense with some of the coffee I've had. And I sure need something in my stomach to counter the effects of the coffee grounds that snuck past my teeth. Let's take five."

As they all rose to leave, Kathy knocked on the door. Opening the door, Mike asked her to place the tray of breakfast burritos on the table and have some fresh coffee brought in.

Upon returning a few minutes later, Rick waited until everyone had a cup of coffee and a burrito before he said, "We'll wrap up the briefing with Major Fleenor. Jerry, would you please update us on the implementation of the plan?"

Jerry rose and passed a folder to each member. "I have notified one of our close associates in Washington to be prepared to disseminate this information within the hour. He has assured me that his contacts within the Washington correspondent's field will have it on national news as soon as he receives it.

In your folder, you have the names of our contacts, his news contacts, and the names of the local correspondents we will contact. All the news correspondents have been notified that additional information is forthcoming and to be ready to broadcast it when it is received. Copies of all the photos have been prepared for encrypted transmission.

On the documentation issue, I have arranged for the ticket reservation computers at American Airlines to have a ticket purchase under the name of Mohammed Al'jazera entered as if purchased ten days ago. If the records are ever searched, that ticket will appear to have been purchased just like the rest of the tickets sold that day.

We have gone through all the TSA computers and made a note, dated September 10, that collaborates a disturbance resulting from a passenger being denied boarding. The name of the officer actually involved has intentionally been left off.

We also have several people that will testify to the incident, if need be," Jerry said as he finished his presentation. "Do you have any questions, sir?

"Only a couple. First, have you checked the compatibility of your encryption with those you are transmitting with? Second, are all the points of contact within the other agencies even remotely aware that this is not what it seems?" General Modelle asked.

"Regarding your first question, I'll let Karyn answer. The agencies mentioned have only been told that information has been uncovered from several sources that prove our story regarding the fifth hijacker team is factual. Information supporting this has been placed within all their computers, predated to bear out our story," Jerry answered. "Karyn?"

"Sir, I have had my communications specialists go over all your equipment with your men. They are completely compatible. Additionally, we will be using our internal encryption equipment for all communications during the search. This will simplify the flow of information between the teams and our command post. It will also prevent any information transmitted to Washington from possibly being caught by our local teams, and their transmissions can't be picked up by Washington, nor anyone else," Karyn said.

"Sounds good. You have my approval to implement the program immediately," Paul said as he stood. "Rick, I assume you are running the Command Post. I will contact you when I want any updates. I know you will get the mission accomplished, so don't feel you need to get any further approval for your actions.

Amy, I'm sure you are correct in your theories. I appreciate all the hard work.

Jerry, good job. If you need any horsepower to make it happen, don't hesitate to call me. President Bush can push a lot of buttons if need be.

And you, Karyn—this is an outstanding plan. I want you to know that we all appreciate your efforts, and although neither you nor any of the others will ever get public recognition, it has been duly noted and at the very highest level.

Mike, you've got a great team here. You've all done well. Now, I'd like a real breakfast. Why don't you and I go somewhere quiet and talk over a Spanish omelet," Paul said as he picked up all the material he had been given. "I'll check back with you guys after we return. Again, if you need any assistance on any issue, call. Ready, Mike?"

CHAPTER 36

Butch came driving in as Marrion and Merna Duffy were coming out of the pasture. As he got out of his truck, he told his daughters, "Come on, girls, we've got a lot of work to get done. I didn't let y'all stay up all night drinking and take you to a wonderful breakfast just to have you lay around on your butts."

The girls got out of the truck as Marrion and Merna were walking up. "Morning, Butch. What in the world are you doing to these poor little girls?" Merna asked as she walked over to them.

"Morning, folks," Butch said. "These lazy heifers just want to play all night and sleep all day. Don't know where they got that attitude from."

"Could that have been you?" Marrion said as he hugged the girls. "How have you girls been?"

"Pretty good, Marrion," said Jeannie. "Daddy's getting as grouchy as old Mike Jackson. Pretty soon, he'll be known as the grouchiest man in the county instead of Mike."

"I think it's because he's getting too old. He just can't run with the big dogs now. Guess he just better stay on the porch," Mischelle said as she punched Butch on the arm. "He's the one that taught us everything we know, at least about partying. Guess he can blame himself for the way we are now."

"Jeannie," Butch told her, "You better tell your big sister Mischelle to be nice to her pappy. I may not be around much longer to sponsor her evil habits. And I'm leaving everything I have to the unwed mothers' home."

"You should," she answered. "You've tried to fill it over the last few years. You need to send them a check every week. I hate to think that there may be any more of your kind loose out here."

"You girls have a good trip in?" asked Merna. "I saw that the FAA had stopped all the flights. How did you get here?"

"We were already in San Antonio. When our flight was canceled, we rented a car and drove up. We had to get here and try to straighten Daddy out," Jeannie said, grinning.

"You done riding?" Butch asked Merna. "And did you bring me any cookies? Girls, she makes the best macadamia nut cookies in the world."

"No cookies today," she said. "Guess you'll have to wait until Friday and get them at the bank."

"I guess. At least those fine ladies at Woodhaven Bank treat me nice. Some days, they even give me milk with my cookies."

"They spoil you," Jeannie said. "Everybody around here is way too nice to you. One of these days, they will find out what a rotten man you really are."

"Somebody has to be nice to me. My own girls are mean and evil little urchins. No respect for their elders."

"We've got to run, folks," said Marrion. "Bring the girls by before they leave when we have more time. Girls, it's been a pleasure to see you again. Keep him in line if you can."

"Nice you see you again," said Merna as she walked with Marrion to their truck. "Maybe I'll make some cookies for tomorrow, just for you girls."

"Bye," said the girls as they turned and followed Butch into the barn.

"We need to put a couple of round bales out in the pasture. I told Steve to put the forks on the skid-steer. Let's see if he did."

Steve and Gene came in the other end of the barn as they were walking down the aisle.

"Morning, ladies," Steve said. "Your daddy making y'all go to work the minute you get here, I see."

"Yep, a slave driver. We get no rest, won't feed us, I'm calling the child protection people," Mischelle said.

"There are laws for people like him."

"I'll get you the phone number," Steve said, grinning. "Tell them how hard he makes me work, too, while you're at it."

"Got the forks on so these girls can move that hay?" Butch asked.

"Yep, ready to go."

"Good. Jeannie, you can take the first one out. You remember how to drive it and how to work the forks?"

"I think so. Where is the hay, and where do you want me to take it?"

"I'll start it, and y'all can ride on the forks. You can show Mischelle how it operates when you take the first bale out. Just try not to knock down the fences or run over the horses."

Butch climbed into the skid-steer and started the diesel engine. After he had it running, he said, "Come on, girls, climb on. I'll drive over to the bales and let you have it there."

They stepped on the forks and held on. It could be a rough ride since there were no springs, and the ground was pretty bumpy. "Ain't this fun?" Butch yelled as they bounced over to a row of one-ton bales of hay. "You don't get this kind of excitement up in Seattle or Baltimore."

"Thank God," they both said, hanging on as they slid to a stop.

Butch climbed out and told them, "I'll open the gate and make sure the horses don't get out while you're moving the hay. Put the first one kind of on one end of that little hill and the next one on the other end.

Just keep them about one hundred yards apart so the horses don't bunch up and fight over who gets to be king of the hay."

Jeannie climbed in and told Mischelle to get in beside her. "You steer it with these handles on each side and work the forks with your feet. Your left foot raises the forks up and down. Your right foot makes it tilt up and down."

As she drove up to the bale, she said, "Just drop the forks on the ground, get them level, and then drive up to the bale so the forks just slide under it.

Then, use your right foot and push with your heel so it tilts the forks up a little. After it slides a little to the back, use the heel of your right foot to lift it up a few inches.

Now is the hard part. Since you can't see right in front, you have to drive by watching the sides. Just follow the gravel on the road until you see the dumpster on your right, and start turning right through the gate."

Once they were through the gate, she said, "OK, now just head across the pasture. It's easy to see the trees, and Daddy doesn't care exactly where we put it just so there is a lot of room between them.

To drop the bale, just lift it a little, tilt the forks down like this, and the bale will slide off. Now, just back up with the handles, and we're done. You can drive back," she said as she climbed out of the seat. "It's pretty easy to drive. Push both handles forward to go forward. To turn, either push one further or pull back a little on one in the direction you want to go. Just drive around a while out here. Daddy can stand by the gate while you practice. Kind of fun, isn't it?"

"Yeah," Mischelle said. "Kind of like driving the mower. I'm going to play with the forks as we drive so I can do it right while everyone is watching."

After moving the second bale, they drove back to the barn as Butch closed the gate. Steve and Gene were still cleaning stalls when they entered the barn.

"How's it going?" he asked.

"Fine, same old shit," Steve said. "Gene's about to get his Ph.D. Piles of Horse Dung. Maybe an MD. More Dung."

"Gene, these are my girls, Jeannie and Mischelle. They're both worthless, but they're mine. Kids, this is Gene. He's working here while Steve runs off and plays."

"Hi, Gene," they said.

"Nice to meet you," Gene replied as he quickly nodded and went back into the stall.

"The girls want to go to Decatur and spend my money. We'll be back in a couple of hours. If you need me, I'll have my cell phone. We are going out to Red's tonight. Karaoke night. Girls just love to hear me sing. They have dollar hamburgers also. Gene, why don't you plan on going with us? Let you see why I'm not a country singing star. Anything we need from Decatur?"

"Not that I can think of," Steve answered. "Sheril and I need to leave about five or five-thirty to get down to Waco tonight. My family will be there, and Mom wants to eat by seven o'clock. That OK?"

"Sure. Matter of fact, the girls and I will be here by four, and we'll help Gene get the horses in and fed. You can probably leave then if everything else is taken care of."

"I told Gene to stay in the house while we're gone," Steve said as he pushed the wheelbarrow back from the stall he was cleaning. "That way, he can sleep in the spare bedroom and have the shower. Sheril has made the bed and left a towel and stuff out."

"Good. That's much more comfortable than the couch in the office. I'll see you when I get back," Butch said as he and the girls walked out to the truck.

Gene wondered if he should go out, especially to someplace where more people would see him. But he didn't want Butch or Steve to think he was any different than anyone else. And he needed to stay here another few days until he determined why this place seemed so important to him.

"What's Red's like?" he asked as he continued to scoop the manure and shavings from the stall.

"Oh, it's just a little bar up in Bridgeport. Not too many people on a Wednesday night. Normal little country bar. You know—few guys drinking beer, dark atmosphere, some pool tables. Butch likes to sing some. Sometimes, he'll dance a little. Kind of a fun place. You ought to go. You'll enjoy it."

"Guess so. I just don't like big crowds."

"Don't worry. They don't often get a really big crowd. Usually, it's the same old bunch. Never any trouble. You really ought to go."

CHAPTER 37

Kathy greeted Mike and Paul as they walked toward his office. "How was breakfast, gentlemen?"

"The best one I've had all day," responded Mike.

"The best one I've had in years," said Paul. "Those damn Yankees just don't know how to make a good Spanish omelet. I haven't seen a fresh jalapeno since my last visit here; what, five years ago?"

"Been a long time, sir," Kathy noted, "too long. Colonel Erickson asked me to let you know they are in the communications area. I think he'd like for you to stop in as soon as you can."

"Thanks, Kathy," Mike answered. "Please give him a call and let him know we will be there in about five minutes. General Modelle needs to freshen up a bit and put on something a little less formal. This could be a long day."

"Yes, sir. General Modelle, do you need anything?"

"No thanks, Kathy. Mike, I'll meet you in your office as soon as I get changed."

Paul walked off toward his quarters as Mike and Kathy entered his office. "I'm sure we will be eating here for lunch. Could you please call the Officer's Club and have them make up several trays of sandwiches? Ham, turkey, roast beef, or whatever you think. Have them make some potato salad, coleslaw, and several bags of chips. Get a big jug of iced tea, too. Have Major Romine pick it up at about eleven or so. Just charge it to my account."

"Yes, sir," she said as she went back to her desk. "Mustard, mayo, catsup?"

"Yes, and some pickles and fresh jalapenos."

Kathy sat down and picked up her phone. As she was dialing, she called out to him, "You may want to see Channel 4. It looks like there was supposed to be another airplane hijacked. I think all the channels are covering it. Something happened at DFW the other night, too. Not sure what it's all about. I haven't had time to watch it all."

Mike quickly turned on the set at the far end of his office. The scene was of a local newscaster with the exact picture of six bearded Middle Eastern-looking men he had seen less than an hour ago. "Rick's not wasting any time," he thought.

He rose from behind his desk and was just leaving when Paul came in. "We need to get down to the communications room ASAP. Something's on the news I think we need to see," Mike said, knowing Kathy would overhear. "Looks like there was another planned hijacking."

Entering the communications room, they saw a large screen showing at least ten differing pictures. Each of the major broadcasting networks—CNN, FOX, ABC, NBC, and CBS—was being monitored on the screen. Along with them, five local stations were depicted. The sound was switched between stations as they watched.

Rick was talking on the phone as they saw the same pictures they had seen before, some with single photos, all in varying stages of telling the story of the breaking news.

As he hung up the phone, Rick said, "Let's listen to the locals for a minute. All the announcers are sticking close to the transcripts we provided. Most of them are verbatim. The local folks have just now started zooming in on the DFW part of the story."

The sound from Channel 4 came on, and the scene shifted to a reporter standing just inside Terminal C of DFW. In the background, you could see the bank of magnetometers used to screen the passengers.

Several TSA agents could be seen standing around waiting for the FAA to lift the restrictions on civil airline operations.

The reporter described how a passenger, bound for Boston, had been turned away the evening before the destruction of the World Trade Center, the crash into the Pentagon, and the crash in Pennsylvania. As he discussed each of the crashes, an insert on the screen showed the latest films of the areas.

Then, he began to describe how the FBI had learned of the other team, released the information about the DFW passenger, and provided photos of all involved. He then brought the photos of Gene into the screen and told the camera everything he had been told of this particular terrorist.

He described how 'Mohammed Al Jazeera' had been denied boarding by alert TSA agents and had subsequently left the terminal. As the screen changed to show the picture of Gene in a baseball cap and T-shirt, the reporter continued to describe him and said that intelligence had been found showing that this individual had been using the alias of 'Gene'.

He implored anyone knowing any information regarding this individual or having seen him to please contact either the local police or the FBI. As the picture zoomed in on the photo of Gene, a series of phone numbers appeared below the photo.

"It's a good start," Mike said. "What are you doing to route all the calls regarding Gene to us?"

"We have directed all local entities to contact the FBI number and route the calls to them after they obtain the appropriate information on names, phone numbers, and sighting location.

The FBI number then plots the location of the individual calling, verifies it through the 911 system, and transfers any calls to us. We take the information again and contact our field agents to investigate.

So far, we have had about a dozen sightings, some as far away as Waco. But we are limiting our agents to the west currently until we get a confirmed sighting in any other direction.

We are letting the local police handle those calls within their jurisdiction under our FBI authority. If it is determined to be a valid call, one of our teams is dispatched to verify the sighting. All local authorities have directed their officers to report and maintain surveillance only.

It has only been thirty minutes or so since the news was broken. I'm optimistic about getting a confirmed sighting within the next hour or so. That is if Gene tried to leave the area where Vicki said she dropped him. The only other thing he could have done was stay around and hide under one of the bridges or in one of the parks.

Even then, someone will eventually spot him. It may take considerably longer since there are no televisions in those areas. I still think Amy's right. He's going to be moving. And the more he moves, the more people he will come in contact with."

Paul and Mike watched for a few more minutes. Looking around, Paul asked, "Where's Karyn?"

"Right here, sir," she said as she came from behind a bank of computers.

"Nice job. If I didn't know better, I'd be looking for him myself. I'm positive this plan will produce the results we desperately need as fast as possible. Thanks again," he said.

"Thank you, sir," she replied. "Major Fleenor certainly deserves the credit for getting it on the screen. It was his contacts and ideas that made it visible to the public. I just made up some pictures.”

“Well, you both have done excellent work. I don’t mean to shortchange anyone here, but the plan was yours, and it appears to be working. I’ll be back in a while. Mike, I’ll let you know if I need anything later. Keep up the good work, folks,” Paul said as he left the room.

CHAPTER 38

It was a little after twelve o'clock when Butch and his girls drove back from Decatur. As they got about a mile from the road leading to the stables, Butch asked, "You girls want to go up and see where the spaceship crashed over a hundred years ago?"

"No, Daddy, you've shown that to us already. I still don't believe it ever happened. It's just another of those bullshit stories that only illiterate jerks like you believe," Mischelle said. "If you can't have a good story to tell, you'd make one up."

"How can you say that? I've shown you the documentary from the History Channel, haven't I? And you've seen the little body lying there by the wreckage. What are you going to believe—me and an official documentary or your alcohol-soaked little brain?"

"How could they have a film of something that happened back in 1897? They didn't have cameras like that back then. Explain that!" she said.

"You two quit it. You always want to argue about that. Mischelle, don't let him get you into one of his 'intellectual' discussions. You know he's got Alzheimer's," Jeannie said as she turned her head and tried to ignore them.

"Intellectual? This is a fact. Even the great state of Texas says it is. Why, right down that road is the cemetery where the kind folks of Aurora buried the poor little fellow. You've seen the authentic historical marker with your own eyes. How can you not believe it?" Butch said as they passed Cemetery Road.

"Never mind. I've read the sign, too. It doesn't say an alien was actually buried there. It just says that 'supposedly' an alien was. That sign doesn't prove anything," Jeannie said.

"If the great state of Texas says it happened, then it happened," he said. "Maybe the state you live in tells you lots of lies, but not Texas!"

"Bullshit. There are more liars in Texas than in any other state. Things are bigger in Texas—yeah, bigger liars."

"Don't you talk like that about Texas. We don't even come close to having as many liars as Oklahoma. Nothing but liars and thieves up there. Hell, you've got to count your fingers every time you shake an Okie's hand. They'll steal them right off your hand and then lie to you and tell you they found them.

Why do you think we put the Red River up there? To keep those damn Okies out of Texas! Unfortunately, some fool built a damn bridge, and here they came," Butch said as they turned into the stables.

"Now, don't say anything about Okies to Steve. I think he has kinfolks up there and is too ashamed to admit it."

They stopped by Steve's house as they pulled in. "Y'all just wait. I'm going to get Gene, and we'll go get a burger for lunch. Be right back," he said as he got out of the truck and walked to the door.

"Come on in, Butch," said Steve. "How was the shopping? They melt your credit cards, running them through the machines?"

"Well, they gave it a good try. Hey, Gene, are you ready to get something to eat? Thought I'd take you with us.

The girls wanted a hamburger, and not just any hamburger; it's gotta be a Whataburger.

They don't have them in Seattle or Baltimore, so every time they come down here, they have to have one. They *are* good. Best burgers in Texas. I don't think they are anywhere besides Texas, anyway."

"Yes, sir," Gene said as he was getting up. "Steve said he needed to go get something Sheril wanted in town, so I guess I don't have anything to do right now."

"All right. We'll have to drive back up to Decatur after we stop by the house and drop off the stuff they bought. I guess they didn't like my selection of food. Sure are picky little things. Don't know if I'll ever find them a new momma—they are just too picky for anyone but me to put up with. Destined to be orphans, I guess. See you in a while, Steve," he said as they left. "We'll be back in an hour or so.

The girls and I will stick around to bring in the horses, so if you and Sheril want to leave early, that's all right. Gene's figured out how to take care of things. Now, if you start getting lazy on me, I'll have someone ready to take your place," he said, smiling as they walked to the truck.

"When we get to Decatur, we can go to Wal-Mart if you need anything, Gene," Butch said as they turned onto FM 718. "I'm going to fill up the truck here at Kountry Korner before we go. I don't like to get too low on diesel in this thing."

As Butch stopped by the diesel pumps and got out, Mischelle asked, "You lived around here long, Gene?"

"Fort Worth," he said. "Haven't been up here but a couple of days. Your dad offered me the job yesterday so that Steve could take a few days off."

"Well," she said, "he's kind of fun to hang around with. Just don't believe a word he says, though. He likes to joke about everything. 'Course, he probably won't be with you yet. He's got to get to know you before he starts giving you a real hard time.

Just remember he really doesn't mean any of it. Just likes to kid people."

"I've noticed," he replied. "Most of the people I've met out here seem really nice. Your daddy does give a lot of them a hard time, but they don't act like they mind."

"No, they know him too well. Most of them just give it right back. He's a lot different when he's up visiting us. A lot quieter. Sometimes that's a blessing," Jeannie said. "Too bad he can't be that way down here. But that's the way he is."

Butch came back from paying, climbed in, and started the truck. As they drove across the road into his driveway, his two horses came running along the fence toward the house.

"Lucky's getting kind of fat, isn't he?" Jeannie said as they watched the horses stop beside the fence in the back of the house.

"Just a little," Butch replied as he got out. "He can gain weight on dirt. Poor old Bud has to eat a bale a day to keep weight on. Some horses are just easy keepers like Lucky.

They're a lot like people. Some folks can eat all day and never gain a pound, while others get fat just by looking at a picture of a pickle. 'Course, a lot of the fat ones don't just look at the picture; they gotta eat everything they see.

I was in this little bar the other night, having a beer with one of the boarders. There were so many heavy old gals, I told him that if it were an auction, we'd have to buy them by the head. I couldn't afford to buy them by the pound."

"See what I mean?" Jeannie said. "He's got to have some witty little saying all the time. At least he thinks it's witty. I think it just rhymes with witty. And he's full of it."

"Be nice to your poor old pappy. Now get your stuff in the house while Gene and I go give the horses a treat. Don't listen to them, Gene. Little liars. I think they must have been born in Oklahoma!"

Butch went into the garage and got a handful of large pellets from a feed sack. Taking them to the fence, he held one out in his hand to the biggest one. As the horse reached over the fence to take it, he said, "This is Lucky. Best rope horse I've ever owned. He's about sixteen hands and weighs almost 1,400 pounds. By the way, horses are measured in hands, and one hand is four inches. You measure from the ground to his withers. Lucky'll pull seven-hundred-pound steers around all day when we're roping and never gives up. Got a lot of want-to in him."

Holding out another pellet to the other horse, he said, "This one is Bud. He's a good horse but basically lazy. Lucky wants to give you 100 percent every time. This guy, you gotta have spurs on to make him give you what he's got. It just pisses Lucky off if you spur him, kind of like he's thinking that he's already giving you all he's got.

Bud will start pushing it after a couple of hard pokes and will keep it up as long as you keep the spurs on. You don't have to use them after he knows you've got them and will use them. But if you take them off, he's back to being lazy again."

"When are you going to be roping again?" Gene asked. "I'd like to watch sometime."

"Probably not until spring. I hate cold weather, and all the steers I had were getting too big. I'll get some more about next March or so."

"How long do you keep them?"

"Depends. As soon as they develop bad habits or get too big, it's off to Taco Bell."

"What do you mean, bad habits?"

"Well, cattle do learn things. I work with them for a week or so, teaching them to come running out of the chute as soon as it opens. I usually have to use a *hot shot* the first couple of times.

Then you have to show them the way to the alley where the stripping chute is and where you get your rope off after you and your heeler have roped—that is, if you caught him. I'll get a couple of guys to help, and we'll push them down the arena and force them into the alley at the end.

After a few times, the cattle figure out that if they run straight to the opening, they get to go lie down in the holding pen just through the stripping chute, and we won't bother them again.

After they've been roped a lot, they know you're about to rope them, and they will either drop their heads or stop just as you get ready to throw your loop. Or they will try to sit down and drag their butts on the ground so the heeler can't catch the back legs.

I always tell them—play nice, and they can eat nice green grass all day and only get roped two or three times a week. Don't play nice—they're off to the hamburger farm. They just don't listen. Sooner or later, they get bad habits."

"Let's go!" Mischelle said as they came out of the house. "I'm starving. I'm going to tell everybody I see how you're mistreating us. It's inhumane!"

"Never have kids, Gene," Butch replied. "Get a good dog. A good dog will always be your friend, never treat you mean like children do when they think they're as smart as you, and you can put it down if it turns evil on you as my kids have done. Let's go get a Whataburger."

CHAPTER 39

It was shortly after one o'clock that afternoon when Kathy knocked on General Modelle's suite door. "Come in. The door's unlocked," Kathy heard from within.

She opened the door and questioned, "General, do you have a minute?"

"Yes, how may I help you?"

"Well, sir, Colonel Erickson asked me to see if you could come to the communications room."

"Certainly. Tell Rick I'll be there in less than five minutes. Thanks, Kathy."

General Modelle resumed talking on the phone as Kathy softly closed the door. "Yes, sir, Mr. President. I have full confidence in General Nelson and his staff. As a matter of fact, Colonel Rick Erickson has just sent for me. I believe they must have made some significant progress. They would not have disturbed me otherwise.

Certainly, sir. I'll contact you if it warrants your attention. I'll use the com-sat phone from the plane if I believe we need to discuss specifics."

Paul listened for another few seconds and replaced the phone. The room was sparsely furnished, much like most temporary officer's quarters. A standard double bed and nightstand dominated the room. An adjoining bathroom opened beside the open closet doors, which covered one wall. Opposite the entry door stood a small television on the edge of a dresser with six drawers. The headboard of the bed was on the opposite wall, and two stuffed chairs with a small table between them sat against the wall opposite the bathroom.

Due to being two floors below the hangar floor, there were no windows, and the only light was from the fluorescent strip lights on the ceiling or either of the two table lamps.

He closed and locked his briefcase and turned off the television. He had been monitoring all the news channels as he had reviewed the reams of material the staff had provided him this morning.

There had been a continuous stream of reporters and well-known national broadcasters replaying the same information throughout the morning. Paul knew there would be no real break in the capture of these phantom terrorists until they gave the word.

Anxious to hear if there was any breakthrough in the spotting or location of Gene, he hurried back to the communications room.

Colonel Erickson was talking on the secure phone as he entered. He stood beside the desk as he listened in.

"All right, have the Tarrant County Sheriff's Office send one of their most experienced officers to question them. If there is any certainty of the report, have the officer remain with them until one of our teams replaces them. Have the Tarrant County people let me know when the officer arrives and use our discreet frequency for all further communications."

Rick replaced the phone, stood, and walked to a large map of the Dallas-Fort Worth Metroplex mounted on a large portable divider.

"General, if you'll step over here, I think we may have our first confirmed lead. I've sent it to General Nelson. He should be here by the time I get my next message from the search teams."

They stood in front of the map, and Rick took a yellow tack and stuck it into the map just north and west of Fort Worth. There were several yellow tacks and a few green tacks scattered across the map.

Beside the map of the DFW Metroplex was a map of the state of Texas. All across the state were hundreds of yellow tacks.

Several green tacks were scattered from El Paso in the west to Texarkana on the east border and from Houston, at the Gulf of Mexico, to Amarillo, up in the Texas Panhandle.

"Each yellow tack represents a contact that reported seeing any of the six broadcast photos. The green ones represent contacts that have been closed with no evidence of Gene being there.

Some of the green tacks represent reports of sightings based on the photos of one or more of the other individuals. Since we know they are not actually in the United States or are already in custody, only cursory contact is made at those locations. Usually, a local policeman drops by to ensure the public is assured that we are actively pursuing each report.

This tack represents a location where the caller says without a doubt that Gene was there. Both the husband and wife agree and state that the husband, Mr. Ray Downey, picked Gene up at an all-night service station and convenience store located near the intersection of Highway 183 and 199, the Jacksboro Highway.

The location is well known as a place where local ranchers pick up day labors, usually illegals, and return them at the end of the day. I have sent one of our team to question the owner or manager, but I don't expect they will admit to having seen anything. And I'm sure they never look at these people unless they come into the store."

"Isn't that somewhat different from what Vicki told us?" Paul asked as General Nelson entered and joined them at the map.

"Well, yes and no. It is possible for her to have dropped Gene, which she said she did, and he either caught a ride or walked around 820 to this location.

However, due to the distance, I believe he either caught a ride or Vicki lied. Personally, I think she lied."

"I think you are right, Rick," Mike said as he looked at the map.

"At the time of day when most of the locals get the workers from this location, Gene would have little chance of getting there even if he caught a ride almost immediately after Vicki dropped him off."

"A lot of sightings," Paul remarked as he looked at the green tacks spread across the state, the majority of which were centered around Fort Worth and its closest communities.

"Yes, and most of them have been reports of Mexicans seen at locations similar to the one where Gene was reported to have been picked up. Some, of course, were just people making false reports due to some personal issues.

But this one is different. They were adamant about him being there for quite a bit of time, and they both talked to him."

"What do you know of the area?" Paul asked as he studied the map. "Does it have any significance to him as Amy suggested it might?"

"The ranch where the Downeys live is just north of Azle on Highway 730. There is nothing in Azle itself that could be tied to Gene, but continuing north on 730 into Wise County, he would be about three miles from Aurora," Rick answered.

"And as you know, Aurora does bear significantly on Gene's genetic makeup. Amy could have been absolutely correct. With this report having a high level of confidence, it would appear that she was off only in which site provided the majority of influence on him. We'll certainly know more after interviewing the Downeys."

"What is your plan if this is a confirmed sighting?" Mike asked.

"We will refocus our effort more north than west. I will shift all team members to the area around the 183 and Jacksboro Highway intersection so we can respond quicker if need be. Of course, I will leave one member on the west side for sightings in that area. He will remain at the motel until we call for him to respond if one of the local police reports happens to need further investigation."

Rick's phone gave a sharp ring, and the light on the handset blinked.

He quickly stepped over to the desk and answered, "Colonel Erickson."

After listening for only seconds, he looked at both Mike and Paul, nodding his head enthusiastically. "Have the officer remain there, and a member of our FBI team will relieve him within fifteen minutes. Under no circumstances is the officer to leave until he is replaced, and direct him to make no additional reports. I do not want any further mention of this location being transmitted by any uniformed officer from any jurisdiction. Is that understood?"

"Good," Rick said as he replaced the phone and turned to face the two Generals. "An officer from the Tarrant County Sheriff's Office confirms that the Downeys did see Gene. They described his shirt, said he told them his name was 'Gene Morales' and spent over an hour at their location. I'll have one of our members expedited to the Downeys' location. I want to get the county boys out of there while we question them.

The only inconsistency in their stories involves the direction Gene took when he left. Our people will try to resolve that issue when they arrive. I want to keep as much information on Gene's travel out of the local's knowledge as possible."

"I agree, Rick," Mike said as he turned back to the map. "Paul, if you follow 730 north of Azle about fifteen miles, this little town here is Boyd. Has a population of what, Rick, about one thousand?"

"That's about right."

"Aurora is about three miles east on Highway 114. If Gene is headed in that direction, we should be able to find people in the Boyd area who may have seen him.

Most of these small towns are acutely aware of any strangers, but they are used to seeing numerous Mexican workers all over the place. There has been a lot of new construction out in that area, and all the framing crews, concrete contractors, and so forth use lots of them.

Due to the large numbers of Mexicans passing through that area, it may hamper our efforts, especially since Gene does appear as much Hispanic as he does Middle Eastern. Without the beard and Arab-type clothing, he could easily pass for just another Mexican working on any number of projects or hitchhiking to a job.

If his going in that direction has any drawbacks, it is that those people seldom give a second glance to another Hispanic working in the community. As long as he stays out of any business location, he is virtually invisible to the locals."

Rick's phone rang again, and he moved to the desk to answer it as Mike finished speaking. Turning to Rick as he replaced the phone, Mike raised his eyebrows, silently questioning him.

"Our man is on location. He will report on sat-com after his interview. We should have a better idea of Gene's plans when he finishes. All we can do now is give him a chance to do his job and call us."

Mike turned toward the door and said, "Kathy has provided a bunch of sandwiches, chips, and stuff for lunch.

It's about time, and there isn't much more for us here right now. What say we put on the feedbag? With this good piece of news, Dr Peppers are on me. If you want something else to drink, you're on your own."

"Call me at the conference room as soon as you receive any news from the Downey interview, please," Rick said as he followed Mike and Paul out of the room.

CHAPTER 40

As they left the stables and turned left on Highway 114, Jeannie said, "I thought we were going to Decatur and Whataburger. Why are we going toward Boyd?"

"I wanted to take the back way. Highway 730 is a prettier drive, and Gene needs to see something besides an interstate road. We'll come back down 287 to the stables."

During the three miles to Boyd, Gene looked at some of the familiar sights he had seen when Butch had first driven him from Azle to the stables. He recognized the place where large cats were kept, and as they passed a metal building on the left, he saw someone waving at them.

"I think someone over there wants you," he said as he pointed to the building."

Quickly slowing as he looked to the left, Butch made the next turn into the driveway. "That's old Mikey Carmichael. You girls remember him. Has a ranch out by Jacksboro. His ranch motto is "Raising Beef for the Elite."

As they pulled up in front of 3 Way Trucking, Mikey came over to the truck. "How's it going, Butch? What in the world are you doing with these two pretty little gals riding around with you?

Hello, girls," he said. "You keeping your pappy out of trouble?"

"Not a chance," Mischelle said. "We don't have the time or energy that requires. He seems to find trouble everywhere he goes."

"I think it's the company he keeps," replied Jeannie, smiling. "It could be men like you that keep stirring him up and laughing at his crappy jokes."

"Oh, your daddy doesn't need any encouraging. Besides, we only laugh just to make him feel that we like him. Say, did I tell you my old lady caught me sneaking in again the other night?" Mikey asked, smiling.

"I'd just stopped off at Red's for a beer or two, you know. Somebody made me play a couple of games of pool, and before I knew it, they were turning all the lights on bright and telling us to go home.

Really, it wasn't my fault. I tell you, that wife of mine has ears like a bat. She can hear a cricket fart a half a mile away."

"Hell, you should have seen the ears of my ex-wife. She could hear a man's zipper going down almost a mile away. She'd hear that and go on point like a good bird dog in a covey of quail. She had to be a mite closer to hear those button-fly jeans, but her ears would perk up, and she'd slobber like a newborn calf on a tit."

"Daddy, stop it," both girls yelled at once. "That's our mother you're talking about!"

"Yeah, I know. Bless her little old cold heart. That, sure enough, was your mother. Well, Mikey, I've got to get these girls to Whataburger before they faint from starvation. Take care."

"You too. Say, ya'll going to Red's tonight? One of my exes says she's going and wants to sing 'I've Got a Tiger by the Tail' for me one more time."

"We had planned on it, but if that old hide is going to be there, I think I'll just stay home and pound nails through my toes."

"I was just joking. I think I may stop by for one beer before I go home. Maybe play a little pool."

"You might better get home to Mama tonight. Another night like last night's one beer and pool game, she might just cut off your end of the table and let you eat with the dogs."

"Yeah, you're right. I reckon I'll be a good boy and go home tonight. You sure you don't want a wife, Butch?"

"No thanks, Mikey. I don't mind a wife for the night, but I'll just leave that permanent stuff to you boys. See ya."

Pulling back onto 114, they continued into Boyd and turned right on 730 toward Decatur. As they drove north, Gene could see herds of cattle grazing out the window and asked, "What type of cows are those?" pointing to a pasture on the right side.

"They're called cattle. A mama is a cow. A young female is a heifer, a young male is a bull calf unless he's been cut, and then he's a steer. The big males are bulls. So, the cattle you see there are Black Angus.

Up here on the left, a couple of miles, you'll see a herd of longhorns. They're on a real pretty ranch with a lot of oak trees and a nice big pond in front.

The Angus cattle are raised for beef, like steak, but the longhorn is skinnier and usually is used for cheaper meats. We might even get some of one at Whataburger. My cousin sold a couple a few months back. She named them Rib Eye and T-bone. Should have named them Hamburger and Helper since I'm sure that's where they wound up."

As they passed the longhorn herd, Gene could see why they were named that way. About fifty head were grazing along the fence as they drove by. Some of the larger ones had horns curving up, out, and back down, stretching six feet from tip to tip.

"You ever rope one of those?" he asked as he watched them try to stick their noses under the fence for the grass outside the pasture.

"Yeah, but I have to keep cutting the ends of the horns off so they can fit through the chute. Kind of like trimming your toenails. The girls got to help once. It's kind of a bloody job. There's a vein down the middle of the horn, and it will really spray you if you're not careful."

"Gross, Daddy," Jeannie said. "Let's not talk about eating cows we know or how much blood squirts out when you cut off the horns. I think I'll just have a salad when we get there."

"Too bad they don't have calf fries. You'd like those," Butch told Gene.

"What's a calf fry?" he asked.

"It's bull balls," Mischelle said. "Rocky Mountain oysters. And I will not eat them!"

"Hell, it tastes just like chicken fried steak, but more tender. Maybe I'll call Mikey and have him bring some over tomorrow. We'll fry them up and invite everyone over. Guess we better stop and get some more beer. I'm sure you girls didn't leave much after last night anyway."

Driving on into Decatur, Gene was amazed at the different types of cattle along the way. Just before reaching town, he saw a herd of dairy cattle, and one place even had a bunch of goats running through the pasture.

He had seen a lot of these things, but only pictures or videos. Seeing them alive and in the pastures was certainly different. Even the smell of the air still excited him. Everything was so different than the filtered and artificially controlled environment where he had spent his life up till now.

Joining Highway 287 at the edge of Decatur, Gene saw hundreds of new cars and trucks as they passed James Wood Motors. He had never seen so many in one place, and all under huge red awnings. This was his first time to see the type of businesses that were in these towns. His trip from the base to where Vicki had dropped him off had been mainly residential, and it was also dark.

The little he had seen of Boyd didn't provide much to see either. Just a few businesses along the main street, mainly small restaurants and gas stations. Here, there were large buildings set apart from each other, motels, and other commercial businesses in every location.

As they exited 287, Butch turned left to go under the road, and they pulled into the Whataburger parking lot. Getting out of the truck, Butch said, "Well, girls, here's your one chance for fine dining until you come back again. You might want to take a couple of napkins with you so you'll have a token of this event and to dry your eyes when you have to eat at one of those crap burger joints up north."

Entering, they went directly to the ordering station. "Not much of a line when you're an hour after everybody else eats. What do you want?"

"Whataburger Jr. for me, and fries," both girls said.

"I'll have a Whataburger with cheese and jalapeno. Onion rings, too, please," Butch told the cashier. "Put it all on one ticket and four Dr Peppers. Gene?"

"I'll have what you ordered also."

As the cashier was turning the order in, Jeannie said, "Aren't you going to tell them not to overcook your onion rings?"

"Nope, I know when to keep my mouth shut. You should learn that maybe?" he smiled as they went to a booth.

As they were waiting for their order to be delivered, Gene asked, "How do you guys know how many cattle you have and keep track of them?"

"I guess there are several ways," Butch responded. "I've got one friend who's a real whiz at mathematics. He runs all the cattle in a big pen and down an alley to his corrals. As they go by, he counts the legs, and when the last one passes him, he just divides by four, and that's the answer.

Now, another buddy, who isn't quite as smart, does it by counting the ears and dividing by two. He says it's twice as fast.

Me, I just count the heads. Guess I was never too good at high math anyway," he said, chuckling.

"Ignore him, Gene," Mischelle said. "If you ever want a straight answer, never ask him around other people. He thinks he has to be so witty!"

"Come on, girls, let your poor old pappy have a little fun. I just might not be here to entertain you much longer, you know. The doctor told me just the other day that I might not live to be a hundred. What will you do then?"

"Cry all the way to the bank. Driving your Corvette, too!" Jeannie smirked.

"I knew it. Bunch of little vultures. I tell you, Gene, get a good dog! Let's eat and get back so Gene can earn his pay."

CHAPTER 41

Standing in the conference room, having their lunch, they couldn't help but glance at the television tuned to one of the local stations. It constantly showed Gene's pictures and talked about the massive search that was taking place throughout the area and across the state.

One of the newscasters had a large map of Texas as a backdrop, and numerous locations across the state had small lights glowing to represent each potential spotting. As he talked, the screen would switch to an expanded view of the Dallas and Fort Worth areas as well as the towns within twenty-five miles of the center.

"Looks like everyone in the state is giving us a hand," General Modelle said as he finished a bite of his sandwich.

"That's one of the benefits to Karyn's plan," Mike said as he set his Dr Pepper down. "Here in Texas, there isn't any love lost for the radical Muslim crowd after what they did up in New York.

Texans don't especially care for New Yorkers, but when it comes to America, they become family. Most Texans see themselves as Texans first and Americans second. And just like any family, it's OK to fight your own brother, but they will defend the same brother against anyone else."

Rick was just getting a fresh jalapeno from the plate when the phone rang. Taking a large bite from the pepper, he answered it, saying, "Colonel Erickson." As he listened, he finished the jalapeno and took a drink from his can of Dr Pepper. "We'll be right there," he said as he replaced the phone. "Reports coming in via data link with the Downey place. It looks like it was Gene."

Everyone quickly finished what he or she was eating and left for the communications room. This looked like the first real break in the search had happened. It had been just over twenty-four hours since Gene had been taken out, and with some luck, they might have him back within the next twenty-four hours.

Entering the communications room, Rick went directly to the printer connected to the data link. As he pulled the first pages from the printer, he said, "Confirmation has been received. Positive identification by both sources. There is only one discrepancy between the two. Mr. Ray Downey stated that he did pick Gene up where it was reported and said Gene had planned to visit a cousin in Boyd after the job.

Mrs. Myrtle Downey stated that Gene told her he was returning to Fort Worth as he left the ranch. She did not actually see which direction he took but only watched him as he left the house and walked back toward the road.

The barns and buildings were all searched, and nothing was found that provides information as to Gene's intentions. But he did leave the area.

Gene was already gone when Mr. Downey returned, and he stated that he did not see him along the road coming back from Azle. Gene could have been in another car headed south and not have been seen, though.

Unless there are any objections, I am directing each member of the search team to deploy to separate locations, starting at the Downeys' and going north toward Boyd," Rick stated as he handed the copy of the data-link printout to Mike.

"There are several places where he may have stopped along the way before he got to Boyd. We will have the teams go into each business along the way as we work northward.

Even if there are televisions in the stores, the employees may not have seen any of the broadcasts but still have seen Gene. Showing his picture in each location may prove he is heading north."

"How much time do you think the search as far north as Boyd will take?" Paul asked as he looked at the map on the board.

"With ten men searching, it could take up to ten hours. I still want to keep one at the motel, just in case we need to send him in another direction, and one to continue to question people in Azle in the event Gene *did* catch a ride back toward Fort Worth. We also need to consider that Gene may well have gone north just to mislead us while he reverses his direction and heads west toward Roswell."

"I agree," Mike said, nodding his head. "The plan all along may have been to be seen heading in one direction to divert the search. Gene is highly intelligent and certainly knows we will mount a massive search immediately upon discovering his absence."

"OK, I'll send orders to the team leader and let him develop his search plan to use ten of his men. I'll have him provide us with a list of the members and where each will be going. I'll also have a more detailed map showing each area, such as Briar or Center Point. We can follow their progress and be ready to send them further north if we get any hits from the local police in any other area."

"Do you think you need to advise the sheriff or police departments located north of Azle of the sightings?" Karyn asked.

"No," Rick answered. "I don't want any rush of civilian officials into the area. Any increased activity may spook him, and more people would mean an increased chance of some Barney Fife type trying to gain a reputation by catching him.

That information might also cause a slowdown of effort in other areas, and I want the same level of intensity in all directions. Just in case Gene is trying to throw us off his trail. All things considered, I think we are making progress as fast as possible, and I sure don't want to jeopardize the plan just when we are showing some progress.

I think we will know a lot more when we get our next confirmed sighting. At that point, we may issue guidance to focus civilian authorities in that area, but I still have my concerns with their professionalism when it comes down to backing off if he is spotted.

As I said before, some of these officers are itching to prove their granddaddy was Wyatt Earp, and they want their fifteen minutes of fame. Some of these small towns don't get the brightest individuals on their force, and I'm sure the training isn't as we are used to in the military."

"I agree," responded Paul. "Things are moving our way, and the plan is just starting to bear fruit. I think it's way too early to make any shifts in our strategy. There are several drawbacks to focusing civilian attention on where we think Gene is going, and not a lot of benefits. This is just going to take a little time, and we knew that when we started. It's more important to maintain absolute control than it is to rush it and have some other agency capture Gene and determine what is really going on.

We must remember that the primary reason we are looking for Gene is the effect knowledge of his existence would have. So, as we discuss differing strategies, it's imperative that we don't forget the major concerns in our rush to recover Gene.

I'm positive that everyone involved with this project, from President Bush on down, would rather have it take an extra day or two to capture Gene than run the risk of him falling into the wrong hands."

Everyone there nodded and reflected on the General's message. They all knew that sometimes the desire to get the mission accomplished could doom it by rushing into it without taking every facet into consideration. This first big break had caused them all to become overanxious and want to intensify their efforts.

Paul looked toward Mike and asked, "Well, Mike, I guess we'll have to wait for the next break. In the meantime, I've got a couple of calls to make. Old George W. might appear calm, but I know for a fact that this has him more worried than any of those ragheads overseas. He knows we can defeat that enemy sooner or later, but if this got out, there's no telling what might happen.

I don't suppose you have a bottle of Jack Daniel's hidden in that office of yours, do you? I think I would enjoy a taste or two after I get off the phone."

"I'll do even better," Mike said as they walked toward the door. "I just happen to have a brand-new, never-been-sipped bottle of Gentleman Jack. I'll have Kathy get a bag of shaved ice, and we can have a little taste of heaven right here on Earth. I'll see you in my office when you're ready. Rick, good luck, and keep us posted."

"Yes, sir," Rick said as the Generals left the room.

CHAPTER 42

As they climbed into the truck, Butch turned to Gene and handed him $100, saying, "Here's your pay for yesterday and today. Is there anything you need before we go home? There is a Wal-Mart right down the street. It's no problem to stop before we leave."

"If it's no trouble, I *would* like to get a couple of things. Just some socks and stuff," Gene answered.

"No problem," Butch said as he started the truck. "I'll go in and help you. I've finally learned where everything is in the store. Seems like just when I had it all figured out, they moved everything. I used to be able to get my shopping done in thirty minutes, then after the move, I had to search each aisle just to find one item.

At least they have a good selection of most stuff," he continued as they pulled into the parking lot. "They even have Slim-Fast. Of course, from the looks of most of the big old gals you see here, not much of it is sold.

A buddy of mine from Bowie always said he came to Wal-Mart before he went out to the bars around here. Said after seeing the big butts in there, the gals he saw in the bars even looked slim in comparison," Butch said, smiling at Jeannie.

"Well, maybe the girls at the bar do that too," Mischelle said. "I know who you are talking about, and he might need to lose a hundred pounds or so himself."

Looking shocked, Butch said, "Really? Just because he can't see his feet without a mirror? I hope he doesn't know you would talk about him like that. It would break his little heart. He's sensitive, you know."

As they entered the store, Butch pointed at the greeter and told Gene, "Fellow there is a retired fighter pilot. Since there's no better job than flying a fighter, most of them just give up and hang around, hoping they can tell war stories to pass their time."

"Why aren't you a greeter then, Daddy?" Jeannie asked. "You're retired. What happened, you get fired for telling all your bullshit stories and pissing all the customers off?"

"Nope. I decided to go fly a big bus full of rude, obnoxious, ill-mannered passengers through the sky. Sacrificed my pride for money. But then, I had to support you two little shits, didn't I?"

After finding the menswear section, Gene quickly picked out a couple of pairs of socks and a new shirt and asked about the jeans.

"Well, I like Wranglers," Butch said. "They fit good and wear well. Just get a pair about two or three inches longer than those you're wearing so they look right with your boots."

Jeannie looked down at Gene's boots and cried, "Those are mine. Why did you give him my boots, Daddy?"

"Poor guy didn't have any, just sneakers. I couldn't let him work around those horses in soft-toed shoes like that. Besides, I bought you a new pair last time you were down here. If they're getting worn too much, we'll go to Justin tomorrow and get another pair. You should be more generous anyway. Haven't I always told you to be kind to the less fortunate? Hell, don't I dance with the fat ones when they ask?"

"You're such a jerk sometimes. You may dance with them, but you come back to the table and moan about how they dislocated your shoulder or broke your arm when you tried to spin or something," Mischelle said disapprovingly.

"Well, it's true. Had to wear a back brace for a month after I tried to dip one at the end of a dance last year. Doctor told me to never try to hold three hundred pounds while bent over like that again! Got everything, Gene? Let's get out of here before these girls get me into trouble."

As they walked toward the check-out counters, Butch said, "Let's use the self-service things. Lines are too long everywhere else. At least they widened the aisles to accommodate these big old butts when they moved everything. Guess they got tired of having to put stuff back on the shelves after one of them bumped their way down through it. Some of them even had to smear Crisco on their hips to squeeze through anyway."

"Don't listen to him, Gene. And never agree with him. He'll just get you into trouble," Jeannie said as she shook her head and walked off.

After returning to the truck, they drove out of the parking lot and turned right on FM 51. About a mile later, Butch pointed to the right and said, "There is David's Western Wear. Most of the time, when I come up here, I stop in and look around a little. They've got some nice saddles and stuff. Nearly always buy my hats here; ropes too. The guy that owns it has a real nice arena just south of town.

If you ever see something called National Ropers Supply, it's the same thing. They give lessons and have clinics and stuff at the arena. Real nice facility."

After stopping at the traffic light, they turned left and came to Highway 287. As they merged with the traffic headed south, Gene watched as large trucks with tarps covering the trailers passed them.

"Why are there so many of these trucks everywhere?" he asked.

"Rock haulers. There's a big rock quarry just west of here at Chico. They haul rocks and sand all over the place for roads, concrete, or whatever's being built. The bad thing is that they always lose a rock or two driving down the road. Lots of broken windshields. Always stay way behind them. Just like that," Butch said as they saw several rocks fall from the truck and bounce along the road, one barely missing them.

Gene could see several new housing developments as they drove on for the next few miles. Just like he had heard, the country was filling up with new houses, and he could see hundreds of workers in the developments. He could tell that most of the laborers were Mexican. "Maybe I'll blend in out here well enough to not be noticed," he thought, "Nobody seems to pay them any attention."

As they arrived at Rhome and turned west on 114, Butch said, "We'll help you get the horses in and fed, and then we can clean up a little and go to Red's. Maybe the girls can teach you to do a little two-step while I'm amazing the crowd with my spectacular singing."

"It's spectacular, all right," Jeannie said. "It's spectacular that there's anyone left in the bar after hearing you."

As they stopped in front of Steve's house, Butch told Gene to drop off his new clothes and meet them at the barn. "We'll start bringing them in. When you get down there, just fill the feed buckets and check the water. We'll give them some hay when we come back," he said as Gene got out of the truck.

As he parked in front of the barn, he told the girls to get a couple of lead ropes and meet him at the gate to the stall area. As he walked through one of the corrals beside the stalls, he noticed nearly every one of the horses standing just outside the gate. They were constantly laying their ears back and charging each other or turning and kicking.

"Looks like they're anxious to be the first one in tonight, don't they?" Butch said as the girls came into the alleyway between the corrals and the stalls. "Jeannie, you guard the gate and let them in a couple at a time. I'll take the ones going to the barn and let Mischelle open the gates for those staying in these stalls."

As Jeannie opened the gate, Butch told Mischelle which stalls the horses belonged in as he caught a solid black gelding and led him toward the barn. "Wait till I get back before you let any more in," he said as the horse walked along his side into the barn.

As he was closing the stall door, Gene walked in. "You remember which feed to use on each horse?" Butch asked.

"Yes, sir. Only two in here get their own special feed, and it's in the cans in front of their stalls. And this one gets alfalfa instead of coastal," Gene said, pointing to one of the stalls.

"That's right. I'll finish bringing the rest of them in, and you can feed the outside ones while I let the girls pretty up at the house. You'll have plenty of time to finish feeding and get a shower before I come back. Sure takes women a lot more time than men to get presentable. They gotta paint and primp till they look like a peacock's tail. We just knock off the worst of the dust, and we're ready to go," he said as he walked back to where the girls were waiting.

"Okay, Jeannie, give us another couple. Mischelle is getting bored just standing there. I want to get done and hustle out to Red's. My fan club's probably making up a list of all the songs they want me to sing."

"They're probably bribing the karaoke guy to lose all the songs, you mean," said Mischelle as she closed the gate on a large bay mare.

All the horses were put in their stalls in about fifteen minutes, and Gene was starting to take the feed and hay to the outside stalls as they walked to the truck.

"Be back in about thirty minutes, Gene. Don't get too pretty. Folks at Red's don't always look as nice as we do. Being so good-looking is a burden I have to bear," Butch said, smiling as he got into the truck and drove off.

CHAPTER 43

Paul and Mike entered the office as Kathy was hanging up her phone. "I've told my husband not to expect me for dinner tonight. I figured you gentlemen might need me around for a while. Is there anything I can do for you?"

"Would you please ask Cory to get us a bucket of shaved ice from the Officer's Club? Paul and I are going to relax for a minute before we get back to work. Have you heard anything new on the raghead that was denied boarding at DFW the other night?" Mike asked, reinforcing the concept that their mission centered on capturing terrorists instead of its real purpose.

"The news has shown lots of reports all day. There have been hundreds of sightings, but I don't think there have been any arrests," she said as she picked up her phone to call Major Romine. "I'm just glad he was stopped; otherwise, we would have had another terrible accident."

"Never call this an accident," Paul said, shaking his head. "This was an obscene, criminal act by a group of radical idiots that think they have to destroy anyone who feels differently than they do. The leaders of their religion need to quit perverting the teachings of Mohammed and stop trying to kill not only each other but every other established religious group."

"I don't mind them killing each other," Mike replied, opening the door to his office. "If they want to fight among themselves, let them. But when they attack the United States, it's not just criminal; it's an act of war. If they want to fight, let them stand up like real men and fight, not take a cowardly way of hurting civilians who could care less whether or not a Sunni or a Shiite is right. They are all a bunch of pussy shitheads as far as I'm concerned.

I've had to work with Iranians, Iraqis, Kuwaitis, Jordanians, Saudis, and lots of other Middle Easterners throughout my career, and I wouldn't trust a single one of the lying bastards. Bunch of gutless, worthless throwbacks to precivilization. Still living in the Dark Ages. Without Western influence, they'd still be cooking over camel shit and living in tents."

"Feel rather strongly about that, do you, Mike?" Paul asked as they entered the office and closed the door.

"Yes, I certainly do. I realize the tremendous political pressures on our government to appease certain groups in the Middle East, but we need to ensure they realize the repercussions of acts of terrorism. If the ruling governments can't or refuse to, control their citizens, then the rest of the civilized world needs to take care of the problem," Mike said as he sat behind his desk.

"Now, don't get me wrong—I've known quite a few Middle Easterners and Muslims that are as fine a bunch of folks as you could ever meet. They hold the same basic values we do. But they are also at fault for letting the fanatics hijack their religion and pervert it to further their own agenda. As far as I'm concerned, every one of them is responsible for today's attacks, either because of their actions or, possibly even worse, their inactions. At this point, I blame them all, just as I'm sure the rest of the nation does. I'm sorry to say this, but today I hate every damned one of them."

"Guess you won't be running for any public office anytime soon, will you?" asked Paul as he sat in one of the leather chairs facing the desk and picked up a crystal glass. "I can't say I disagree with you, but we can't blame an entire nation or a religion for the acts of a few zealots. Hell, even the Christians and the Jews have their share of religious bigots. Now, how about a sip of that Gentleman Jack while we're waiting for the ice?"

As Mike poured a shot of the amber liquid into two cut-glass tumblers, he said, "Hell, I'd never have a chance at public office. I couldn't get elected as a dogcatcher. I've got too much of a tendency to say what I think, and dealing with the public like that, I'd piss off three-fourths of them. You already know how I am. I think that's one of the reasons you chose this assignment for me. Not only do I not have to deal with the local community, the project almost forbids it."

"Yeah, I know how you are. I've always respected that about you. You certainly stand up and let people know how you feel. I'll admit it has gotten you into a few scrapes with some very senior officers over the years, and I've been criticized more than once for sponsoring you. But as you so eloquently put it, this job was perfect for a man like you. Here's to our speedy success," Paul said as he raised his glass.

As Mike raised his glass and took a healthy swig, he said, "To our success. And again, my thanks to you for your support of a hardheaded old ass like me. Not a lot of our modern officers would put up with some of my ways."

As Paul set his glass on the oak desk and leaned back in his chair, he said, "Mike, you know as well as I do that if this fails or if the wrong people find Gene before we do, neither you nor I will survive the fallout. All joking aside, this is about the deepest river of shit either of us has had to swim out of. Even a successful conclusion may not protect our careers, maybe not even our lives."

"I know, Paul. If this destroys my career, I just want you to know I want the buck to stop right here. My folks did absolutely nothing wrong. I'll never let them suffer for my mistakes. When you talk to the boss, please make sure he understands that. If he needs Presidential approval to favorably resolve that, I would like you to do it."

"You know I will, Mike. We go back too far, and regardless of what the current head of MJ 12 thinks, I still have faith in you and all your people. I'll do everything in my power to protect all of you. I've already talked to President Bush and gotten his guarantee that one mistake in over fifty years of working this program will not result in punishment of anyone that did not overtly commit the acts that led to our current dilemma."

There was a knock on the door, and Mike said, "Yes?"

Kathy opened the door and walked in with a container of the shaved ice they had requested. "Anything else?" she asked as she set the ice on a table next to the coffeemaker and cups.

"No, Kathy," Mike answered. "Guess that will be it. Why don't you go on home and surprise that tall Texan of yours. Plan on being back by six o'clock tomorrow morning. If anything comes up before that, I'll give you a call. Thanks."

"All right," she responded. "I hope y'all have a good evening, and don't worry about calling me if you need me. I want those sorry little sneaky assholes caught as much as you do."

As she turned to leave, Paul said, "Why, Kathy, I've never heard such language! Now I know I want you to quit your job here and come to work for me."

Turning back to face the General, she said, "General Modelle, I'm sure you've heard worse, but I do appreciate your offer. My only problem is that I'll never leave Texas. It took me long enough to get here, and after living in this little piece of heaven, I don't think I'd ever be happy anywhere else."

As she closed the door behind her, Paul said, "Hell of a good woman. Take good care of that one, not many like her. Now, let's get a glass of that shaved ice and enjoy one more glass of this wonderful nectar before I go try to grab a couple of winks. It may be a very long night."

"I bet you're right about that," said Mike as he rose to pack ice in their glasses. "This waiting around is the hardest part."

Returning to his desk, he poured each glass full and sat back after handing one to Paul. They both sat quietly, sipping their drinks and wondering how this would play out.

Both of them knew the stakes were higher than any other mission they had been assigned, and they had less control over the results than ever before.

CHAPTER 44

Butch finished showering, shaving, and put on a starched hunter-green pearl-snap wrangler shirt with the equestrian center logo stitched over the left breast pocket. Taking a pair of heavily starched Wrangler jeans from his closet, he had to force his feet through the legs and peel the fabric apart. As he took a pair of ostrich-skin boots from the floor, he yelled through the closed door to the girls to hurry up and get pretty.

Buckling his belt, he walked out of his bedroom and pounded on the bathroom door where the girls were fixing their hair and makeup. "Come on, girls, there's fun to be had. I just know Old Red is looking at everyone coming in, hoping it's me," he said as he walked to the entryway to get his black felt hat.

Taking a small brush and removing a little dust from the hat, he set it squarely on his head and went into the kitchen. As he opened the refrigerator, he asked the girls if they wanted him to make them a drink. "Jack and Coke," came the answer as they emerged from the bathroom.

"I see you're wearing your new black hat tonight," Jeannie mentioned as she took her glass from his hand. "Guess that means you're going to be bad. You always told your mother that you wore the silver belly when you were going to be good and the black one when you weren't."

"I may be bad, but then again, I'm so good when I'm bad that it's difficult to pick a hat that matches my mood every time. The black one goes better with this shirt anyway."

Mischelle came into the kitchen where they were standing and spun around, asking, "What do you think, Daddy? Pretty enough to be seen with you?"

"Of course you are. You two will be the prettiest girls there and the skinniest too, I would bet. I'll probably have to fight the boys off you, most of them anyway. There are a few there that like the full-figured type, and there will be plenty of them, some of them fuller-figured than the rest. Just hope they're driving at least a three-quarter-ton truck if they hope to take them home. I've seen a few of them that flatten the springs on a half-ton."

Raising his glass, he said, "Girls, I want you to know that I sure enjoy y'all being here. Real nice of you to spend time with your poor old daddy. One of these days, you'll realize that you can only be happy living in Texas. I've lived all over the United States and overseas and traveled just about everywhere, and there's no better place. The greatest people in the world live in Texas. Y'all need to get back here real soon. Maybe you can help me find you a new mama so you won't be orphans."

Hugging him, Mischelle said, "I do love you, Daddy, but it's too damned hot down here in the summers, and I'd just as soon not hang around you while you keep looking for love in all the wrong places. You know you'll never get married again— you don't want someone else living in your house."

"I'm only looking for a mother for you girls," Butch replied. "I just can't stand thinking that when I die, you'll be all alone. That's why I want to find a real pretty one just a little younger than y'all. That way, she'll be around after I'm gone to keep you straight."

"You'll probably outlive us anyway," said Jeannie. "You're too damn mean and ornery to die. You'll probably live to be a hundred and fifty, still making jokes about fat women, ex-wives, or whatever you and your friends joke about all the time."

"Didn't I just tell you that the doctor said I may not live to be a hundred? You girls will only be in your sixties when I die. I gotta find you a mama to take care of you. Maybe I better wait until I'm about eighty, find a pretty little twenty-year-old, and marry her. That way, when I'm about one hundred, you'll be almost eighty; she'll be only forty or so and can take care of you during your elderly days. Now, that's a plan."

"Oh yeah, that's a plan. Guess you need to go to the nursery room at the hospital and start picking one out right now. That way, you'll know who she is when you're eighty because you won't be able to see very well and might just pick an ugly one," Mischelle said as she finished her drink and set the glass in the sink.

"I can handle ugly," Butch replied as he sat his glass on the counter and poured another healthy shot of Jack Daniel's in the glass. "I just can't do fat. Ugly goes away in the dark, but a big old hail-damaged butt doesn't."

Jeannie shook her head and put her glass in the sink as she started for the door. "Let's go. I'm ready to get there so I can listen to someone else for a change. I've heard all of your shitty little sayings too many times today. I hope Gene doesn't pick up any of your foul manners and insensitive jokes."

As they walked out to the truck, Butch remarked, "I have good manners. I always say something pleasant to everyone I meet, I tip my hat when I meet a lady, and I always say thank you. I had a good upbringing, you know. How can you say I have no manners? Insensitive?

Nope, I'm very sensitive. Don't I always compliment large ladies on how nice it is to find someone to provide shade enough for twenty on hot days? I tell you, I'm so sensitive that some days I look for fat gals just to compliment them."

Driving out of the house, the sun was just setting behind a group of large pecan trees, and pink and gold rays stretched across the horizon. Several squirrels could be seen running across the pasture and up the trees. As they came to the end of the driveway, Butch turned left on 718 and looked at the white pipe fence running along his property. "Sure changed a lot since I bought this place fifteen years ago, hasn't it?" he said as they passed the gate going down to the roping arena.

"Yes, you've done a lot of work cleaning up this place. Built a lot of fence and made me paint it," said Jeannie as she watched the fence slide by as they drove. "Starting to need some new paint in a few places."

"I know, but finding time to do it is the problem. You can't find too many people that will work that hard out here. I'll still pay you $10 an hour, just like last time. Free room and board, except this time, you buy your own whiskey and beer. You damned near broke me with your bar tab last time. I seem to remember your bar expenses cost me just about the same as your salary."

"I'm worth it," Jeannie replied. "It's worth more than that just to have somebody around who'll put up with you. I'm sure most of the people around here only tolerate you because of me anyway. 'Cause I'm so sweet, and you're so mean."

As they continued driving through the Aurora Vista development, they looked at how much the area had changed in the last five or six years. Houses valued at $500,000 and higher lined both sides of the winding road. Set on one-acre lots, most were two stories with brick and stone exteriors, lights shining on the shrubs, and front doors. It was a dramatic change from the houses that were in the rest of the community.

Trailer houses sat just outside the southeast corner of the development and ran down 718 toward Newark, only five miles away. Land prices had risen sharply in the area as people left Fort Worth or Dallas and moved to the country. Most of the longtime residents of the area wanted to keep the country rural and remain the small community it had always been. But as more and more people moved out here, they saw the inevitability of progress, and several sold their land and moved further west.

Exiting Aurora Vista and turning right on Old Base Road, it was almost dark as they pulled into the stables. As Butch stopped the truck beside Steve's house, Gene came walking down the steps. "Looks like a midget cowboy, doesn't he, girls? Got that bull-rider look. Short in size and short on brains, but full of guts. I think I'll stick with roping. I don't have enough brains left to let some snot-slinging bovine knock the remainder out."

"Looks like you're ready to dance with all the pretty ones, Gene. Jeannie and Mischelle got all spruced up, so you'll have some arm candy when you walk in. Start off by making all the other ones jealous. Some of them you may have to drink pretty, but the lights are dim enough that it normally only takes a case or two," Butch said as Gene got into the back seat of the truck. "Sun's going down, and we're going out. That's nature's plan, you know. Even the squirrels and rabbits party at night.

It's true—I've seen them in their little holes in the trees or the ground. Got lots of tiny little lights shining while they sip acorn whiskey or carrot beer. The damnedest thing you ever saw. Squirrels can really shake their tails, but the rabbits do something they call the 'bunny hop.' Guess that's cause they got no tails to shake."

"Oh, Lord, here he goes again," Mischelle moaned. "Daddy can come up with the most amazing line of bullshit about anything you can imagine. Just remember, we warned you. Don't believe a word he says, and it gets worse the more he drinks, and the more people are around. There's no telling what you'll hear tonight."

CHAPTER 45

As Mike and Paul were contemplating the last of the Gentleman Jack in their glasses, the phone gave a sharp ring. Keeping his glass in his left hand, Mike picked up the receiver and answered, "General Nelson."

He listened for a minute and replied, "We'll be down in a couple of minutes, Rick. Thanks." Replacing the phone, he leaned back in his leather chair and told Paul, "That was Rick. Not much new to speak of, but he wants to discuss a little strategy with us. Karyn's still there, along with Jerry. Looks like a good time to take stock and adjust if they have any good ideas."

"Whatever you and your staff think, I'm sure it will be thoroughly reviewed, and I'll approve it. Did Rick say how far north they have covered?" Paul acknowledged as he drained the last drop from his glass.

"No, he said he would fill us in when we arrived," Mike answered as he set his glass on his desk and stood. "I think we should go out and bring some food back after we talk to Rick. I'm getting a little hungry, and I'm sure everyone else is also."

"I sure am," replied Paul as he rose and started for the door. He set his empty glass back on the table and reached for the doorknob.

As they neared the communications room, Rick was just coming back from the restroom. He held the door open for them and continued into the room. He went directly to the map and pointed to the hundreds of tacks now littering the state.

"We have been receiving calls all day, as you know. The majority of them have dealt with the other five attempted hijackers. Several have just been calls reporting terrorist cells operating almost anywhere, but we've quit contacting anything south and east of Dallas.

It is rapidly becoming too much of a burden on most of the local police and sheriff's departments. I have discussed this with Karyn and Jerry to get their initial impressions, and Jerry has contacted his people in Washington. I'd like to take a couple of minutes and tell you what I have planned and what we will do to implement it."

Mike and Paul studied the map for a couple of minutes and could see how large the problem was becoming. Looking back at Rick, Mike told him, "All right, let's hear what you have in mind."

Rick stood to the side of the maps and pointed at the large map of Texas. "There have been hundreds of reports throughout the state that we know for almost absolute certain could not possibly be Gene, even though a great many of them made that report.

The majority of these reports are coming from fairly isolated rural areas, which is natural since that is where most of our Mexican population works. Those areas where predominately Mexicans live, such as just east of Main Street around Exchange Avenue in Fort Worth, have had surprisingly few reports. I attribute this to the fact that most of them know who their neighbors are and don't see any similarity between our Middle Easterners and themselves.

My plan would be to begin providing information to the news media announcing that five of the six have been apprehended. The reason I would like to get this implemented quickly is to ensure it runs in tomorrow morning's papers, especially the local editions."

"What do you need to do to implement your strategy?" Mike asked.

"Pretty simple, actually. The majority of the work was convincing the nation that there really was another group of hijackers. Removing several of them from the continued search is just a matter of a few phone calls and some data entries into governmental computers. I'd like Karyn to discuss what she has planned and for Jerry to brief you on the required data entries."

"Before you continue, Paul and I were wondering how far north of Azle you have covered and if there have been any sightings worth further investigation," Mike said as Karyn walked up to the map.

"The team has been in every open business up through Briar. They have personally shown the full array of pictures to everyone in those stores. A few have reported they think they saw one of the fictitious hijackers, and they have been assured we will find him. There have been a couple believing they saw Gene in a pickup yesterday morning, headed north toward Boyd, but wouldn't swear to it.

One of the ladies working in a convenience store in Briar says she saw someone walking along the road north of the Downeys' place that morning when she was going to work. She said she had not seen a television since arriving at work, and the photos the team member showed her were the first time she had known about the fifth group of terrorists.

She continued to say that had she known, she certainly would have called the Tarrant County Sheriff and told them. She did pick Gene's picture of him in a T-shirt and ball cap out without much hesitation," Rick concluded.

Paul nodded and said, "Well, it looks as if Gene is headed north as we suspected and not trying to mislead us. At least not yet."

"I believe you're correct in that assumption, but he could change directions when he reaches Boyd. I agree that North is the best choice until we finish our interviews in the Boyd area. Maybe then we can determine if he is changing direction. Go ahead with your brief, Rick," Mike said, nodding his head.

"Karyn, would you please show them your press releases and tell them where you plan to have captured each of the individuals?" Rick said as he turned toward her.

"Here is a copy of the release we intend to forward to the major news organizations from our FBI office," she said as she handed a folder to Mike and one to Paul. "We have staggered the captures so that they would appear to have been separate incidents. There will be three captured in the Boston area first.

I believe it will be more credible that those would be captured first since they were supposedly there waiting for the rest of their group. I have coordinated with Jerry to have plans to ensure the local police records show calls of their sighting in the area, and records will be modified within the FBI files to support the capture.

I will then have two more captured in Methuen, Massachusetts. It's about forty miles north of Boston along I-93, just short of New Hampshire. That release will come out about thirty minutes after the first.

With five of the six captured, we can restrict our search to just Gene. We have another press release ready for the local papers and news organizations that show Gene again and state we are intensifying the search for him and believe him to still be in the state.

This should provide a great deal of relief on the local law enforcement departments since all they need to concentrate on are calls relating specifically to Gene sightings," Karyn said as she concluded.

"Jerry, how are you coming in coordinating with Washington?" Rick asked as he turned to him.

"I have contacted our computer hacker and described where we want our information placed, and he has already opened several files within the FBI's computers in anticipation of receiving our entries. He can have it done within seconds of receiving them. He is also prepared to insert any of our information into the Boston police and Methuen police files showing erroneous calls reporting the captured individuals. Since thousands of sightings were actually reported, it will be quite simple to add a couple more logged phone calls in case anyone ever goes back and checks for authenticity. Those calls will show to have been routed to the FBI, and as I stated, their files will be altered to show the receipt and actions taken regarding each call," Jerry said.

Rick walked to the other side of the map to attract their attention and stood beside the large map showing Fort Worth and its outlying areas. "With only one left to capture and our teams covering each building and store along 730, I think we can expedite his capture or at least verify his destination. Most of the businesses along 730 will be closing soon, except for a couple of clubs, some all-night convenience stores, and two liquor stores by the Wise County line.

We have covered just about everything else, and after nine o'clock, there will be very few left. It's mainly a rural area from Briar to Boyd, and we will complete our search through Briar tonight. Most of the businesses in Boyd will be closed when we get there and will not reopen until after six o'clock tomorrow. I think that releasing the news of the captures will concentrate the local population's focus on Gene and will improve our chances of receiving another report.

It will also allow us to rule out the extraneous reports quickly. Karyn mentioned the local newspapers—which include the *Wise County Messenger* and what they call the *Daily Update*. By getting our releases into those papers, we ensure the good citizens of Boyd have copies of Gene's picture. If he is indeed up there, one of the less than one thousand people in the town will have seen him.

I plan on directing three members of the team to be in Boyd at six o'clock tomorrow morning. There are a couple of places open that early. One is called the Pit Stop and caters to early morning workers, and a few of the locals sit with their coffee before they start the day. Another is the Long Island Express, which is a convenience store and gas station. Several of the local police departments and highway patrol officers stop there for morning coffee.

Besides those two, there isn't much to cover early in the morning. However, the few people that do frequent those two locations will probably know if a stranger has been hired within the community. It's a pretty tight-knit group up there, and they tend to look out for each other," Rick said as he lowered his arm from the map.

"I agree, Rick," said Mike as he eased closer to the map. "There isn't much up there to cover, especially late at night. Are there any all-night businesses?"

"Just the Long Island Express, as far as I can determine. There is one cantina, though. It's actually a private club, but it's open until midnight. A place called Double K. I can have two of the team precede the other one and check on those two as soon as they finish Briar."

"Let's do that. And with your permission, General Modelle, send out your news releases," Mike said as he turned to Paul.

"You've got my approval. I think this is an excellent adjustment to the plan. You folks are doing an outstanding job. Mike and I are going out to get a minor celebration dinner to bring back. Since I'm buying, I'll pick the menu. I'll bring back a few dozen homemade tamales, tacos, and a cold case of Dr Pepper. I've already figured out what you Texans like. Just let us know how the releases went when we get back and if you need any help from my boss or his. I'll brief both of them when I get back, and you have assurances of the program's implementation," Paul said as he started for the door. "Coming, Mike? I may be paying, but you gotta carry it."

"Right behind you, sir. Where the hell is a good Lieutenant when you need one?"

CHAPTER 46

The drive from the stables to Bridgeport took them through Boyd again. It was just getting dark as they passed across the railroad tracks on the east side of town. The one stoplight, at the intersection of 730 to the south and 114, was red as they approached. Slowing from the posted thirty-five miles per hour, Gene looked left out of the truck's window. It seemed so long ago that he had traveled up that very same road from Azle, but it had been less than forty-eight hours.

Having seen no one expressing any unusual interest in him, he felt a tentative safety being out here. Knowing that a massive search was taking place, he was astonished that no one had said anything about his disappearance. He had assumed that his picture would be posted everywhere and policemen were scouring the country looking for him.

However, he had not seen television or read a newspaper since having seen the attacks on New York City on the day of his escape. Maybe, he thought, the country was so determined to find the hijackers that there was little manpower left to search for him. If this was true, just maybe he could remain at the equestrian center for a few more days. He still wanted to figure out why he felt so drawn to the area. He did enjoy his newfound freedom and believed that the people he had met were the friendliest and most helpful he had ever seen.

When the light turned green, Butch continued through Boyd, and Gene could see the few stores in town. He recognized the Southern Delight Restaurant as they passed and noticed how few cars were on the streets, even though it was still fairly early. The whole town seemed to close once the sun went down.

For the next ten or so miles, the countryside was slowly becoming completely black, with a few lights on in the houses set well back from the road. It appeared that it was almost a mile between the houses out here. Having only Fort Worth and Decatur to compare with, it seemed almost desolate. Up ahead, he could see another small town coming into view.

As he slowed again to the posted fifty-five mph, Butch said, "This little town is Paradise. I've got a cousin that lives out here, not within the town, but has a Paradise address. Her husband finally fulfilled his promise to her he made when he proposed many, many years ago. He told her that if she would marry him, he would ensure they lived in Paradise for the rest of their lives."

Stopping at the single stoplight in Paradise, Butch told them, "When I moved out here fifteen years ago, there was one stoplight from Roanoke to Bridgeport. Now, there are five, and probably should be more. If they would hurry up and stick a few more on 114, maybe those damned rock trucks would find another road around us instead of through Boyd and Rhome. Maybe a windshield would last longer than a month without having them drop rocks all over the road."

As soon as the light changed, Butch accelerated quickly and told them, "Just another five miles or so. I hope the crowd isn't too upset about me not being the opening act."

"Not as upset as they will be when you start singing, I bet," Jeannie smirked as she punched him in the shoulder. "Maybe a few will actually stay around after you start. I think the owner wishes you'd never come on karaoke night."

"You are sooo wrong, little missy. I know for a fact that she worships the very ground I sing on," he responded as they approached Bridgeport. "You just wait—I think her hormones run rampant every time I walk through the door."

"You mean run amuck, don't you?" Mischelle giggled. Turning left off the road, Red's sat just on the south side of 114. After pulling into an empty parking slot, Butch said, "Okay, kids, it's showtime! My fans are waiting, and all I need is a cold Budweiser to smooth out the kinks in my melodious voice, and then the magic begins."

"I think the magic is the disappearing act the crowd does," remarked Jeannie as they shut and locked the doors of the truck and started toward the front door.

As they entered, Gene could see that it was indeed dimly lit, and very few people were inside. Most of them sat on stools against the long bar running along the wall. A few people were playing pool, and the tables away from the bar were almost vacant. He decided that with his hat, boots, and long-sleeve shirt, he probably would not be noticed. He observed that most of the people paid no attention to them as they walked past the bar and sat at a table around the corner.

A lady with red hair came over as they sat down, saying, "Butch, where did you get these folks? Bringing your own cheering section?"

"Nope, Gay Lynn, these two little ladies are my daughters, Mischelle and Jeannie. This other one, Gene, works for me at the stables while Steve and Sheril take a little vacation."

"Hello, girls. I'm glad to finally meet you. Your daddy talks about you all the time and says what perfect children he has raised. I still can't believe that he can raise anything but hell. Nice to meet you, too, Gene. What can I get y'all to drink? I know what you want," she said, rubbing Butch's shoulders.

"Jack and Coke. Just don't let Daddy have anything except Budweiser—he's the designated driver," they said. "Gene, you want to try one?"

"I guess that would be all right," he replied. "I'm not much of a drinker." He wondered if he was doing the right thing since he had never had any alcohol, but he thought he at least needed to have a drink sitting in front of him. It would seem very strange to be the only one not drinking.

"Be right back. You gonna sing, Butch?"

"Real soon. As quick as you can soothe my parched throat. It was a dusty ride out here, and I almost died of dehydration."

As Gay Lynn returned with their drinks, she brought two women over to the table. "I hope you won't mind, but these two ladies are trying to celebrate tonight, and they don't know anyone here. I told them what a nice guy Butch was, and I was sure the rest of you wouldn't mind the company, especially if he started telling his tales. They also said they like to dance, and your daddy is about the best one here."

"No problem," Butch said as he stood and tipped his hat. "Ladies, I'm Butch North. These are my daughters, Mischelle and Jeannie. And this fellow is Gene. Sit down. We'd love to have your company."

"Thanks, I'm Leslie Barber, and this is Stacy Hyden. Stacy is from Bowie, and it's her birthday. I'm from Arlington. Stacy and I have been friends for years. We always celebrate our birthdays together, and since this is hers, she got to pick the place," one of them said as they took seats beside Gene.

"Very nice to meet you ladies. Let me buy you a drink for your birthday, Stacy. Gay Lynn, please put their drinks on my tab. We need to show these ladies that we appreciate them choosing our little country bar," Butch said as he stood up. "Now, if y'all will excuse me, I've got to go turn in my song list."

Gay Lynn returned with the drinks and told Stacy and Leslie, "Butch will make sure nobody bothers you. Just pretend you like his singing. We all know it's horrible, and so does he, but he sure enjoys it."

"What birthday are you celebrating?" asked Mischelle as she took a sip of her drink.

"Yesterday, I was 25, but Leslie couldn't get off work early enough to come out, so we're having our little party tonight. Do both of you live here?" Stacy asked.

"No. Jeannie lives in Seattle, and I live in Baltimore. We tell everyone that we moved as far away as possible from Daddy and couldn't listen to his tall tales. I better warn you—he does like to stretch the truth and jokes about everything, especially when he's had a couple." Mischelle said as Butch was returning to the table.

"My girls been lying to you ladies?" he asked as he sat down. "Don't believe a word they say. I'm just too nice to them anyway, and they take advantage of me every chance they get."

"They just said that you may stretch the truth a wee little bit, but you were pretty harmless," Leslie said as she swallowed almost half of her drink. "What do you do, Butch?"

"Well, you may not believe this, but I'm a famous writer of country music," he said, trying not to laugh. "I've got a couple that I'm sure will make it to the top of the charts. Wanna hear one?"

"Sure," said Stacy, winking at Mischelle. "What's the title of the first one?"

"It's called, 'There's Nothing Slim in this Bar but the Pickings.' Would you like to hear it?"

"This has got to be good," Leslie said, laughing. "Sure, go ahead."

"Oh, shit," Jeannie moaned. "You don't know what you've started."

"Here goes. Now you are going to have to remember—I don't have the music, so just imagine that George Strait or Toby Keith is singing it," Butch said as he started singing . . .

"I wasn't really looking for love,
I wasn't looking for romance,
I just wanted a cold beer,
And maybe a chance to dance.
I looked around at the ladies,
As I listened to the local band.
The sight was really disturbing,
I saw the biggest girls in the land.

There's nothing slim in this bar, but the pickings,
And there really ought to be a law,
To make them look in a mirror,
And see what I just saw.

I've never seen so much denim,
Stretched across a single tail,
It must have made the farmers happy,
'Cause each pair took a bale.

There's nothing slim in this bar, but the pickings,
And there really ought to be a law,
To make them look in a mirror,
And see what I just saw.

If I tried to pick one up,
You know it'd be just my luck,
'Cause to carry a load like that,

I'd need a one-ton truck.

There's nothing slim in this bar, but the pickings,
And there really ought to be a law,
To make them look in a mirror,
And see what I just saw."

"I told you, didn't I?" Jeannie said, holding her head in her hands. "You just had to get him started. Now he won't quit."

Both Leslie and Stacy were looking at Butch and laughing, "Where in the world did you ever come up with that?" Stacy asked.

"Oh, I was sitting in a little cantina in Boyd awhile back, and there were these three rather large ladies sitting on stools at the bar. And one of them had one of those T-back undie things on, and it was showing above her jeans. All three of them had the plumber's-butt-crack thing going on, but the sight of that T-back was the final straw. I thought, 'There's nothing slim in this bar but the pickings,' and sat there writing it out on a napkin. What do you think?"

"Sounds like a country song to me. What about the other one?" Leslie said as she signaled for Gay Lynn to bring Stacy another drink.

"Well, I wrote this one about an ex-girlfriend. The title is 'I Can't Get Over You Till You Get Out From Under Him.'"

"Now, that's a country song," Stacy said as she laughed and drained the remainder of her drink.

Jessica, who was running the karaoke show that night, finished singing and called for someone else to come to the stage. As they were crossing the dance floor to take their turn singing, Butch asked if either of the girls could two-step.

"Of course we can," answered Stacy. "We were both born in Texas, went to college in Texas, and live in

Texas. You can't do all of that and not know how to two-step! Do we look like damned Yankees to you?"

"No, of course not. I can tell by the way you're dressed that you're Texan. But since one of you is from Arlington, and that's close to Dallas, and Dallas thinks it's a suburb of New York, I just didn't want to embarrass either of you out on the floor. If that guy up there getting ready to sing selects a good song, I'd be right proud to have a dance with either one of you lovely ladies," Butch replied.

"Since it *is* Stacy's birthday party, I'll let her go first," Leslie told him. "Stacy, you take him out there and show him some of us city girls can two-step with the best country boy around."

As the music started, Butch stood up and put his hand out to Stacy, saying, "May I have the pleasure of this dance, ma'am?"

"Why, certainly, sir. It would be a pleasure to dance with a fine gentleman such as you," Stacy answered as she took another drink and stood.

"Leslie, you and Stacy are gonna swell his head so big that he'll have to get a larger hat before the night is over," Jeannie told her. "Gene, do you dance?"

"Not really," Gene answered as he watched Butch and Stacy out on the floor. "Looks like fun. Is that the two-step they are doing?"

"Yeah, come on. I'll give you your first lesson. It's easy. Daddy taught Mischelle and me years ago, and we can't keep up with him when he starts turning and spinning, but we can keep time to the music and go around the floor."

Gene had drunk almost half of his Jack and Coke. Since it was his first taste of alcohol, he was beginning to feel a little lightheaded, and a sense of security was settling over him. For the first time since leaving Vicki, he felt like smiling. "Okay, I'll try it," he said as he stood up and took Jeannie's outstretched hand.

"I'll lead to start. You just follow and kind of slide your feet along with the beat of the music. Don't worry about what anyone else thinks. Just relax and enjoy it," Jeannie said as she showed Gene where to put his hand and began to move to the beat of the song.

As the two couples moved around the dance floor, Gay Lynn came over to the table and sat down to visit with Leslie and Mischelle. "What do you think?" she asked Leslie.

"He's a nice guy. I think we'll have a lot of fun. He does like to make fun of overweight women, doesn't he?"

"Yes, that he does. Guess he figures that if he can stay in shape at his age, the younger ones should too. He doesn't just make jokes about the women; he's pretty hard on the guys, too. But he says that if you can't have pride in the way you look, you probably have no pride in anything else."

"That's Daddy, all right," Mischelle said, nodding her head. "He's sort of pigheaded about some things. Honesty, integrity, pride, and respect are a few things he considers important. He claims it's important to stand for what you believe in and never compromise when it comes to those things. He'd never intentionally hurt anyone's feelings, but sometimes, he gets carried away with his joking. Jeannie and I have given up on changing him. He's really a very thoughtful man once you get to know him, but then again, his little witty sayings get worse the better you know him."

Gay Lynn stood and nodded her head. "That's your daddy, all right. I'll be back in a few minutes. You girls need anything?"

"You better bring Daddy another Budweiser, and I'd like another Jack and Coke," Mischelle answered, and the music ended, and Butch led Stacy back to the table.

"You're picking this dancing stuff up pretty good, Gene," Butch said as he held Stacy's chair out for her. "And this lady certainly does know how to dance. If Leslie is even half as good, I'm gonna wear out a new pair of boots tonight. Not to mention shining my belt buckle so much it'll sparkle like a diamond in a goat's butt. Well, Jessica just called me. I think I'll sing a little Moe Bandy song. I was going to sing an old Hank Williams song and dedicate it to my ex-wife—'Your Cheatin' Heart.'"

As Butch walked to the stage, Stacy asked Gene if he would like to dance. "Sure," he replied. "I'm just learning, though."

"No problem. Between all of us girls, you and Butch aren't going to sit out many songs tonight. Come on, he's singing 'Bandy the Rodeo Clown,' and I love that song. Order us another drink, please, Leslie."

Throughout the evening, they continued to dance to almost every song and swap stories about where they lived, college days, jobs, and tell jokes. Gene, now having had two drinks, was certainly feeling no pain, and the grin on his face seemed to get bigger with each story that was told.

As it got closer to eleven o'clock, Butch told them they had to go. "Morning comes early, and those damned horses don't care how little sleep I've had. Ladies, it's been a real pleasure." He stood and walked to the bar to pay his bill.

"Gene, if you'd like to stay a little while longer, Stacy and I will be glad to drop you off when we leave. We can go right through Boyd on our way to Bowie. I'd love to have someone to dance with for a little longer. Do you think your daddy would mind?" Leslie asked Jeannie.

"No, he wouldn't care at all, as long as Gene's there in the morning ready to work."

"All right. What do you say, Gene?"

"I think I would like that. This is the first time I've had this much fun in forever. You sure Butch won't mind?" he asked Mischelle.

"I'm sure. If there's one thing Daddy likes, it's for people to have a good time. But like Jeannie said, he expects you to be up and working by eight o'clock. If you can do that, stay and have fun."

Butch came back to the table and said, "Ready?"

Jeannie and Mischelle stood up and told him, "Leslie and Stacy want Gene to stay a little while longer and dance. They said they would drop Gene off at the stables on their way back to Bowie. Is that all right?"

Butch looked at Gene and the girls for a second. "You Okay with that, Gene? And y'all promise to get him home safely?"

"I'd really like to stay and dance a little more if that's all right with you," Gene replied, grinning at him.

"And we promise to take good care of this little cowboy," Stacy said as she put her arm across Gene's shoulders. "We're only staying another hour or so. I made Leslie quit drinking so she can drive."

"Okay, y'all have fun then. I'll see you in the morning. I've got to hit the head before I leave. Here, Jeannie, take the keys, and I'll meet you at the truck," he said as he walked toward the men's room.

A couple of minutes later, when he arrived at the truck and got in, he said, "I'm not positive, but I think I just saw Gene and Stacy getting into a white pickup parked over by the fence across from the bar. Maybe Stacy's planning on more celebration than I thought. Hope Gene knows what he's getting into. But like I've always said, if you're over twenty-one and weigh more than a hundred pounds, you're big enough to make your own decisions."

Butch started the truck, and they drove back toward Boyd. As they passed through town, Butch told them he needed to stop at the Long Island Express, and since long tradition existed with coming home from an evening out, they needed to get a corndog on a stick before they went on home.

As they parked near the front of the store, they noticed two black Suburbans with very darkly tinted windows. On entering the store and choosing their corndogs, they saw two men in dark suits questioning the cashier and showing her some pictures. After getting a couple of packets of mustard and some napkins each, they walked toward the front of the store as the men were leaving.

"Evening, Butch," the cashier said. "You've been out partying again, I guess. I know—that's the only time you stop and get one of those things to eat."

"Guess you're right. My girls and I need something to settle our stomachs before we go to bed. Who were those two guys?" he said as he laid a ten-dollar bill on the counter.

"Said they were FBI. Out looking for some raghead that was supposed to have been part of another hijacking plot but couldn't get on a plane at DFW. Showed me some pictures, but I told them I haven't seen anyone around here that looked like that. Just your usual Mexicans and the late-night drunks like you."

"Shit, I haven't heard about that. Guess I need to watch television a little more. No telling what I've been missing these last couple of days. Thanks," he said, taking his change. "Have a good evening."

As he lowered the tailgate for them to sit, he ripped open the mustard package and squeezed it across his corndog. "Well, girls, a perfect ending to another perfect day in Texas. We gotta do this more often." They finished their corndogs and placed the empty mustard containers and napkins in the trash as they saw the two black vehicles pulling out from across the street.

"Bedtime, ladies," he said as he got into the truck. "Wonder what the FBI would be doing way up here looking for some camel jock. Guess because they seem to run every 7-11 in the country now."

CHAPTER 47

Mike and Paul returned about an hour later, their arms laden with boxes filled with Styrofoam containers overflowing with tacos, tamales, and a medley of Mexican sauces and side dishes. The aroma filled the air as they entered the communications room. Setting the boxes on the table holding the coffee pot and cups, Mike told everyone, "General Modelle wanted to buy almost everything on the menu from the La Paseo restaurant up in Azle. He says that if you don't like what he's brought, you must be a damned Yankee!"

"That's not exactly the way I phrased it," Paul retorted. "I said that you can't find this quality of Mexican food up in Yankee land and that I could understand why you Texans love it so. Please, dig in and relax for a few minutes."

Mike took one of the plates from the stack, picked up a packet containing a fork, spoon, knife, and napkin, and placed two tacos and two tamales on it. As he moved to the side, he asked, "Any word from the field team?"

"They called in just before you arrived," Rick answered as he filled his plate and took a can of Dr Pepper from the cooler on the floor beneath the table. "They have finished working their way through Briar and have started driving toward Boyd. They should get there within the next fifteen or so minutes unless they need to inspect any of the houses along the way. I think they plan on going to the Double K restaurant for dinner when they arrive."

Karyn finished filling her plate and placed it on one of the desks after moving a stack of papers out of the way. "I've completed forwarding all the news releases through Jerry's contacts, and they will appear in the morning edition of almost every newspaper in the country. All the major television networks have already started airing the reports of the capture in Boston. The locals are picking it up for their late-night broadcast also."

"When do you plan on releasing the other captures?" Mike asked as he poured *picante* sauce on his tacos.

"We will send that information to the same sources in about another ten minutes. Isn't that correct, Jerry?" Karyn said as she bit into a tamale.

"Eleven minutes, to be exact," replied Jerry, and he took a swallow of his Dr Pepper. "The timing was determined by the speed normally used to travel from Boston to Methuen. That would provide the most plausible scenario for our story. We could have made it quicker, but we figured that our terrorists would probably not have been stopped on the interstate and most likely would have driven at the speed limit to avoid detection."

"That sounds completely reasonable," Mike told them as he read the label of the *picante* packet. "Thank goodness they use *Pace Picante* sauce. I think some of the other restaurants use something from New York City."

Smiling around his half-eaten taco, Paul said, "I've seen that commercial, too. We do happen to have *Pace Picante* in Washington, by the way. And I agree that it is the best commercial sauce I've found. But some of the restaurants down here make their own and do a hell of a good job."

As everyone refilled their plates and enjoyed the excellent cuisine, they made no further mention of the ongoing search for Gene. They were all acutely aware that the majority of their work had been done until another spotting occurred. Although it was impossible not to have it on their minds, the mutual feeling was that this small break in the constant level of energy was like a mini vacation. Time to relax for a minute and just enjoy the meal.

Major Jerry Fleenor placed his empty plate in the trash container, wiped his mouth, and finished his Dr Pepper. As he tossed the empty can in the trash, he checked his watch and walked to Karyn's desk. "Let's get the news on the line about the other miraculous capture. By the time it's passed to the newscasters, it should just make the close of the late-night news."

Karyn nodded as she wiped the *picante* sauce from her chin and took another drink of Dr Pepper. After wiping her hands, she removed a folder from within her desk and removed a compact disk from its protective envelope. Placing in into the encrypted data transmitter, she entered the numbers corresponding to the FBI centers that would then release it to the authorized news agencies. As she waited for the disk to stop spinning, she picked her drink up and drained the last of it.

When the disk finally slowed to a stop, Karyn nodded at Jerry, and he picked up the receiver on the secure telephone on her desk. Entering a series of numbers, he spoke briefly to each person and repeated the call several more times. Laying the receiver back in the telephone's cradle, he turned to Rick and said, "It's done. All data banks have now been altered to show the times and events necessary to enact the capture."

"What's next?" inquired Mike as Rick thanked Karyn and Jerry.

"We wait again. I've tuned the televisions to CNN, Fox, CBS, NBC, and two of our local stations. We should begin seeing the news within the next few minutes."

Even as he was finishing, all of the national news channels stopped in the middle of their programs and began delivering the breaking news of the capture of two more of the thwarted hijackers. Then, they showed pictures of the five captured and of the one remaining, Gene.

As they were watching the national stations, one of the locals told the breaking story, followed within seconds by the other. Switching channels to include every local station, they saw replays of the scenes from the national organizations.

The secure phone on Karyn's desk began ringing, and a red light flashed on the dial. Stepping over to the phone, Rick answered, "Colonel Erickson." Listening for a minute, he said, "Fine, go on back to the motel and plan on being back in Boyd at six o'clock tomorrow morning. Thanks."

As he hung up, he turned to Mike and said, "Two members of the team ate at the Double K. While there, they showed Gene's picture to the waitress, cook, and owner. Also, a couple of local people were dining there. No one reported seeing Gene, but they were told that another cook and waitress would be there when they opened at six o'clock tomorrow morning.

They also went to the only open convenience store before leaving and showed the picture there with the same result. They left one of the pictures of Gene dressed in the T-shirt for them to post on their counter and received assurance that it would be there for the morning shift. There were very few vehicles in the town, and only an occasional rock truck passing by. The only vehicle at the convenience store came up just as they were about to leave. It was driven by one of the local cowboys, who appeared to have a couple of his daughters with him.

Other than those contacts within Boyd, the town was practically closed down for the night. The first store to open in the morning is a place called the Pit Stop, and both it and the Double K will open at six. That is also the time the shift changes at the Long Island Express, where they left the photo.

Most of the other businesses open between eight and nine. As you heard, I told them to return to their rooms for the night and be back at six. I will make sure all eight members of the team arrive in Boyd at six to hit every store, gas station, or restaurant the minute they open. If Gene is indeed in the Boyd area, we will know by the time the sun comes up."

"With your permission, sir," Rick said as he threw his empty Dr. Pepper can in the trash, "I would like to send everyone here home for the night and have them all back before six in the morning to be ready for any reports coming in. I don't see any reason to sit around here for the next six or seven hours, staring at the maps or listening to the same broadcasts we've generated."

"Let's all go get a little sleep," Mike replied as he finished his Dr Pepper and tossed the can into the trash. "Paul, do you have anything to add?"

"No, I'm ready to get a couple of winks myself, and as Rick said, there's nothing more productive to be done in here tonight. I guess he'll even have his cowboy coffee ready when we get here, don't you think?" Paul said as he placed his long-empty plate and utensils into the trash.

"Without a doubt," Karyn smiled. "But I will make sure there is some good coffee ready in case anyone doesn't want acid burns and coffee grounds in their stomachs."

They all cleaned up their plates, drink cans, and napkins as they were preparing to leave. As the last of them were going out the door, Rick held Karyn back for a second and told her that he would remain here for the night, just in case any reports from the area west of Fort Worth came in. As he told her goodnight and to go on home, he settled down into the most comfortable chair in the office, placed his feet up on the desk, and closed his eyes.

CHAPTER 48

At six o'clock on September 13, 2001, ten black Suburbans with extremely dark tinted windows drove up 730 and entered Boyd. One stopped at the Pit Stop, where 730 intersected with 114. Two others turned right onto 114, one of which made a left turn into the parking area at the Double K restaurant and the other continuing to the Rock Island Express convenience store. Two more turned left when the light at 114 turned green, one of which stopped less than a block later and parked as the other one continued on through town.

Of the five remaining vehicles, two went to the east and west, two went to the ends of town, while the fifth stopped just north of town on 730, leading to Decatur. These turned around as they reached the city limits and faced back toward the town, waiting for further instructions.

The driver stopping at the Pit Stop got out of his car and entered the building, noting as he went in that a couple of pickups were at the gas pumps, and several were parked beside the store. Tables sitting a short distance from a coffee station were filled with men wearing coveralls and boots, some with cowboy hats and others with baseball caps. Every one of them looked up as he entered, wearing a dark suit and black shoes.

He walked directly to the cashier and placed a picture of Gene on the counter. "Have you seen this individual around here in the last couple of days?"

"No, I don't think so. You might ask those men over there," she said, pointing to the tables.

"Thanks," he replied as he turned back toward the men drinking coffee around the small tables. Walking up, he told them he was an FBI agent, showed his identification, and asked if any of them had seen the man in the picture he laid on the table.

As everyone looked and passed the picture, each shook his head and denied having seen anyone around who looked like him. "What's he done?" asked a man wearing a pair of bib overalls.

"He's wanted in connection with the hijackings of airplanes from the eleventh," came the reply.

"That's the same guy I saw on the news last night, isn't it?" another asked. Several others took the picture again and nodded, saying they had seen the news photos also.

After determining that no one there had seen Gene or was admitting it, he returned to his car and made a short radio call.

The agent parking at the Double K restaurant entered as soon as the front door was unlocked and opened. Once inside, he spoke to the waitress who had opened the doors, asking her if she had seen anyone looking like the man in the photo he held.

Taking the picture from his hand, Kay said, "Oh, my God. This is one of those guys the FBI is looking for. I saw this on the news last night but didn't really pay attention to this one. I swear to you—he was in here a couple of days ago. Sat right there and ate lunch."

"Was he alone or with someone?"

"He came in, I think, with—no, I'm positive— Butch North. And Mike Jackson came in and sat with them. I know it was him. Have you called Butch?" Kay asked as she stared at the photo.

"No. Could you tell me where he lives?"

"Sure. Just go east on 114 to the traffic light at 718, turn right, and his place is on the left. About one hundred yards or so off 114. Has his brand over the gate, Check Six, and a big *BN* on the gate. It's right across the road from the Kountry Korner. That's the gas station and feedstore there on the corner."

"Have you seen him back in here—either the man in the photo or Mr. North?"

"No, I don't think so. I just remember the one time two days ago."

"Okay, thanks. You've been a big help," he said as he quickly returned to his car. Opening the door, he reached for the microphone attached to a compact transmitter sitting in the front seat.

On the west side of town, one of the black Suburbans pulled into the Southern Delight Restaurant. Entering, the agent walked to the woman who was opening the register. "Excuse me," he said as he laid the photo of Gene on the counter. "Have you seen this man?"

Picking up the photo, Nannette's eyes opened wide as she exclaimed, "Why that's the guy who came in here with Butch North the other day. I'm positive that's him."

"Where can I find this Butch North?"

"Just east of town, across the road from Kountry Korner, right there on 718."

The agent started to speak when his pager attached to his belt buzzed. Seeing the numbers on the illuminated face, he said, "Thanks," and hurried out of the restaurant. His phone was ringing as he climbed into his car and turned the key in the ignition.

Back in the communications room, Colonel Erickson had just finished making a pot of his cowboy coffee when the secure phone on Karyn's desk began to ring. Picking up the receiver, he said, "Colonel Erickson," and listened for less than a minute before telling the caller, "Get every member of your team and find the exact address of this North fellow. Have every car placed on all the roads leading into his place. I'm calling up a map on the satellite link and will provide real-time data to your screens. Call me back when everyone is in place."

Replacing the phone, Rick picked up the local phone receiver and began to punch in the numbers written on a sheet beside the phone. As he was dialing, Karyn walked in, carrying a pot of freshly brewed coffee, and set it on the table. Listening to Rick telling someone thanks and hanging up, she asked, "Any word?"

Continuing to dial other numbers, he replied, "We've got two positive identifications in Boyd and the name of an individual he was seen with both times. I'll tell you more when everyone is here."

Within minutes, both General Modelle and General Nelson were standing with a cup of coffee in their hands as Rick told them of the latest developments. "I've called Colonel Amy Moore and told her to be here as quickly as she can. Major Fleenor should be here within another minute or so. I want Amy to be in Boyd with the team when they pick Gene up. She knows him better than anyone except Vicki and should be there in case of any problems."

Jerry walked in the door and was quickly briefed on the impending capture of Gene. As he listened, he told them that he had already set up the necessary data to enter into the local FBI data banks for the capture of Gene and would have it inserted as soon as Gene was back within the security of the facility.

"General, could you please arrange for one of the base helicopters to take Colonel Moore to rendezvous with the team? I'll have a location as soon as all the team members are situated. Looking at the map, I plan on blocking 718 from the intersection at 114 down about a mile toward the town just south called Newark. The landing site will be somewhere on 718. I'll know definitely when we get a report on the power lines along the road," Rick asked Mike.

"I'll have it ready within five minutes," Mike said as he left for his office.

At home, Butch was just making coffee and turned on the television. Taking a cup of orange juice, he walked back through the house and went into his bathroom. Finishing, he noticed the door to the bedroom where Jeannie and Mischelle were sleeping was still closed, the bathroom door open, and no sounds came from the bedroom.

"Lazy little shits," he thought as he smiled and took a sip of his orange juice. "Keep me up half the night and then want to sleep all day. I swear they're trying to send me to an early grave."

As he poured a cup of the coffee that had just finished brewing, he walked back into the living room and sat down in his recliner. Placing the cup on a coaster on the table on his right, he picked up the remote and selected CNN on his satellite receiver. Taking a sip of the black coffee in his cup, he glanced at the screen. As he saw the photo displayed and listened to the newscaster, he suddenly sat forward and exclaimed, "Son of a bitch, that looks just like Gene!"

Turning the volume up, he set his cup back down, got up, and went to the girls' bedroom. Pounding on the door, he called, "Get up, girls, you won't believe what's on the news! Come on, hurry up!"

"Oh, Daddy," he heard from inside, "I don't want to get up yet."

"I don't care what you want, get up. They've got a picture of Gene on CNN. Something about a hijacker or terrorists. Come on, get your butts up!"

As he was returning to his chair in the living room, he heard the unmistakable sound of a helicopter flying overhead. Sitting down and picking his cup of coffee up, he listened to the reporter talking about the capture of five known terrorists and that only one remained at large as the picture of Gene was enlarged to fill the screen.

Just as the picture was showing, Jeannie walked in, still in her pajamas and rubbing her eyes. As she saw the picture on the screen, she stopped and exclaimed, "That's Gene!"

"I know it," Butch said. "I just don't know how he could be involved with those crashes up in New York. He's not some raghead or Muslim shithead, he's just a Mexican guy. There's got to be something wrong."

At that moment, there was a loud knock on the front door. Getting out of his chair, Butch walked toward it and told Jeannie to get Mischelle up. Opening the door, he saw a man in a dark suit holding an identification badge in his hand.

"You, Mr. North?" he asked.

"Yes, and who are you?"

"I'm with the FBI. May I come in for a minute?"

"Sure, come on in. What's this about?" Butch said as he led the way into the living room.

"Do you know the man in this picture?" he asked as he held Gene's photo up.

"Yes, I do. I just saw the same photo on the television. What's going on?"

"Where is this individual right now?" he asked Butch as Mischelle and Jeannie came walking into the living room.

"He's over at my stables," Butch replied.

"Where is that?"

"It's about a mile away, over on Old Base Road. One-half mile south of 114, on the right."

"Okay, wait right here. I'll be back in a minute," he said as he walked back out of the house toward his car.

"Girls, you better get dressed. I'm not sure what's going on, but it sure doesn't look good for Gene. I think we better be ready to go over there and find out what's going on.

Hurry up; get some jeans and a shirt on. I don't want these guys showing up over there without me being there."

Both Mischelle and Jeannie ran back to the bedroom and shut the door to get their clothes on. As Butch was looking at the television, the agent walked back into the house and said, "Sir, I'm going to have to insist that you and your daughters come with me. Are there any other people in the house?"

"No, just us. Where do you plan to take us?"

"We need you to accompany us to the stables where Gene is," he answered as Butch saw a helicopter rising from 718 just outside his fence.

He could also see what looked like several black vehicles parked just outside his gate. He turned toward the hall leading to the bedrooms as Jeannie was coming out and Mischelle following her.

"Girls, we have to go over to the stables with this guy." Butch turned back to the agent and asked, "Is it all right if I follow you in my truck?"

"No, I'm afraid that you'll have to ride with me. If you're ready, we need to leave right now."

"I guess so," Butch said. "Come on, girls, it'll be all right."

As they neared the Suburban parked in the driveway, Butch saw a lady in an Air Force uniform sitting in the passenger seat in the front. Opening the door to the rear seats, he told the girls to get in and got in beside them. The agent that had knocked on their door walked to the other side, got in, started the car, and spoke quietly into a phone sitting on the seat between him and the lady on the other side of the front seat.

CHAPTER 49

Rick hung up the phone and told General Nelson, "That was the team reporting in from Mr. North's house. Mr. North and his two daughters appear to be the only ones at the house. Mr. North says that Gene is in a house located about one mile away at some stables that he owns. The team has taken him and his daughters, and they are driving over to 700 Old Base Road.

I directed him to have one of the men make a quick search of North's house before following to verify that the house was empty. They plan on blocking Old Base Road on both the north and south sides of the address once they arrive. I have also directed the helicopter to remain over Mr. North's property until the search of his house is complete and then to follow the convoy to the stables."

"What did Mr. North tell your agent?" Mike asked as he turned to look at the enlarged map of the Boyd, Aurora, and Rhome area.

"Just that Gene was at the stables. The agent reported that Mr. North seemed genuinely surprised about seeing Gene on the television and in the photo. I'm sure he will get a few more answers when they arrive at the stables."

Karyn came walking back carrying a computer printout, and as she handed it to Rick, she said, "I had a quick computer search run on Mr. North. This may surprise you."

Rick took a quick look at the printout and handed the first sheet to General Nelson as he started reading the second page. "Looks like our Mr. North is a little more than some country turd kicker. He served in naval intelligence during Vietnam, transferred to the Air Force, where he was stationed in Korea working with an Army group up on the demilitarized zone, and spent some time in the test program of the F-5 before retiring. Following that, he retired as a Captain after flying for American Airlines."

Handing the second page to Mike, who had handed the first page to General Modelle, Rick said, "I better make sure the team is aware of this man's background. If he's half as smart as he must have been to have the careers he's had, he could present a problem. I doubt if he will buy our story about Gene being a Middle Eastern terrorist. Especially if he's been around him these last two days."

"We better have him brought in, along with his daughters, when they bring Gene in," Mike said as he handed the second page to Paul. "I would bet that he would doubt our story, especially since it shows in this report that he taught most of our Middle Eastern 'allies' during his time as an instructor in the Air Force. He will definitely know the difference between the standard raghead and Gene."

"What do you plan to use as a reason? Especially with his daughters? You better come up with a good one because this fellow will probably see right through any bullshit story," Paul said, handing the report back to Rick. "He is probably the worst man possible to have found Gene. I think I'd rather have had the local Barney Fife catch him. At least Deputy Dudley Dumb-ass wouldn't question an FBI agent's authority and wouldn't know the difference between a Shiite and shitpile."

"We'll just tell him that we want an official statement from him attesting to where he found Gene, where they went, if Gene used any telephones, or contacted anyone else. We need to know this anyway, and it will provide the necessary cover to get him in here. I also recommend that his statement be taken somewhere else on base. General Nelson, would you please contact General Brown at JRB and arrange for a conference room? We'll provide the stenographer and security guards."

"I'll have Kathy do that right now," Mike said as he picked up the phone.

Karyn switched one of the televisions to a dedicated satellite system to display a map depicting real-time images as the team approached 700 Old Base Road. "Looks like they have blocked the road, and one of the units is going into the stable area."

As they were watching, they could plainly see one of the black vehicles stop beside a trailer house. Both Butch and the driver got out and walked up the steps and were lost from view as they went beneath a roof over the porch of the house.

Mike replaced the telephone's receiver and told Rick that there would be a room available as soon as the team returned. "I think we should bring them back in the chopper. They can land in the pasture there," he said, pointing to a large open area just outside a barn. "We can have Amy, Gene, Butch, his daughters, and two of the agents fly back and land here. That would get Gene here as quickly as possible and allow us to question Mr. North and his daughters a lot faster than driving them back. When we're done, we will fly the two agents and the North family back and pick up the cars then."

"That would be my preference, also," said Paul as they watched the agent and Butch come back toward the car and get in. "It may also alleviate some of Mr. North's potential concerns if he believes that this is an official Air Force operation in conjunction with the FBI. Mike, I want you and

Rick in your dress blues to be at the interview as witnesses only. One of the agents will conduct the actual interrogation, but having a couple of high-ranking officers there may give us a little help. I'm sure he still respects the uniform, especially since both of you have silver command wings on your chest and your Vietnam Service Ribbons."

As they continued watching the satellite monitor, they saw the black Suburban drive from the house to the barn, and once again, Butch and the agent got out. As they saw them enter the barn, they watched as both rear doors opened, and the two daughters exited the car and went into the barn after their father. Within just a few minutes, they saw the agent hurrying back to the car, and the phone on Karyn's desk began to ring.

"Gene's disappeared," Rick said as he hung up the phone.

"Oh, shit!" General Nelson said as he stared in disbelief at Rick. "All right, let's get Mr. North's ass in here as soon as we can. And I want a comprehensive file on him and both his daughters on my desk before they land. General Modelle, I think we better make a couple of very disappointing phone calls."

CHAPTER 50

As they entered the driveway leading to the stables, Butch told the driver, "Pull over there by the trailer. It's still too early for him to be down in the barn feeding the horses. I'll probably have to wake him up."

He got out of the car and started toward the house as the agent driving slammed his door and followed. Climbing the steps to the porch, Butch saw that there were no lights on in the house. Reaching the front door, he opened the glass storm door and knocked on the closed door of the house. After waiting a few seconds, he knocked again, much harder. Still with no answer, he opened the door and shouted, "Gene, are you awake? Come on, it's time to get up."

Hearing no answer, Butch entered the house, followed by the agent. Again, he called out, "Gene, are you in here? Gene, come on. Time to get up."

Butch walked down the hall and looked in each room as he went. Every door was open, and no one was in any of the rooms. "I better check the back bedroom, too," he said as he came back up the hall and through the living room and kitchen. Coming to the open door to the master bedroom, he entered, noted that the bed was made, and went into the bathroom. Seeing no one there, he stepped past the agent and said, "Looks like he may have gone down to the barn early.

He may have decided to sleep down there instead of here in the house."

They quickly exited the house, got back into the car, and drove the one hundred yards to the main barn. The doors were still closed, and they saw that no lights were shining through the crack between them. Butch pushed one of the doors open and stepped into the darkness. Reaching to his right, he found the light switch and turned on a series of fluorescent lights running half the length of the barn.

As the lights came on and they started down the aisle, Jeannie and Mischelle came into the barn, asking, "Daddy, where's Gene? I thought he was going to spend the night in Steve's house."

"I don't know, girls. Maybe he decided to just stay on the couch in the office for tonight," Butch said as they reached the end of the row of lights.

The light switch for the office was located on the wall just outside the door, and he switched it on as he opened the door and looked inside. The couch was empty and had obviously not been slept on. The blankets and pillow were still stacked where they had been yesterday morning when Butch had come over.

"I don't know where he could be," he said as he walked down the aisle to the other end of the barn. By now, the horses were all neighing and banging their feed buckets. As Butch reached the end of the aisle, he turned on the remainder of the lights and walked into the horse-walker area. He looked around, turned left, and walked to the covered arena. Seeing nothing, he led as the girls and the agent followed close behind.

"Beats the hell out of me," Butch said as they returned to the office. "I'll check the phone for any messages, but I don't think he even knows the number here."

As he looked at the phone, the agent could see that there were no message lights illuminated and said, "Stay right here; I'll be back in a minute."

As the agent left, Butch pulled a chair out from the desk and sat down, and the girls took seats on the couch. "I hope Gene and those girls didn't have an accident or something. It could be that they went up to Decatur after Red's closed to get something to eat, but they should have been back here by now, even if they did."

Neither of the girls said anything as they sat there waiting for the agent to return. Butch looked at them and said, "Girls, I don't mean to sound suspicious, but I just can't imagine Gene being a terrorist. I'm positive that he isn't some type of Arab, and he doesn't have any accent or anything that would make me think he would be."

Jeannie looked at him and replied, "I don't know. He seems like some quiet young man, kind of like he's bashful or something."

"Well," Butch said quietly, "I'm not sure exactly what's going on here, but I don't think it has anything to do with terrorists. Whatever happens, all we knew about Gene was that he appeared to be an illegal Mexican and was never out of our sight until we left Red's. Since that is the truth, just stick to it, and don't volunteer any information that you don't know. Understand?"

"Of course. I don't think Gene was a terrorist or anything, either. What do you think they will do with us now?" Mischelle asked.

"Not sure, but you can bet they will want to ask us a shitload of questions. They probably believe right now that we know more than we do, maybe even helped Gene escape, and it will just take some time to convince them that we have no clue as to where Gene is, and we certainly did not help him go anywhere. We'll just have to wait and see."

The agent came back into the office and told them, "I'm sorry, but you are going to have to come with me to the base at Fort Worth. There's a helicopter landing right outside that will take you, the Air Force lady that's in the car, and two of my agents to the base. Please don't resist. You have

to go with them. We will bring you back as soon as you've
made your statements and signed them. Just wait here until
the chopper lands, and I will escort you to it."

CHAPTER 51

After Butch, his daughters, two agents, and the female Colonel boarded the helicopter, the pilot lifted off from the pasture and turned south toward Fort Worth. Both due to the noise and nervousness, Butch did not speak to either the girls or the Colonel. The agents quietly sat watching them as the helicopter continued to climb to just about five hundred feet above the ground and accelerated to 150 miles per hour.

The Colonel leaned back in her seat with her eyes closed, a look of resignation on her face. Butch glanced at her nametag on the right side of her uniform and saw her last name was Moore. He noted that she did not wear pilot wings, nor did she have many service ribbons on the left side below her medical badge.

"That's rather strange," Butch thought. "Sending a medical person instead of a security officer. Why would the government be more concerned with the medical condition of a suspected terrorist than with additional security?"

Less than ten minutes after liftoff, Butch could see out the left side that they were approaching Azle, and the NAS/JRB was obviously their destination. The pilot was beginning to descend and swing around to the east. The traffic on 820 was almost bumper-to-bumper with early-morning commuters as they crossed overhead. It appeared that they were indeed landing at the JRB, and Butch could see two black Suburbans identical to those he had seen back at the stables parked by the large circled H denoting the helicopter landing area. He could also see several men in dark suits standing beside the vehicles as they got nearer the landing site.

"They are just arriving," Rick told General Nelson as he replaced the phone's receiver. "The agents will take them to the Base Commander's conference room. I suggest we be in place and wait for them to arrive."

Mike was adjusting his tie and smoothing out the lapels of his uniform. His silver command wings shone brightly over several rows of multicolored ribbons above his left breast pocket. As he tugged the hem of his jacket, he glanced at Rick's uniform and asked him, "What do you think of the biography of Butch North and his kids?"

"He seems to be a normal American man, with exemplary service while in the military, an outstanding record with American Airlines, no records of reprisals, and well-liked within his community. Has plenty of financial assets to live comfortably for the rest of his life. No excessive habits such as alcohol, no drug use, really nothing that would lead me to think he would be involved with our suspected terrorist. I don't think he has any idea that we would suspect him of anything.

Both girls seem completely normal as well," he continued. "Mischelle is married, has no children, and lives in a middle-income home in Baltimore. College degree, stable financial situation, husband works, and no mention of either drugs or alcohol. Jeannie is single, has a college degree, an average-paying job, and no drug- or alcohol-related issues. They all seem to be average citizens with no history of misconduct. All appear to be of above-average intelligence, social status, and citizenship. Only the daughter, Mischelle, has any left leanings. She's the only known Democrat." Rick smiled as he finished. "I just hope they can give us a clue as to where Gene went."

"All right, gentlemen," General Modelle said as he inspected both men's uniforms and nodded his approval. "I think we all agree that neither of these people committed any violations, and we would be hard-pressed to hold them any longer than necessary. I certainly do not see any need for 'disposal' due to their accidental involvement. That would only further complicate matters. I want them treated with respect and proper consideration for their assistance in finding our fugitive. If we have to convince them of Gene's involvement in our terrorist plot, Karyn has provided documents showing that Gene was born in central California to a Hispanic father and a Korean mother and had ties to a Muslim mosque in the San Francisco area before going to Afghanistan in the mid-1990s. If he suspects, as we've discussed, that Gene is not of Middle Eastern descent, this will explain his physical appearance.

They will be told that the reason for misdirecting the public was to give us time to locate his family and set up surveillance in the event he tried to contact either them or his associates at the mosque. Our interrogator is one of the best in the business and has been told that he can improvise as necessary. We can provide documentation to cover any issues needed to prove his story. The President has given us full authority to maneuver as necessary with respect to Mr. North and his family, short of extreme prejudice. If you're ready, transportation is waiting."

Butch and the girls were escorted to the black vehicles, placed in the rear seats, and waited for the driver and another man to get into the front. He saw the female officer get into another of the cars and leave as the driver of their car started the engine and began to drive toward what he assumed was the base headquarters.

As they pulled into a reserved parking slot beside the building, he saw two more men in black suits coming out of a side door toward them. They walked to both sides of the car and waited until their driver had shut off the engine. As the driver and front seat passenger opened their doors to get out, the other two men opened the rear doors and stepped back, waiting for Butch and his daughters to get out.

"If you will just follow me, sir," the passenger from the front seat said as he turned and walked toward the side door. The driver preceded him to the door and held it open for them as the other two men followed closely behind Butch and the girls.

After entering the building, they followed a brightly shining tile floor to a door just short of what appeared to be the main hallway of the building. Butch could see several uniformed individuals walking through the building, pictures of past Commanders, trophy cases of awards, and the general activity he had seen during his Air Force career at every military installation.

Entering a door on the right side of the hall, they walked into a spacious conference room with an oval oak table and several leather chairs arranged around the sides. Standing behind one side of the table, Butch saw an Air Force General and a Colonel standing in their dress blues. He noted the wings and ribbons and nodded his head in respect as he looked into their eyes.

There was a well-dressed man, wearing a dark suit but having no insignia, nametag, or other means of identification, sitting just in front of the officers. On the table in front of him sat an open briefcase, a pitcher of water, and several glasses. As they approached the table, he rose and said, "Mr. North, Jeannie, Mischelle, if you would please have a seat, I hope we can conclude our questioning as soon as possible and have you on your way back home."

As they took their seats, each girl on either side of Butch, the man took his seat and asked, "Water?" as he poured a glass for himself.

"No, thank you," Butch said as he leaned forward and placed his elbows on the table. "Just what is the reason for taking me and my daughters from my home, bringing us here, in what I perceive as more of a kidnapping than a request for information?"

"I'm sorry it had to be handled this way," the man said, taking a drink from his glass. "Please excuse what we have had to do. We would love to have taken care of this in more relaxed surroundings, but due to the sensitive nature of the situation, we had to guarantee absolute security. I hope you can appreciate that, especially with your background. By the way, I apologize for not introducing myself at the very start. My name is Kevin Johnson. Please just call me Kevin."

"Okay, Mr. Johnson," Butch said, intentionally not using his first name as requested. "You obviously have done a little research to be able to discuss my background," Butch said, leaning slightly more forward. "Why don't you just ask your questions? We'll all try to provide the most truthful answers we can, and you can take us back where you got us."

Kevin looked at Butch for a second, reached into his briefcase, and took out one of the pictures he had been provided of Gene in the T-shirt and baseball cap. As he passed it across the table, he asked, "I believe that you know this individual, isn't that so?"

Butch glanced down at the picture and looked into Kevin's eyes, saying, "You already know that. Your associates showed us the same picture almost an hour ago, and my daughters and I told them that we did. If that is your only question, I believe you've gotten your answer."

"No, sir, that is not my only question. I just want to hear each answer for myself. I don't want there to be any mistakes when I forward my report to the FBI headquarters. If you would please bear with me, there may be some questions repeated, but it's for my sake not to doubt your integrity or question your honesty. I just need to know for my own certainty that I have asked the right questions and gotten the most truthful answers. Now, if I may continue, what was the nature of your contact with this individual?"

Butch leaned back, looked at Kevin for a minute, then up at the two officers standing behind him. "I think I would like a glass of water. You girls want anything?" he said as he returned his gaze back to Kevin.

Both Jeannie and Mischelle shook their heads and said, "No thanks."

Kevin picked up the pitcher of water and slowly poured it as Butch continued to stare at him. Filling the glass, Kevin looked directly at him and passed the glass across the table. "Here you are, sir. Is there anything else before we continue?"

Butch accepted the glass and set it in front of him, leaned back again, and simply said, "No."

"All right then. When did you first meet Gene, where was he, what has your contact with him been, where did you go, and who else had any contact with him?"

"I picked Gene up just north of Azle on Tuesday morning, about ten or ten-thirty. He was walking along 730 toward Boyd, and I stopped to give him a ride. He told me he was going to Decatur to see if he could get a job with a cousin, I believe he said.

I then told him that I needed someone to replace my hand at the stables for a couple of days and asked if he wanted the job. He told me that his last job involved stable work, and he accepted my offer.

We stopped at the Double K restaurant for lunch—part of his pay was room and meals—went to the stables where I introduced him to Steve, my hired hand, and left him there to learn his job.

He never left the stables that I know of without me, and I know of no contact he would have had with anyone else. Except, the Duffys came by while he was there, but I don't think he spoke to them. He spent the night on the couch in my office and was there Wednesday morning when I arrived.

I took him to Decatur a little after noon for lunch and stopped by Wal-Mart for some socks and jeans. We came back, worked until about six or six-thirty, and I went home to clean up before we went to Bridgeport. We all went to Red's Take 5 Sports Bar—by that, I mean my girls, Gene and I. We stayed there until about eleven or so, and the girls and I left to go home. He was supposed to get a ride home with two ladies we met there. And that was the last time I saw him.

The first time I heard or saw anything about him was this morning on CNN, just before one of your men knocked on my door. Until then, I figured he was just another Mexican doing day labor around the county."

"Who were the ladies at Red's?"

"One said her name was Stacy something. Hyden, I think. Is that right, Jeannie?"

"Yes," Jeannie said. "And the other one was Leslie Barber."

"That's right," Butch said, nodding his head. "They said they were from Bowie and Arlington and were going back to Bowie after they left Red's."

"Are you positive their names were Stacy and Leslie, and which one was from where?" Kevin asked as he picked up his pen and began to write.

"No, I'm not positive that their names were Stacy and Leslie. I am positive that they told me their names were Stacy and Leslie. Nor am I sure where they are really from, just that Stacy said she was from Bowie, and Leslie said she was from Arlington. I have known women to lie about their real names or where they are from in case they don't want to be contacted later. So I'm only positive of what I heard, not what their names may actually be or where they are really from."

"Do either of you girls have anything to add?" Kevin asked as he looked at Jeannie and Mischelle.

"No," said Mischelle. "Except that I think their real names are Stacy and Leslie. Even after they had drank a couple of drinks, they responded to their names, as you would normally expect. They did not hesitate and looked at each other, trying to remember who was who. I think they were using their real names."

"Okay, anything else?" Kevin asked as he looked at them.

"Gene did say he had not drunk much before, and he seemed a little higher than most people would be after just one Jack and Coke," Jeannie replied.

The questioning continued for another thirty minutes or so. "Here's my card. Call this number and ask for me if you think of anything else," Kevin said as he handed his card to Butch and replaced his notes and the photographs back in his case, and closed it. As he stood and turned, looking at Mike and Rick, he nodded and started for the door. "I'll have some of my men escort you back to the helicopter and take you back to your house. Thank you for your cooperation, and if I have any further questions, I'm sure you will be available to provide the answers," he said, slightly turning back and looking at Butch. "That is to say, I assume you aren't planning on going anywhere any time soon."

Mike and Rick turned to follow Kevin as two agents entered the room and asked Butch and the girls to follow them. As they got out of their chairs, Butch let Jeannie and Mischelle walk in front while one of the agents waited to follow him out.

The same car, driver, and passenger were waiting where they had initially parked. After getting into the car, they drove directly back to the helicopter, where the pilot sat waiting in his seat with a couple of ground personnel standing by for the start.

After starting the engine and waiting for clearance to lift off, they rose slowly from the concrete pad and began to fly west as they gained altitude. Butch sat quietly and watched the two agents traveling with them. After a short fifteen-minute flight, they landed in the pasture beside the house, and Butch and the girls got out. Never stopping the rotors, the helicopter rose quickly and swooped across the house, heading to the east in the direction of the stables.

"Well, girls, it's been an exciting morning, hasn't it? Y'all go on inside. I've got to get back to the stables and feed the horses. I'll be back in a couple of hours, and we'll talk."

Back at the conference room within the deep walls of the Facility, a very disappointed group of individuals sat discussing the impact of the current events. "Looks like we're back to square one," Rick said as he looked at the map."

"I'm afraid that we're way behind square one," Mike replied. "I think we may have lost Gene. If he has disappeared into either Arlington or Bowie, we could be in for a very long search. In the meantime, I guess I better relay this to Washington. General Modelle, would you accompany me to my office, please?"

Without another word, they turned and walked slowly out of the conference room as the rest of the staff sat with their heads bowed in disappointment. They all knew that their careers were hanging by a thread and that catching Gene could now take months, even years. And if the wrong person were to ever contact Gene, the world could soon have to acknowledge what, up to now, only a handful of supposed fanatics believed. There was another life form out there, and now it was here.

EPILOGUE

Nine months later, in the local clinic of a small town about an hour's drive north of Fort Worth, the only doctor and his nurse were rushed back from their homes while they were eating dinner. As they arrived at the hospital, a waiting Texas Highway Patrolman was standing just outside the double doors. As the doctor got out of his car and started up the sidewalk, the Patrolman came down to meet him.

"Evening, Doc; sorry to have you brought back in from dinner, but I stopped a speeding car just north of town, and the lady inside needed to get here in a hurry. I'm surprised that she didn't have that baby in my car driving here."

"Got yourself a real emergency this time, did you, Thomas?" said the doctor, who had known him since he was a little boy growing up there. "Must beat sitting up there waiting for drunks coming back from the casinos on the reservation."

"Yes, it sure does," answered Thomas as he held the doors open for the doctor.

"Amber here already?" the doctor asked as he walked into the waiting room. As he looked around, he asked, "Where's the patient?"

"Amber got here just after I did, and we took her into the examination room. If you don't need me anymore, I better get back on the road before some damned Okie tries to sneak over," Thomas said as the doctor continued on down the hall.

"No, guess that will be all. Thanks, Thomas. You be careful out there, and tell the little lady I said hi and to bring your daughter in next week for a checkup."

"Sure thing, Doc," he said as he turned and left the building.

Entering the examination room, he saw that his only nurse, Amber, had prepped the young lady lying on the table. As he walked up, he nodded at Amber and asked the young lady, now in a standard white patient gown, "Well, young lady. I hear you think you're ready to have a new baby. Is that so?"

As she let out a scream, she yelled, "Yes! My baby, it's coming! You gotta do something now!"

The doctor went to the end of the table, lifted the gown, and told Amber, "She's right. Get me a sterile sheet and my delivery instruments. Hurry, this one is ready to greet the world."

As Amber returned with a white cloth over her arm and a tray of instruments, she heard the doctor say, "Here it comes!"

Rounding his right shoulder, Amber saw him put his hands between the woman's legs and accept the new life. The doctor looked down as it was born, and his eyes opened wide in amazement. "Holy shit!" he exclaimed as Amber got her first glimpse of the newborn. Looking down at the doctor's hands, she gasped, dropped the tray of instruments, and placed her hands over her mouth. "Oh my God," she whispered through her splayed fingers.

AUTHOR'S BIOGRAPHY

Jim West was born in Texas, raised in a small town in the Texas Panhandle, and continues to live in the great state of Texas. Of all things one can say of him, it is that he is truly a Texan.

Following several failed attempts at finishing his education after high school, he served in the U.S. Navy as a photographic intelligence analyst during the Vietnam War. Using the GI Bill, he returned to college back in Texas and completed his bachelor's degree in business. After graduation, he joined the U.S. Air Force and began pilot training immediately following Officer Training School (OTS).

Assigned throughout the United States and Korea, he retired after flying his entire career, which included training both U.S. and foreign national pilots from the then-allied countries.

Following his retirement from the armed services, he joined American Airlines and flew both domestic and international routes for over sixteen years. He retired as a captain in 2005 and began his next career, writing.

Always going back to his roots as a Texan, he operates an equestrian center, competes in roping events, and raises cattle. Throughout his life, he has always tried to maintain a sense of humor, help his community, and cherish his friends and family.

DNAlien

DNAlien is the story of a secret government program to develop life by combining DNA taken from alien bodies with a normal human embryo. Taking place within an ultrasecret facility hidden on the Naval Air Station Joint Reserve Base located in Fort Worth, Texas, success ultimately occurs.

Years ahead of their civilian counterparts, the military and government scientific personnel finally hit upon the magical combination of alien DNA and human embryonic tissues that resulted in a being that hopefully will possess the traits desired from both sources.

Gene, standing for Genetic Embryonic Nucleus Enhancement, grows under the constant care and watchful eyes of a small group of individuals assigned to the Fort Worth base. Knowledge of his existence is so closely guarded that only a handful of very high-ranking people, including the president of the United States, are aware of him or the program.

DNAlien follows Gene in a rural community north of Fort Worth after he escapes the facility and tries to evade the massive clandestine search for him during the worst terrorist attack on the United States, the days following the attacks on the World Trade Center in New York City.

Copyediting By Richard Leo V. Blanco

Reviewed By Richard Leo V. Blanco

www.ingramcontent.com/pod-product-compliance
Lightning Source LLC
Chambersburg PA
CBHW072105300726
48975CB00003B/711